An Adoration

First published in Canada in 2003
By McArthur & Company
322 King St. West, Suite 402
Toronto, Ontario
M5V 1J2
www.mcarthur-co.com

National Library of Canada Cataloguing in Publication

Huston, Nancy, 1953-
[Adoration. English]
An adoration / Nancy Huston.

Translation of: Une adoration.
ISBN 1-55278-373-1

I. Title.

PS8565.U8255A7513 2003   C843'.54   C2003-904010-0

Composition and Design by Tania Craan
Cover image: © Ron Fehling/Masterfile
Printed in Canada by Friesens

The publisher would like to acknowledge the financial support of the
Government of Canada through the Book Publishing Industry Development
Program, the Canada Council, and the Ontario Arts Council for our publishing
activities. We also acknowledge the Government of Ontario through the
Ontario Media Development Corporation Ontario Book Initiative.

10 9 8 7 6 5 4 3 2 1

An Adoration

Nancy Huston

McArthur & Company
TORONTO

for Linus

for Nora

"Realism is an illusion of reality,
every character is the author,
every object is a character, and therefore the author,
this tree I'm looking at and describing
has been touched by culture, it is Joan of Arc
and the retreat from Moscou,
our ancestors the Gaulois,
the Mona Lisa, it is my eye."
— ROMAIN GARY

"Only you are real."
— RAINER MARIA RILKE
to Lou Andréas-Salomé

THE NOVELIST *(To the Reader)*

This is a true story, I swear.

Oh, I've changed the names, of course; I've changed the setting, the time frame, the jobs, the dialogues, the order of events, their meaning, and so on and so forth. It nonetheless remains that everything I'm about to tell you is perfectly true. It's a hearing, as per usual — a phantasmagoria, as per usual; the witnesses, filing past you one by one, will do everything in their power to convince you, dazzle you, take you for a ride... I'll lend them my voice, but you're the one they're counting on to understand them; the one they need in order to exist. So pay close attention — it's important, because in the final analysis, only you can judge. As per usual.

First Day

Fiona

The first time I met Cosmo, Your Honour, was in my mother's eyes. True, all sorts of people inhabit my mother's eyes, my mother lets just about anybody penetrate her — of course, when I say penetrate I mean in the psychic sense of the term; she lets other people's souls seep in and mingle with her own, it makes me want to puke, Your Honour, I don't see why I should have to share my mother with every country bumpkin who plunks his ass down on a stool at *La Fontaine*, she looks people straight in the eye and they realize, with a surge of delight, that they'll have the right to pour their whinings and bitchings and complaints into her ears — that's all people do around here, complain and bitch about each other, it's their favourite activity, everything rubs them the wrong way, their lives, life itself, the weather, the passage of time, their neighbours and the rest. My mother doesn't mind chatting with the customers of *La Fontaine,* and her boss Mr. Picot encourages it because talking makes them thirsty; when they finally get up to leave they give her a big tip because, Mama says, they're glad to have been listened to, and that way the amount of unhappiness in the world has been diminished by a fraction. Not only does my mother *listen* to other people's stories, she *remembers* them — whereas, personally, I find them depressing, boring and monotonous, monotonous, monotonous, if I say monotonous a hundred and fifty thousand times will you interrupt me, Your Honour, or will you allow me to pursue my statement to the end? I'm not yet quite certain what we have the right to do and say in here, I know our purpose is to get at the truth, but where does the truth begin and where does it end? You must admit that it's not an easy question; if we really wanted to tell you *the whole truth* we'd need to go back to Cro-Magnon and you'd run the risk of losing the thread.

Here's the thread, as far as I'm concerned — that Sunday morning when I came to cuddle up in bed with my mother, the minute she turned to look at me I saw that someone important had set up housekeeping in her eyes. They were gleaming. You've noticed it, haven't you? Look at her, everyone. Come on, Mama, you're proud of it, don't be modest, go on, stand up and show them all.

See that gleam in my mother's eyes?

That is Cosmo.

Where is my father, you want to know. Oh, you're so pre-dictable. You disappoint me. You pain me. Yes of course, I should have begun by standing at attention and stating my name in full, my qualifications and status, after having had my fingerprints taken, not to mention my mug shot, full face and profile — yes, Your Honour, my name is Fiona, my height is this and my weight is that, I was born on this day of that month in the other year, in such-and-such a place, the daughter of Mr. and Mrs. So-and-So, but surely you must be aware that things aren't so simple anymore, the nuclear family no longer exists, it has exploded like the bomb of the same name. Nowadays, wherever you look, people are separating or divorcing or moving away or breaking up or stabbing each other in the back or cheating on each other or fighting or getting adopted or adapted or cloned or sowing their wild oats and if I may say so, Your Honour, I doubt that even *you* grew up from birth to adulthood with your two biological parents, if you did it would be something of a miracle... Yes, I know. You're the one who asks the questions around here. All I meant to say was...

Okay. Okay, I'll tell you about my father. Here goes...

No, I can't do it. It would make me cry and I refuse to cry in here. I'll give you nothing of myself in the course of this hearing, nothing at all from the inside of my body — there are limits, fortunately, to what I'm obliged to reveal in here. The inside of my body belongs to *me*; it is my solitude and my pride. Mama says that solitude is the most stubborn illusion of the human species. She says that in fact our minds don't belong to us, because they're filled with the words received from other people and there's nothing we can do about it, no way we can hoard them for ourselves, no way to pretend we don't understand them, as if they were pure music or geometrical patterns, it's a pity, Your Honour, don't you agree? It would be so marvellous to be able to love words for their sheer auditory or visual beauty and not allow them to join hands and organize themselves into sentences, paragraphs, square dances, grandiloquent choreographies... The only words I like are long, difficult ones — *antidisestablishmentarianism* for instance — words that are so heavy as to be almost opaque, like objects. I collect them.

Okay. I'll let Frank tell you about our father.

Frank

Fiona's older brother. Five years older. Yes, I know my kid sister's a bit obstreperous, but the two of us are thick as thieves... I don't know whether you yourself have a younger sister, Your Honour... Uh... sorry.

Our father Michael was an animal photographer. I say *was* because we haven't seen him in ages, but he probably still *is* an animal photographer, somewhere on the surface of the Earth. Fiona can't bear to talk about what he did, but I don't mind telling you, man-to-man as it were. You must have strangled cats or sliced open lizards or dissected live frogs when you were a little boy — now, come on, all little boys do that, it's perfectly natural, there's nothing to be ashamed of... Anyway, our father Michael, ex-husband of our mother Elke, back in the days when he still *was* her husband... well, he turned strange. He'd never managed to feel at home in this part of the world. It was, and is, foreign to him. He hails from a land of dizzying cliffs and sapphire lakes, blinding snow and vast empty skies, soaring ambitions and high-leaping prayers. Whenever he would indulge in his favourite pastimes — hiking and jogging — the peasants would look at him askance. Going out of doors for the mere sake of being out of doors is considered suspicious around here. Moreover, the local weather made him desperate. Did you know a man could be made desperate by the weather, Your Honour? Winter in these parts — the penetrating damp, the fog and mud, the dull grey skies, the dun-coloured fields — all these things drove him mad. *Biting* cold he could handle, forty below with blue

skies and brilliant sunlight, but the constant icy drizzly greyness sapped his soul, his appetite, his vitality. Each year in
April he'd tell Mama that he refused to spend one more winter
here, but the following year he'd be even more diminished,
even less capable of taking initiatives and decisions. His career
began to stagnate; he suffered from the turgid hostility of the
locals towards any idea or activity that threatened to disturb
their habits. *The greatest force of this region,* he would tell visitors, *is the force of inertia.* Or again: *You know what the local
motto is? If anything moves, kill it and go back to sleep.* At first
he'd say these things as a joke, but gradually the joke soured,
and within a few years he stopped laughing altogether. His
anger slid towards his loved ones, Fiona and myself, especially
Mama. He would yell at her for trifles — for not having dinner
on the table at seven sharp, or for reading to me beyond my
bedtime, or for rolling around on the living-room rug with
Fiona. My father appreciates order and punctuality — he was
raised that way; it's not a crime. The direction his life had
taken made him sullen and sulky; we scarcely saw him around
the house anymore, he divided his time between the forest and
the dark room.

I'm not trying to make excuses for him, but since we're
here to explain what occurred as fully as possible — well,
without going all the way back to Cro-Magnon as my sister
facetiously suggested, I think it worth mentioning the fact that
expatriation had made my father miserable. You can choose to
live in a place because you've fallen in love with a woman
there, but within a year or two your childhood will begin to

gnaw at you — and I use the word *gnaw* intentionally; you'll see why in a minute. Yes, love is all very well and good, but there's no way it can take the place of your childhood memories, mother tongue, friends, parents, native sky... Love, in my opinion, is vastly overrated. It's far less powerful than people make it out to be.

Our father felt squashed and squelched by the life that had accumulated around him. People often speak as if they organized their lives on the basis of a series of clear, rational decisions, but for most of us it's more like an accumulation — life sort of piles up around you like so much shit, sticking to your feet and preventing you from moving on. Or to take another metaphor, your choices are like the stakes in a palisade that goes up gradually around you, blocking off your view of the rest of the world so that you can't even bemoan the chances you've renounced... People in exile are a different story. They know there's another world, and they know they're not in it. The stakes of their palisades are driven, as it were, into their hearts. They go berserk with nostalgia. My father had gone berserk — that's what I'm trying to tell you.

I love him. I imagine you love your father, too; it's pretty hard not to. I'm glad for the chance to give him some sort of existence here, however fleeting. All right, I'll come out with it. At that time, the animal photographer, rather than capturing images of quick lively throbbing goldfinches flitting at the pond's edge, or slow worms slithering furtively through high grasses, began to set traps... His purpose was no longer to immortalize the magical instant when the animal's eyes meet those of the human being; it was no longer to capture the fleeting beauty of a crane taking wing from the marsh, or the bright, curious expression of a rabbit... What he now cared about getting on film was the animals' panic, their twitchings and convulsions, their death. Bleeding weasels, mouths agape in a soundless scream, muskrats writhing silently on the ground, keening helplessly in pain, foxes and coypus with mangled paws, young deer with snapped legs... Eyes from which the light is slowly fading. The more visible the animals' suffering, the more our father was entranced by it. No, I have no idea who purchased these new photos of his, or indeed if there even was a market for them. But when our mother came across them, tidying up his dark room one day, she began to weep and vomit at the same time, Your Honour, and I'll spare you the description of her screams. Forgive me for saying so, dear Mama, but you were not a pretty sight that day.

It was shortly after this that the quarrelling began — quarrelling which, over the next year or so, would eventually lead to their divorce. I look at things coldly, Your Honour, and I describe them coldly. Even if I don't torture animals, I'm proud to be my father's son. Women can't understand. I'm sorry, I keep addressing you as if you were a man whereas in fact you might very well be a woman, I know there are more and more female magistrates in our day and age. But I don't need to edulcorate: you've been exposed to the least flattering aspects of mankind in the exercise of your profession over the years; I'm sure you know as well as I do that as a general rule boys prefer to face reality, whereas girls tend to hold their noses, avert their eyes and dissolve into hysterical giggles. Fiona is an exception to this rule. I pretty much raised her myself, and I was careful not to let her turn into a dumb-ass broad. Our mother goes around with her head in the clouds, but Fiona and I do our utmost to remain rooted in reality.

I mean, does death exist or doesn't it? It exists. Is it thrilling, or isn't it? Personally, Your Honour, I can understand my father's obsession with the flame that flickers in a creature's eyes as it slips towards non-existence. How is it possible? One second there's a living creature in there... and the next second, nothing at all. There's something scandalous about it, everyone must sense that. I mean, even a slug protests if you hold a match to its rubbery orange skin; it seizes up in indignation, its whole tiny being rebelling against the pain — Hey, what's going on? Stop that! I, too, have the right to exist!

My father had to leave. He knew it. He had to get away from us. In order to break free, he gnawed off his own paw, just like the foxes that fell into his traps. He left Fiona and me behind. He told me so in as many words: I may be wounded, he said, but I'm free. I may have a limp, but I go where I please. As for the rest...

I've seen my father's final contact sheets. They're sensational. The doe lies there on her side, staring up at you with huge round eyes, your gaze plunges all the way to the bottom of her soul, and what you learn there is unbelievable... I mean, Brigitte Bardot can go jump in the lake, you know what I mean?

Cosmo? Always hated the guy. A phoney, a show-off, a

fucking freak. The fornicating clown is what I call him. I curse the day our mother met him.

Yes, the clerk heard me correctly, he can record my words: *I curse Cosmo*. Put that in your pipe and smoke it.

Elke

My children are still too young to understand, Your Honour. It doesn't worry me. They'll understand some day, I'm sure of it. But please don't forget to take their youth into account as you listen to their statements. Youth is always extreme, isn't it? Just think back to your own... It's funny...

As you can imagine, I have a great deal to tell you about Cosmo, but since we've got to begin somewhere, let me begin by describing the sensation of his hands on my skin. They made me melt, Your Honour. No matter where he placed his hands, it was like snow melting in springtime, rivulets rushing to fill every dip and dent and ditch and ravine to overflowing — or like blood, you understand, like sweet blood trickling from my mouth or my secret hollow — yes Cosmo's hands were like blood, like snow, smooth pink snowblood softening, melting and rushing... He'd remove a single piece of my clothing — just one! — and press his lips to the part of me thus bared, then to the parts of me still clothed, warming me with his breath through the material... Then, very slowly, another piece of clothing would be peeled away, each portion of the body a revelation, never seen or felt before, and I would cry out in surprise to discover that my neck had a nape, or my knee a cap... Oh, I'd known pleasure before Cosmo, Your

Honour, but never the melting rushing joy which he gave, gave and gave, until I gurgled like a brook...

To my knowledge, he was never filmed, recorded, photographed or interviewed while doing things like exploring a collarbone or the crest of a shoulder blade with his tongue... Yet this, too, he did supremely well...

No, strike out *supremely well.* Or rather, since I know nothing can be struck out, insert this: *love is not a performance.* That's what I would tell him, over and over again, when...

The Psychiatric Expert

I would like to point out, if I may, that the expression *exploring with his tongue* is highly significant. The actor had a highly singular attitude towards his mother tongue — it was as if he'd decided to indefinitely prolong its motherliness by refusing to make the transition from oral to written language. As is well known, Cosmo would not allow his words to be separated from his living body. He improvised, reinventing his shows night after night; never did he put the verbal delirium of his performances into writing, nor would he authorize their publication under any form.

I thought it important, Your Honour, that you be aware of this strange mental block from the outset.

Elke

May I go on? After all, I'm the star witness of this hearing... Millions of people saw Cosmo on television, hundreds of thousands saw him onstage, thousands are proud to have shaken his hand or received his autograph... A fair number, like myself, had the immense privilege of being loved by him, but no one in the world — *no one, Your Honour, do you hear me?* — knew Cosmo the way I knew him.

Frank

Ha, ha ha! What a laugh. Dozens of women are under the same illusion, Your Honour. They're out there in the hallway right now, huffing and puffing with impatience to come in and make their statement — each of them privately convinced that *she* was Cosmo's Chosen One... Make no mistake about it, Cosmo was an insatiable seducer, an unrepentant Don Juan; flocks, nay, swarms of women — whether virgins, wives or widows, comely or cacogenic, youthful or decrepit — succumbed to his charms. And towards the end — the words stick in my throat but being under oath I have no choice but to spit them out — the amorous conquests of the fornicating clown were no longer even restricted to women...

I find this shocking, Your Honour, I admit it. It is not a pleasant thing to see one's own mother as a sex object among others, but the sad fact is that Elke was neither the first nor the last to fall into Cosmo's trap. Even today, after all that's happened, she gazes adoringly at her executioner, just like the doe in the photograph...

Don Juan

Objection, Your Honour! This has got to stop. I insist that you *do* something about it! With the utmost indignation and determination, I protest against what has just been said. It is intolerable that my name be invoked every time a ladies' man comes prancing along. It's been going on for centuries and with every passing year my name is further degraded and trivialized... The truth is that my own ambitions were lofty, noble and metaphysical; far from being a guy who scratched his crotch every time it itched, I attacked the hypocrisy of social conventions; I hurled my defiance in the face of God himself; I'm one of the most powerful symbols of individual freedom in the history of the Western World!

As for sexual inversion, the very idea of it makes my heart seize up in horror, like the slug when Frank holds a match to it.

The Doe

I admit to having stared adoringly into the eyes of my executioner as I died, Your Honour, but only because he happened to be bending over me at the time, observing me closely through the lens of his Nikon. He took up my entire field of vision, so of course he meant the world to me — the world I so dearly loved and was now forced to leave... Ah, such a wrenching of the heart! Think of it! To have no choice but to love your assassin, simply because *he* is still athrob with life, because blood is still coursing through his veins, whereas your own heartbeats grow fewer and farther between... weaken... flutter... cease...

Elke

You're right, Your Honour — things are getting a bit out of hand here. Each of us should try to express ourselves fully while we have the floor; otherwise you're liable to get lost. Come now, children, hold your tongues for a while — I've scarcely gotten started; do let me have my say.

Any number of scenes, of course, could serve as an appropriate opening for the story, but being the star witness I have the right to begin wherever I please — and what pleases me, Your Honour, is to tell you how Cosmo and I first met. What could be a more natural starting point? Every time a man and a woman fall in love, the world is reborn.

Fiona and Frank

Stop it, Mama! You're embarrassing us!

Elke

I'm talking to the judge now, children. If you don't want to listen, you can plug your ears. Isn't it comical, Your Honour? We spend the first twenty years of our lives hiding from our parents, and the rest hiding from our children!

So imagine, if you will, a scene straight out of a song by Edith Piaf — *Moi j'essuie les verres / au fond d'un café...* I'm a barmaid at *La Fontaine,* Your Honour. You probably don't know this particular café but you know dozens like it — an ordinary village bistrot, now lugubrious, now cheerful, depending on the customers' moods and the weather out of doors. Unlike the woman in the song, however, I'm never too busy to dream — dreaming is my favourite activity. My hands move of their own volition, dipping glasses alternately into soapy and clear water, shaking off the droplets, grabbing the dishtowel, drying the glasses, and sliding them into their slots above the bar. I blur my vision intentionally, then watch the way the gilded glints enter my pupils and dance on my retina; hanging upside-down, the glasses resemble round, transparent bats, or a long line of dancers at the Moulin Rouge, or the paper dolls my mother used to make, snipping them out of brown wrapping paper with her sewing scissors — and then, once I'd coloured them, taping them in bright, swooping garlands to my bedroom wall! I lived in the capital back then, Your Honour... this was a long time ago.

Josette
The lady waxes literary. My son is dead and she waxes literary.

Elke
Your son loved literature, Josette; surrounding him with verbal beauty is my way of showing him respect.

Anyway, that evening, a Saturday in mid-May, I was working at top speed because the café was packed and the atmosphere electric, not to say explosive. The customers were far more animated than usual. Several of them imitated Cosmo as they waited for him to arrive at *La Fontaine,* reiterating his most comical phrases, gestures and grimaces — quotes and reminders of the performance they'd just attended in the village hall. Sometimes, a single word would suffice to revive a whole number: *Love,* they would say, for instance, or *Tolerance* — and it would whoosh them into high waves of laughter that broke upon the shore in a foam of gasps...

Frank

Objection, Your Honour. Our mother has never seen the ocean.

Elke

Of course I've seen it! I've seen it on television, and this is just how I imagine it — loud and exhilarating, with gales of wind ripping through the waves and stirring them into high motion, the way a conductor stirs an orchestra — so beautiful! Even the townspeople seemed beautiful to me that night because of the anticipation in their eyes, whereas most of them are devoid of the qualities generally associated with beauty, they're neither young nor wealthy, sleek nor elegant, and when I look at them on ordinary days from my place behind the bar, they seem to belong to greyness and hardship as intimately as mushrooms to their treetrunks.

On the wall behind the bar, the multicoloured array of liqueur and syrup bottles formed a complex rippling treasure. They seemed to be reflecting the light more fully, more enthusiastically than usual, as if to take part in this thrilling, unprecedented event — *Cosmo was coming.* Yes, Cosmo in the flesh was about to arrive, he'd promised to join us here after the performance — his first ever in his hometown, in celebration of his thirtieth birthday. Something like half the town's population was packed into the café, a hundred people at least, jostling and calling out to one another, doctors and journalists for once rubbing elbows with peasants... Even Cosmo's parents, who never set foot in drinking establishments, were there, though clearly ill at ease.

Josette

Of course we were ill at ease! How would *you* feel, Your Honour, being a guest at your own son's birthday party? Organized, what's more, by people you'd never even met? It was excruciating!

Sandrine

My name's Sandrine, Your Honour; I'm a district nurse, specializing in home care. More to the point, I'm Elke's best friend, and I thought I should take the stand now because although, as she's said, nearly everyone in town was at *La Fontaine* that evening, *I* happened to be sitting at the counter, inches away from her and... I *saw* the event take place.

It should be mentioned that Elke and her children were newcomers to the village — they'd only moved here the summer before, in the wake of her divorce. Cosmo, on the other hand, had been born and raised on the spot. Half the girls in town (myself included) had endured his advances as teenagers; a good quarter of them (myself *excluded*) had slept with him; and as familiarity breeds contempt we tended to scorn the crowds of his adoring fans... You know, if he comes from around here, he can't be worth much, that sort of thing... Still, despite our legendary stodginess, despite our outward appearance of stunned vegetables, we wouldn't have missed Cosmo's performance that night for anything in the world. The other waitresses of *La Fontaine* would have fomented a riot had they been forbidden to attend, but the owner knew he could count on Elke's placidity. Whence the fact that of all the people in the room that night, she was the only one never to have set eyes on Cosmo.

Elke

But I *had* set eyes on him — just like the ocean! Bits of ink and recorded sound, flickering lights and shadows... Thanks to TV and the radio, newspapers and magazines, Cosmo's image was already imprinted on my brain. I was familiar with his legendary straw stick-up hair, his eyes which always seemed to be focusing slightly above or beyond you. And his voice... what was it about his voice? Cracked, yet soft... And now, unimaginably, Cosmo himself was about to physically enter *La Fontaine*.

I went on working absent-mindedly, revelling in my own sense of expectancy as I poured wine into stemmed glasses, beer into heavy mugs, press-doses of liqueurs and sherries into shot glasses. What could be taking him so long? The show had ended forty minutes ago and all he needed to do was take a shower and change his clothes, the clock said nearly midnight and midnight was late in these parts, this was not the capital, people with animals had to get up at four or five in the morning and *animals know nothing about Sunday,* as they said, peasants never tire of repeating the same truisms about the harshness and tedium of their lives; since their lives never change, there's no reason their wisdom should evolve...

Something in the air quickened, his arrival must be imminent, the noise in the café hitched up another notch then subsided abruptly, as if an invisible soundsweeper had come to prepare the path for his arrival, sweeping all extraneous sounds into the corners of the room — quick, quick, out of the way! The door opened and, preceded by his crew, Cosmo walked in — yes, here he was — truly, fully, in the flesh at last!

The Novelist

For you, Your Honour, unfortunately, it will only be more words. I'll do my best to make Cosmo as real to you as possible, but what is possible in literature, as I'm forced to acknowledge every day to my frustration, is limited to the printed page. However, when you think about it, isn't it preferable this way? If Cosmo — gruesomely, hotly — were to leap from the page, as the hero leaps from screen to theatre in Woody Allen's *Purple Rose of Cairo* — what on earth would you *do* with him? You'd be horrified and helpless. For then you, too, would be forced to exist. You'd have to renounce the reassuring anonymity that protects you as a judge. You'd have stop reading, put down your book and make conversation with this perfect stranger, allowing him in turn to look at you, talk to you, make snap judgments about you... Oh, it's far better this way, believe me. You'll have a deeper and more intimate knowledge of Cosmo when my words have finished with him than you would were you to suddenly feel his material warmth and weight upon your lap.

Elke

There were three seconds of perfect silence — and then, remembering that this was not only a possibility but virtually an obligation, the crowd began to noisily acclaim the hero of the day. Male-shouted bravos soared up over the general clamour and left traces of their trajectory in our ears, as fireworks leave visual traces on our retinas. A woman launched into a high-pitched, off-key rendition of "Happy Birthday" and the song was swiftly picked up by all; after an adjustment of key, the voices gained confidence and began belting out the words with increasing boisterousness — as if this were a military barracks, as if everyone in the room were a drunken sailor on leave. Some of them sensed they were behaving stupidly, boorishly, and that a sophisticated man like Cosmo might take offence at the ruckus — but no, apparently he did not; he had his famous shy crooked grin on his face, so they went on bellowing their way to the end of the song, then burst into applause, then turned away, embarrassed by their own enthusiasm, and pretended they didn't care a whit about the presence in their midst of France's most renowned stage actor.

Now Cosmo crossed the room to embrace his parents, who had risen to their feet and were waiting for him awkwardly, not quite daring to hold their arms out to him but not knowing what else to do with them, holding them, therefore, at an angle of some thirty degrees from their bodies until he reached them. His mother's cheeks turned crimson as he pressed her to his leather jacket. Then, putting an arm around his father, Cosmo turned to face the rest of the room, myself included, and at last I could observe him to my heart's content. I saw that he was just his father's height — not tall, quite small in fact, and slight; his body was almost that of an adolescent. Tawny hair. Thick, bruised-looking lips. High brow, painfully knit. He reminded me of Montgomery Clift or James Dean, one of those bad-boy heroes from American movies of the 1950s, with their wounded eyes and twisted smiles.

As I've said, both his parents were ill at ease, but André's discomfort (though I did not know his name yet) was far more acute and indeed seemed chronic. He kept staring at the floor, muttering under his breath and making odd, jerky movements with his arms.

Josette
My husband isn't here to defend himself, and I will not allow him to be thus maligned by an outsider.

Elke
Ah! Did you hear that? I've been living in these parts since I was six years old, and she still calls me an outsider!

Believe me, Josette, no one was more foreign to your late husband than you yourself, as numerous revelations in the course of the hearing will confirm.

André
Excuse me, but... If Don Juan and the doe are allowed to express their point of view... er... I don't see why I shouldn't have the right...

Josette
Shut up, André! Given the way you chose to die, you've got only one right left, and that's the right to keep your mouth shut.

Sandrine

Here's what happened next.

The two other waitresses leaped into action. The first, Berthe (who has corns on her feet — being a nurse, I know everyone's little miseries), brought in the birthday cake — a blue-and-white, many-tiered affair whose sumptuousness verged on the ridiculous. The second, Solange (who suffers from premenstrual syndrome) swung in with two magnums of champagne. Now it was Elke's turn to steer her way through the crowd with a tray of twenty-odd teetering flute glasses. Her eyes flicked up as she set the tray on Cosmo's table; she caught his gaze and reflected it involuntarily in a smile.

Elke

Sandrine is right. That's exactly how it happened.

Thus authorized, Cosmo's eyes slid briefly downwards and I could feel them moving like hands, passing warmly and rapidly over breasts, stomach and hips, then back up to my face. Though it lasted but an instant, this immaterial caress made me dizzy. Now the champagne was being poured, people were shuffling aside to make way for the town officials; Tabrant, the obese reporter for the local paper, shoved everyone aside with his usual grace and courtesy to take photographs — and at last the mayor, glass aloft, proposed a toast so banal, so predictable, so hopelessly steeped in provincial convention and pretension and cliché that it made me blush.

Josette

What did I tell you, Your Honour? *The woman isn't one of us,* she admits as much herself. She's a shameless hussy, a bastard born in the capital — and now she comes here and presumes to judge us.

Elke

Forgetting that Cosmo was perfectly acquainted with local mores, I stared at him in desperate apology, silently begging him to forgive the mayor's doltishness. This time he not only met my gaze but gave me a broad wink, causing me to dissolve inwardly in laughter.

That, Your Honour, was the first instance of what I earlier referred to as *the melting.*

Sheer felicity. Glasses were raised and the champagne was quaffed, spilled, sprayed, spewed, the champagne rained down on all of us like a sparkling shower, like a million droplets of ocean spume in Brittany, the townspeople went wading and splashing together through puddles of champagne, within minutes it had risen to their ankles, to their knees, mothers had to snatch up their toddlers to prevent them from drowning in champagne, suddenly everyone was young and beautiful and stark naked, their bodies were slick and bright, limber and nimble, supple and sinewy with glistening skin, they began dancing like forest nymphs and satyrs, leaping and whirling in the shower of champagne...

Josette

For Heaven's sake, Your Honour, aren't you going to stop her? How long will you let her go on like this? The woman is raving mad! It's quite clear she's not a reliable witness! You can't trust a person who lets her tongue run away with her like that!

Elke

I know it was all in my head, Your Honour. However, as I hope you are aware, what goes on in people's heads is real as well.

Frank

Calm down now, little Ma.

Well, now you've seen it Your Honour — our mother lives in a state of permanent elation. It's not her fault, that's just the way she is. A childhood tragedy (of which, more later) turned her into an imagination addict. You can't hold it against her, but you have to take everything she says with a grain of salt.

Come to think of it, she and Cosmo were made for each other. Mad love at a distance — nothing could have suited our mother better. It fit her like Cinderella's glass slipper. Yes, it's the Cinderella syndrome to a T — strange it never occurred to me before. Poor, tattered orphan stumbles upon Prince Charming and — since he's not the wooing-wedding-whelping type — contents herself with dreaming about him for the rest of her life.

Elke

Frank, do let me continue.

I returned to my spot behind the bar but Cosmo was still in my line of vision. Even as I moved from customer to customer, I recalled the way his eyes had roamed across my body; this made me jubilant and I played with my own jubilation, pushing it to the back of my mind, then watching as it irresistibly returned to the foreground. He's still here, I told myself. The moment of Cosmo's presence in *La Fontaine* is still now and it's a lusciously long, an endless now, I can use it as I see fit, my mind can caper and jig, flit out to join the motionless owl in the oak tree or go swooping through the forest with the bats, then duck back into the loud bright warmth and still it will be now, now, now, with Cosmo close at hand... Suddenly, as I stood there drying glasses, a fist was thrust before my eyes. The fist belonged to Asimon the blacksmith. I frowned at him questioningly — *What?* His face crinkled and cracked and his lips parted in a huge, gap-toothed smile... Then the fist slowly opened and I glimpsed, folded up small in the dark hollow of his palm, a piece of paper. Again I raised my eyes to query — *What?* His own eyes described an arc ending on Cosmo, the paper slipped from his palm to mine, and he was gone. My hands were dripping wet, they were wetting the paper, I was afraid the ink would run...

Sandrine

She didn't blush, Your Honour. Not for a single second, I can swear to it. Stepping away from the counter, she hastily wiped her hands on her apron before unfolding the paper and I said to myself, at this point I would blush, any normal woman would blush — but not Elke.

Elke

Here's what Cosmo had written: *Have you a car, and will you come to me after closing time, look up at me, say yes.* Beneath the words was a hastily sketched map with an arrow showing his parents' house, which I already knew by sight, and an X on the barn behind it. When I glanced up at him, his eyes were already on me.

Sandrine

Still she didn't blush.

Elke

I nodded, lurching inwardly — as when, in the drifting moments before sleep, one steps off a curb into nothingness. You know what I mean, Your Honour? It's called falling, not for nothing is it called *falling* in love. I was in love with Cosmo and I would go to him later tonight, after closing time; never in my life had I been so happy.

It's true. *This was.* And as I hope you are aware, Your Honour, what *was* is in no way inferior to what *is*.

Can you hear, then, the soft crunch of my tires on the gravel at three in the morning? An exquisitely distinct sound, carving itself out against the background of silence just as the cool, dispassionate mid-May quarter moon carved itself out against the black night sky. Can you feel the poignant suspense of this sweet, solitary instant as I slowly cross the courtyard to the door of the ancient barn? Can you hear the faint scrape of my shoes on the pebbles, the gentle swish of my skirt against my thighs, the soft tap of my knuckles on grey wood?

As if by magic, the door swings open soundlessly and Cosmo lets me in. He's there alone. He and I are alone together. For a long time, we stare at each other, without speaking.

The Novelist
I admit that at this rate, the court hearing is liable to take us several decades.

Elke
Listen to the silence, Your Honour; that's all I ask of you. It's vertiginous. Appreciate the silence between two people who are already madly in love though they don't yet know each other — don't know, that is, the specific details of the past that sculpted this body, this face, this swiftness to answer *yes* to a summons...

Facts are so heavy, you see. So very heavy.

Perhaps it's like an encounter with a prostitute. For the time being, we can still lie, adopt any identity, make up any story we please. I know his name but he doesn't yet know mine; indeed the names we go by, Cosmo and Elke, aren't our real names — what are real names, anyway? The ones inscribed on our birth certificates? It was my ex-husband Michael who gave me the name Elke — because, as he said, I was as slow and placid as the mountain elk he'd so loved as a child. I liked the name and had been using it for years; everyone in the village knew me as Elke, so to all intents and purposes it had become my name.

I feel a bit emotional...

Frank

Let me take over; it'll speed things up a bit. Here, Your Honour, more or less as she must have told it to Cosmo that first night, is the precious story of my mother's origins. The tale of a great, adulterous love affair... A diamanté memory, improbably romantic — oh, embellished upon, no doubt; rubbed and polished into pristine perfection over the years... But don't we all do as much? Aren't we free to use our memories as we see fit?

She was born in the capital, shortly before the war. Her mother was a hatmaker named Yvette. Yes, Your Honour — we're talking about the 1930s, when Yvettes and hatmakers were still extant. Apparently, this particular Yvette had a true genius for hats. By the age of twenty-three, she'd already built herself quite a little reputation. She could turn any piece of silk or felt or even cardboard into a stylish, rakish headpiece, then decorate it with whatever she could fish out of the neighbourhood garbage cans — used feathers and jewels, buttons and sequins, bits of fur and snippets of lace ribbon. She was quite a number. Attractive, too, with full cheeks and light brown hair which she styled with a kiss curl, smack in the middle of her forehead. She was light of heart and light on her feet, graceful and vivacious...

What else, Fiona? Have I forgotten anything, concerning our grandmother?

Fiona
She's dead.

Frank
Oh yes, right, dead, of course — immediately after the word *vivacious* it must be added that she's dead — but for the time being, in my story, she's still young and full of beans, she hasn't the least notion of what's in store for her; she doesn't even know that the love of her life is about to come knocking at her door...

And so, Your Honour, even as you continue imagining the night our mother and Cosmo are spending together in the barn following Cosmo's birthday party at *La Fontaine*, I must also ask you to imagine the en-counter between Yvette and a certain Monsieur Denain. The man has no first name. He's a banker: a wealthy fellow; quite elegant according to the standards of the day, faintly ridiculous according to our own — he wears a black handlebar mustache, three-piece suits and a bowler hat, carries a cane, smells of lilac aftershave, and is driven around town by a chauffeur. To this it should be added that he's married, and lives in a mansion with his wife and their young son in one of the cushier suburbs west of Paris.

So. One day in the summer of 1935, Monsieur Denain came knocking at Yvette's door because his wife wanted a special hat for a tea party she planned to attend the following week. As they sat together in Yvette's cramped little ground-floor flat in the Rue Au Maire, going over the details of the hat (red velvet with black brocade trim and a triangle of white pearls), the banker fell head over heels in love with the hat-maker. This may not sound very original. What's more so, however, is that Monsieur Denain was to go on loving Yvette for seven whole years. He gave her three adorable children and, though not in a position to recognize them legally, he contributed to their upkeep and even took them on Sunday outings to various parks and gardens in the capital.

The family was poor, but its poverty was modest rather than dire. And Yvette transfigured everything she touched — she could make a plate of lentils taste scrumptious and an ordinary pleated skirt look dashing. Have I forgotten anything?

Fiona
The stories.

Frank
Ah yes! Yes, she had the same gift with words. She could take a snippet of any story that came along and shape it into some-thing at which her children could laugh or marvel. Sitting in her window chair with her legs crossed — no, not crossed, *braided,* she was so very thin and supple that she could literally wrap her legs around each other — her hands darting like dragonflies, drawing invisible patterns in the air with her needle and thread, talking through the pins in her mouth, Yvette told her little ones story after story and they listened to her, transfixed...

Then death stepped in — as untimely, incredible, neutral,

unfair and indifferent as always — and dealt a double whammy. First, Monsieur Denain collapsed, the unsuspecting victim of a heart attack; three weeks later, making a delivery on the Boulevard Arago, Yvette was hit and killed by a passing car. The children were abruptly and permanently transformed. Everything vanished — mother, father, stories, hats, apartment, lentils and pleated skirts... The one thing Elke managed to salvage was a pair of gloves of the finest pink silk, a gift from her father to her mother — she's proud of those gloves, and has kept them to the present day...

The three orphans were taken in by the Depart-ment of Health and Social Service. We're talking about 1942, Your Honour, and I hardly need to tell you that conditions in Parisian orphanages during the German occupation were less than luxurious... Within a few months the children were dispersed: Elke and her older brother Maxime were farmed out to foster families in two different provinces; it would be twenty years before they saw each other again. Yves, the youngest, who was only eighteen months old, was adopted; his name was changed, and he dropped out of sight entirely.

I know, I know — it sounds like something out of Charles Dickens. I apologize. Though the part about the passion between banker and hatmaker leaves me dubious, I do have material proof of the fact that in 1943, at the age of six, my mother was sent to this area by the Department of Health and Social Service.

It's more than likely that she spoke of all this to Cosmo, that first night in the barn. Did she so much as breathe a word about us, her children? What does a thirty-six-year-old divorcee tell a man she's just met, and with whom she's already dying to make love?

Elke

I told him a story.

It was one of Yvette's stories, in fact — about a little girl named Alice who gets kidnapped by a fairy. To her amazement, Alice discovers that in the fairy kingdom, all you have to do is think about a flower and it will appear before you. So it was that she found herself first in a field of brilliant poppies, then in a clump of fragrant lilac bushes, then lying in the grass with lush white arum lilies dripping dew upon her eyelids.

And the two of us, here? Cosmo asked me.

Same goes for us, I told him.

Could I have some morning-glory, then?

Here it is. Here's your morning-glory.

How about some mimosa?

Yes, mimosa, too, with its fuzzy yellow balls. And freesia. And fuchsias.

No, said Cosmo. I'm not sure I care to have fuchsias in my home. They're like orchids, they look artificial even when they're real. Take them away.

I'm sorry, I said. We can bring in all the flowers we want, but we can't get rid of them. If you like, though, I can cover the fuchsias over with honeysuckle — soft mounds of honeysuckle with thin yellow, thin white flowers, pink at the heart...

Cosmo had curled up on a rug at my feet to listen to the

story, and after a while I saw that he'd fallen asleep. We were sitting on one of the mezzanines in his barn, which he had had renovated from top to bottom — the granary floor had been removed so that the roof pole was visible some twenty feet above the ground, and a series of ingeniously interconnecting mezzanines had been set up among the rafters. One served as kitchen and bathroom, one as bedroom, and a third, the one on which we were lounging, as a study and sitting room... The ground floor, which served as Cosmo's rehearsal room when he stayed here, was a vast, empty, beautifully proportioned oak parquet, illuminated by spotlights...

I stared down at Cosmo as he slept. He seemed so young, scarcely older than my son. He was breathing through his mouth, and I could just make out the white line of teeth beyond his upper lip. My silence must have wakened him. His eyes opened directly onto mine and he uttered three words — words I shall not repeat here, Your Honour, because people might snort or snicker. I refuse to expose to public mockery the three astonishing words Cosmo whispered to me that night upon awakening, but I whispered them back, the same three words, and they made my heart somersault in my chest.

I left at about five-thirty. It was unthinkable that Fiona should enter my bedroom, of a Sunday morning, and find it empty.

And here's what Cosmo told me, as we stood together in the doorway of the barn: First of all, he said, I'll watch your car pull out of the courtyard and disappear around the bend. Then I'll go upstairs, stand at the window and follow your every movement until sleep. I'll watch you park in front of your house, let yourself in with the key, grope for the light switch in the hallway, check on your sleeping children, then enter your bedroom and turn off your alarm clock and remove your clothes. Yes, for quite some time I'll watch you remove your clothes, over and over again. That will be marvellous. Where do you live?

I told him. He knew the house. This would assist him in his imaginings.

Before leaving, I touched his hair with my hand.

The Novelist

We've now learned a few things about the youth of Elke's parents — and youth, unfortunately for them but fortunately for the rest of our story, was the only period of life they'd get to know. It won't be as easy to get at the past of Cosmo's parents — if only because Josette, incensed by the fact that André committed suicide, has forbidden him to testify. So if you don't mind, Your Honour, I'd like to at least show you this document... a photo of André when, at the age of twenty-two, after six excruciating years in Paris, he returned defeated to his father's farm.

If you study the photo carefully, you can discern — rippling backwards instead of forwards in time — visual echos of Cosmo's own features, now famous the world over. Not innately attractive features — knobby nose and chin, slightly stick-out ears, high forehead...

The eyes, however, are not the same. Cosmo had his mother's eyes, hazel flecked with gold — whereas, as you can see, André's eyes are dark and soulful — baleful, one almost wants to say, like those of the cows he tended as a child.

There's something else in André's eyes though — something Cosmo *did* inherit. Pain. I don't know what else to call it.

The Cosmophile

Pain, yes. There's no other word for it. Pain was indeed the central theme of Cosmo's performances, no matter how much they made people laugh. Take, for instance, the skit he put together shortly after he turned sixteen, when the horrors of the events in Algeria were just beginning to hit the headlines... Two Muslims run into each other in the village square and launch into the usual litany of salutations:

You are well?

I am well, thanks be to God, I'm getting by.

And your father is well?

My father is dead, may his soul be with God.

And your mother? How has she been keeping, since yesterday?

Ah, my mother has also died, God rest her soul.

What about your wife? How is she?

Ah, my wife is dead as well.

And your children — are they in good health?

My children are also dead, their throats were slit last night, God rest their souls, God bless us all, and what about yourself, are you doing well?

I'm doing not too badly, thanks be to God.

And what about your father?

Oh, my father is dead...

Latifa

Speaking of Algeria, I wanted to say... if my turn has come...

The Novelist

No, Latifa, not yet. You don't come into the story until much later on.

The Lebanese Cedar

With your permission, Your Honour, I'd like to evoke something which, on the contrary, dates back to long *before* the events we're currently describing, yet partially determined the course these events were to take. I'm referring to the fact that as a young man, Cosmo's father André had a mystical passion for trees. Almost no one is aware of this, and I was afraid that if I didn't mention it now, it might get left out of the story altogether.

As of his earliest childhood, André belonged to that breed so rare as to be almost a contradiction in terms, the pastoral peasant. As a rule, peasants do not spend their time gazing at the landscape or singing its praises; they're out there working in it from dawn to dusk. The squabbling of city folk over thirty-five- and forty-hour workweeks makes them scratch their heads in perplexity; they work without clocks and sleep without dreams; they can't contemplate a field without thinking of all the work that remains to be done in it; and if at day's end they glance up at the sky, it's less to admire the sunset than speculate about tomorrow's weather. The aesthetic sense can't flourish in a body numbed by back-breaking labour.

André was an exception to this timeless law. Somehow, the

resigned, repetitive genes of his peasant ancestors, leap-frogging in unpredictable permutations from one life to the next, had wound up producing *this* dice toss: Dédé. Even as a toddler, he'd felt a secret kinship with flowers and insects; far from singeing slugs or dissecting frogs in the manner of Elke's despicable son, he observed their precise and enigmatic behaviours, each species its own, sketched them in the margins of his notebooks and remembered them in his evening prayers. He questioned his father and uncles about them — but all the response he got was, on good days, gibes and jeers, and on bad, blows to the head.

He confided all of this to me.

When he got to be about sixteen, André's physical passion for nature became metaphysical. It grew so powerful that the young man could no longer contain it. He sensed that this life of mud, sweat and livestock could not possibly be the only one there was, and that improbable as it might seem, *he*, little Dédé, had a higher calling. The calling was quite literally a *call* — the call of the unknown. And so it was that one dark night, his pockets empty but his heart full to bursting, he fled his father's farm and hitchhiked his way north to the capital. He knew in advance that Paris would make him feel puny and insignificant, but that didn't matter; he needed time and solitude for thinking — both of which were permanently lacking on the farm. He was small, slender and unprepossessing; uniforms looked good on him, and for five years he managed to find jobs as waiter, groom or bellhop in hotels and restaurants. His nights were his own.

He spoke to no one, shared his dreams with no one. Weather permitting, when he got off work, he'd sacrifice his supper to buy a suburban train ticket, travel out to one of the great forests beyond the city limits, and spend long hours, sometimes the whole night, walking and talking aloud to himself in a state of euphoria verging on exaltation. It was there, in the forests, especially when the moon was full or nearly full, that he could hear his *calling* most clearly; he'd be stirred as if by the summons of a disincarnate voice. The branches of the great oak, elm and chestnut trees would appear to him as twisted silent exclamations of glory, arms raised up to the sky in praise. At such moments, the whole universe would seem to move before his staring eyes: not only the trees and grasses, but the very clouds would simmer, tremble and flow silently towards the sky, as if in the throes of ecstasy. Sometimes he would be moved to tears by the ineffable beauty that thus expressed itself to him and through him — yes, for not only was he a witness to the incredible epiphany of nature, he was responsible for conveying it to the rest of the world. As he stood there in the moon's white gleam, enraptured lover of the trees, his being intimately entwined with theirs, his blood their sap, his arms their branches, his legs their roots, the throbbing awareness of life's beauty grew so acute as to become painful. How could other people not feel what *he* so imperiously felt, namely that they were part of the mystery, and that instead of flitting from one petty occupation to the next, treading on each other's feet, distracting themselves with quibble and gossip and grab, they should fall down on their knees...? Compared with the poignant silence of the moonlit trees, human commerce sounded to André like so much barnyard ruckus. Often, approaching a tree in the dark and slipping his arms around its trunk, he would fairly cry out in gratitude and anguish at the immensity of the task incumbent upon him.

One winter's afternoon, he arrived at the Botanical Gardens just as the sun was about to set, and concealed himself in the bushes when the park gates closed. For long hours, he sat patiently in the icy cold waiting for the moon to rise, and then he came to my side and lent an ear to my shadowy whisperings. He'd had nothing to eat since breakfast, and may have had a spell of dizziness — for whatever reason, the grandiose spectacle of the Labyrinth in the moonlight, the black lace of bare branches silhouetted against the sky, the mysterious rustlings of the Gardens, the calm, majestic grandeur of the night — all this crystallized into a strange, powerful vision — so powerful that he was overcome and fell into a faint.

He was found half frozen to death the next morning and rushed to the nearby Salpêtrière Hospital. He awoke delirious and was kept under observation for several days. This, Your Honour, was his first psychiatric internment... and not his last.

Some twenty years later, the new dice toss named Charles Philippe, better known as Cosmo, would inherit not only his father's bone structure but this other thing as well — the terrible, unquenchable thirst for the absolute.

Second Day

Elke

I didn't know André as a young man, Your Honour. With some people, it's hard to believe they were once young. Walking past him in the streets — a small, tense, wild-eyed man, forever muttering under his breath — it was impossible to guess that he'd once aspired to being a spiritual guide...

But to return to my story. After having laid my hand on Cosmo's hair at five-thirty in the morning, in the courtyard where the cool dew was already rising, I got into my car and drove slowly away, keeping him framed in my rear-view mirror as long as possible. He stood there motionless, not waving, and I took a mental photo of his body thus silhouetted against the brightly lit wall of the barn — a photo which, as you can see, I've kept to this very day... Then, as the dirt road described a curve and Cosmo moved out of the frame, my rear-view mirror faded into blackness, the way a movie screen does at the end of a film. That particular episode had ended. I advanced along the thin ribbon of road towards the village, along the thin ribbon of time towards the next episode — my arrival home, where Cosmo had promised to be with me. His words paved the way for my gestures: I did everything just as he had said I would; letting myself in with the key, groping for the light switch, checking on my sleeping children, turning off the alarm clock... Then I took off my clothes and — believe it or not, Your Honour — the mere thought of Cosmo's eyes on my naked body sparked off my first orgasm in three years.

Frank and Fiona
Mama!!!

Elke
I've sworn to tell the truth, my little ones, and I intend to do so because to me Cosmo's truth is the sun itself. Day after day, it brings me light and warmth.

Josette
I cannot let this woman go on talking as if my son's death had not occurred, or as if it were of no importance — a minor detail! Philippe is *dead*, do you hear me? My only son is *dead!* He was *murdered!* He no longer *exists!*

Fiona
You must be wondering, Your Honour, why Josette insists on calling her son Philippe.

It's a funny story. Cosmo was born in 1943 and his family was a miniature France unto itself; his father supported Charles de Gaulle, whereas his mother had a weakness for Philippe Pétain, so they named their son Charles Philippe. Without a hyphen, you understand. It was less a sequence than an alternative, the idea being that they would opt for one or the other only when the outcome of the war was known. Eventually, Charles won out. But when the boy himself learned about

this, applying for a passport some sixteen years later, he figured that if his parents hadn't even been able to agree on a
name for their only child, he'd just as soon choose one for
himself. Cosmo, he told me once, was his favourite character
in *Singin' in the Rain* — not Gene Kelly, the other one,
remember? Donald O'Connor — the one who sings "Make 'Em
Laugh" and keeps falling off the couch and dancing with a
broom and running up the wall...

Elke

I'm crawling at top speed through a tunnel at the river's edge,
the tunnel is bright white with openings everywhere, like lacy
limestone, it's almost impossible to make headway, sometimes
the tunnel gets so narrow that I can scarcely squeeze my way
through but I must advance, I must. Gasping and frantic,
inching forward on my stomach, I emerge at last into a sort of
cave. It, too, is white and brightly lit, and the ceiling is so low
that my head almost hits it when I get to my feet. Glancing to
my left, I see something burning at the centre of the cave — I
rush to put out the fire but it's no use, it's spreading, the light
is brightening and blinding me, burning my face — and now,
off in the distance, I begin to hear explosions and detonations
— oh my God, I think, the whole thing is going to collapse...

No. It was only the sun. Sunlight streaming into my face —
and the sound of television coming from down the hall. Little
by little, I realize it's Sunday morning, the sun is already high
in the sky and Frank is watching cartoons... But *what was
burning in that tunnel?*

Pulling the covers up over my head and closing my eyes, I try to slip back into the dream but church bells from across the street begin to peal and I lose the thread. Ariadne's thread is lost forever, the one that led to the core of my being, to the cavern and the terrifying fire. Still reluctant to begin the day, I lie there balking, clinging to the warmth of my yellow sheets and the memory of the night before. When Michael and I were still married, Sunday mornings were a choice time for love: half asleep, we were still mostly bodies and not yet on our guards, we could roll about in the sheer joy of skin, muscles and hormones without conjuring up citations from the quarrels of the previous day or whetting our tongues for those of the day to come. Three thousand days and nights I had spent with that man — and now, having recovered his precious solitude, he lived in the mountains several hundred miles away and communicated with me only through alimony cheques.

Was it *possible* I'd stroked that face so often? Had I really stared at it close up, close up, close enough to count its individual whiskers? Ah the tensing, the gradual hardening of those handsome, rugged features, the setting of that chiselled jaw in rage... No, this was not what I'd planned to think about when I snuggled back between my yellow sheets — not the slow despair that sluiced through my soul as the months went by and Michael withdrew from all of us. *We're not living together anymore,* I told him once, *we're dying together.* Sometimes — in a chance meeting of the eyes, never in words — we'd wonder what ever had become of the lightness and playfulness of our first years of marriage — and then, turning away, we'd go on guzzling tension as if it were water and we were dying of thirst... But other times, of a Sunday morning, we'd forget who we were, forget we had a checkered past and a dismal present and no future, lock our bedroom door and go at each other like raunchy teenagers. In the last couple of years, though, we stopped touching entirely. Between us, there was no love left to be made. Devoid of lust and even of hope, we lay side by side in bed like recumbent statues.

Divorce. Not easy to explain to a judge, in 1972. No adultery, no drinking, no violence, nothing but a relentless eking away of love — *this* cause for divorce was not in the lawbooks, not foreseen by the statutes.

Whence cometh this eking away? queried the judge, and I threw myself at his feet, thinking to elicit his compassion by the beauty of my long golden hair.

Please try to understand! I wept. It's a matter of snow and sunshine.

Especially sunshine, said Michael...

But no: turning over, I was again startled into wakefulness by the sun. I laughed out loud, remembering the long golden hair of my dream. My hair has never been golden, Your Honour. As you can see, it's dark, nearly black. I did use to wear it long, however: when I was little, my mother use to braid it for me every morning, and weave coloured threads into the braids, and tie velvet ribbons at the ends and kiss me on the nose when she was finished. But the women at the orphanage chopped my braids off the day I arrived and tossed them into the fire; I've worn my hair short ever since.

Sorry about that, Your Honour.

It's hard for me to know what's relevant and what's not.

Fiona

So anyway, that Sunday morning I walked into my mother's bedroom and saw this new gleam in her eyes. Though I didn't yet know where it came from, I had a feeling it didn't augur well for Frank and me. I was wearing a dark blue nightgown, I had my black panther tucked under one arm and as I wriggled in between the sheets I knew exactly what was going on in my mother's mind; she was thinking about my father and saying to herself *This person, this size, this day — how can Michael live without it?* That got on my nerves so I purposely stuck my icy feet between her thighs.

She jerked away with a squeal — and then, taking my feet in her hands and rubbing them, she said, So how's my little black panther this morning?

She's in a bad mood, I said.

Oh? she said. What's wrong?

I don't know, I said.

Here, she said. Let Mama panther lick your head... Does that feel better? Shall we go off to India and hunt us up some antelope?

But I didn't answer her because she was trying too hard to seem normal and I could tell she wasn't and it bugged me. Finally I said, I don't want to keep you from thinking about when *you* were little.

And she said, When I was a little panther, you mean?

And I said, No, when you were a little girl.

She stared at me in amazement and I could tell I'd gone and enchanted her once again, given her yet another pearl of wisdom for her collection. I have to tell you, Your Honour, that this is what bugs Frank and me the most about our mother. She's forever taking mental photos of us or recording what we say on her mental tape recorder, so as to be able to sigh at the beauty of her memories later on. That kind of thing can drive you nuts, you know? You're never allowed to just *exist*, you have to be constantly marvelling at the *fact* of your existence. That's why Frank and I have invented lots of ways of *just existing*, without thoughts or anything else. As I told you at the beginning, Mama claims that people can't exist in and of themselves, they're a patchwork of everything they've seen and done, their heads are teeming with the words and sentences they've heard and read over the years, and personally I can't stand this idea, *I want to be alone* but according to Mama you can't be alone, you can't even think the word *alone* alone because it's a word and people can't invent language for themselves; even to use the word *I* you have to belong to an ancient civilization. She says we're like planets hurtling through space, reflecting and absorbing each other's light, colliding and interacting, whether we like it or not, we're bits of matter swinging through time and being continually transformed, and the only difference between us and other bits of matter is that we're aware of our voyage, amazed by it, eager to describe it to each other, turn it into a story, a history — you tell me your story and I'll tell you mine, your story becomes a part of mine, you become a part of me and I of you, what you've told me enters into me and mingles with what I am as intimately as language itself, and though language doesn't belong to me, I wouldn't be myself and indeed would be nothing without it; it has come down to me from zillions of people in a chain or rather a dense network of chains going back to the darkest mists of prehistory. Thus, Mama says, second by second and century by century, from cavemen to cosmonauts, human words, ideas and stories have been circulating on Earth, and all of this is the food with which we make our minds, just as we make our bodies with the milk we drink and to be a person, Mama says, is to be a part of this ceaseless, mind-boggling circulation of words, ideas and stories that began eons before our birth and will end only when the sun burns itself out, or when we finally manage to smash our precious green-and-blue planet into a thousand new, minuscule, language-less ones.

I say no. I say that even if our brains are usurped by other people, our bodies are our own — and the proof is that when you die, no one dies but you, and when you're in pain, you're the only one who suffers; no one else can feel my pain but me. Not only that, but the mind is vague and fuzzy, it's hard to say exactly where it begins and ends — whereas the body is an object, a real thing, it has limits you can see and touch, which is reassuring. Mama says that when her parents died and she was taken to the orphanage and separated from her brothers, it was like being on the edge of a void, so she used to sing to herself in the dormitory at night, she'd pull the covers up over her head and try to remember *all* the songs her mother Yvette used to sing, stringing them along one after the other without a break, verse and chorus, verse and chorus, weaving them into a net of sound to stretch over the void so she couldn't fall into it — the songs held hands like the paper dolls in her bedroom when she was little, maybe people who talk to themselves in the street are doing the same thing, trying to keep the void at bay, but Frank and I are just the opposite, we *cherish* silence, we *yearn* for the void, we *long* to turn our backs on language once and for all because it doesn't belong to us, it's always other people talking in our heads, so we hurt each other on purpose to make sure that nobody else inhabits our bodies.

When Mama goes off to work at *La Fontaine*, she leaves us alone at home. She says she'd never do that if we lived in a city but there's no danger here, just as long as we don't play with matches or stick our fingers into light plugs. It makes us laugh, the way she goes off to work thinking we're safe whereas we're just itching for her to leave so we can put ourselves at risk. We start with easy stuff. I sit on the kitchen floor, Frank climbs up on the table next to me, he grabs a handful of my hair and slowly, very slowly, pulls me up — the idea is to see how far we can go, someday he'll be able to hold me completely by my hair, the whole weight of my body, and I'll be proud as pie. Then we go down into the garden behind the house. Frank sits on the bottom step of the stone staircase, I pick up a rock and tap him on the head with it, always in the same place, gently at first, then harder and harder. The idea is to give him as big a lump as possible without drawing blood. Frank grasps my wrist, he twists my arm behind my back and begins to pull it

up towards my shoulderblade. He is utterly unsmiling, con-
centrated and controlled, and so am I. I try to feel my pain as
accurately as I can, entering it and becoming one with it and
erasing all the *me* that might still exist around the edges. Frank's
effort is steady and continuous, not jerky, my wrist goes a little
higher every time and if he breaks my arm someday it will be
a victory. Then, taking a cigarette from the visitors' box Mama
keeps in the living room, I light it and start burning Frank. I
burn him in the armpits because the skin is more sensitive
there, and also because the scabs and blisters are easier to
hide. Frank enters into the burning and when he doesn't want
it to go any deeper, he nods briefly and I stop. Each of us stops
the minute the other nods, but we never talk during the game,
that's one of the rules, you're not allowed to say a single word.
You can cry out if you want to — cries aren't words — but
even that doesn't happen often; Papa says animals don't cry
out when they fall into one of his traps. Sometimes just a yelp
of surprise and that's it.

Eyes of stone, body of stone, heart of stone — this is our secret
motto, our highest goal.

Elke

I knew nothing of any of this, Your Honour. I admit it rather
takes my breath away.

So these things were. They happened. Nothing I can do
can make them not have happened...

Let me go on...

It was already eleven o'clock, that Sunday morning, and I

had to hurry if I wanted to get to the market before closing time, so I gulped down some coffee and dashed out of the house. In the covered marketplace, even as I ambled past poultry and pork butcher stalls, registering the limp guinea fowls hanging from their claws, the pigs presented as head cheese, blood sausage, jellied ears and feet, I was also back in Cosmo's barn, comfortably seated in his red velvet armchair and contemplating his face in slumber. *I've seen him sleep!* I said to myself, and the memory of that line of teeth beyond his upper lip made my heart leap for joy; because of it, I greeted the baker rather more warmly than usual.

Hunched over long, low Formica tables, peasant women were packing away their unsold cylinders and pyramids of goat's cheese. I looked at them. Even those that were my own age looked like old women: their bodies were concealed by shapeless dresses and men's jackets, despite the fine weather they'd donned woollen hats and rubber boots, their hair was greyed and thinning, their cheeks ungraced by makeup, their skin puckered and worn with worry. I didn't want to watch their cold red fingers counting up the meagre earnings of the day — I wanted to hear people talking about Cosmo.

Was his voice still ringing in their ears? Were their brains still crackling with his verbal fireworks? I longed to follow Cosmo's caustic humour as it spread through people's minds in successive waves, being deformed and diluted, forming new currents in new rivers — *transforming these individuals* even now, however infinitesimally. Inside of me, his love was like a newly planted seed that would swell and ramify — it made me feel invincible, almost insolent, the way pregnancy does. In my insolence, I purchased the first avocados and strawberries of the season. Though I knew full well they'd be disappointing — the avocados were stone-hard, the strawberries pale and thin — I needed some small symbol of my elation to take home and share with the children.

Over lunch, over the indeed inedible avocados and strawberries, I did my best to interest Frank and Fiona in the events of the night before at *La Fontaine*; I described the suspense of waiting for Cosmo, the hubbub of his arrival, the off-key rendition of "Happy Birthday," the mayor's stultifying speech... but my words fell flat, failing to turn into things; the children remained distracted and unresponsive. Fiona kept staring out the window and playing with her hair while Frank chewed on bread crusts, waiting ostentatiously for the meal to end. I was crestfallen. For some reason, the warm hum was missing — the thing I call the warm hum, Your Honour, and which has to do not with sound and silence but with the lapping and overlapping of presences in a room. Sitting there in the kitchen, we were three people alone. Despite the sunlight pouring in the window, I felt a shadow fall over the table and thicken there. The silence grew ghastly. I didn't remember there being ghastly silences at meals when I was a child — despite the fact that, like Michael now, my own father had been perpetually absent... Had Yvette sometimes stared at my two brothers and myself, feeling us to be a dead weight on her soul?

Whatever became of last night's jubilation? I wondered. *How can I share it with my children if they don't want it?* Parents have no control, Your Honour, over what goes on in their children's heads. No matter how much we love them, we can't keep them company there. The minute they rip screaming from the bloody passageway, the estrangement begins: we give them words and they build their own thoughts with them, just as we give them food and they build their own bodies...

I seem to have wandered off the track again.

Frank

Later that day, the doorbell rang and I went to answer it.

It was a stranger. Blond. Several years younger than our mother. I took a dislike to Cosmo the minute I set eyes on him. He asked if Elke was at home and as I showed him into the living room where she was waiting, I saw her hastily smooth her hair in front of a mirror, the way women do in movies — you know what I mean? — when the man they love arrives unannounced. I got the picture. I threw stones at her with my eyes. Unfazed, she led her young blond man through the kitchen where Fiona was snacking and murmured introductions — but Fiona did't so much as glance up from her Nutella sandwich. I've trained my little sister well.

Mama was worried — would her blond beau still love her, oh dear, oh dear, would he still love her? Rigged out with a glowering son and a listless daughter, was she still the same woman she had been the night before?

They went out to sit on the back steps and, even as I pretended to be watching TV, I listened in on their conversation. They were still in the expository phase. Mama was telling

Cosmo about the fifteen years she'd spent with the Marceaus, her foster family, in a village not far from here. That story, too, Your Honour, I know by heart.

The inordinate number of foster families in this part of the country does not mean that people are more charitable or generous here than elsewhere, it only means that they are poorer, and foster children help them make ends meet. Especially during the war, every penny counted: even the miserable pension of five hundred old francs a month made a difference, to say nothing of the help with farm and house work... The Marceaus treated Elke — who had a different name at the time — like one of their own children, which is to say firmly and unsentimentally.

The family had been tenants on the same farm, father to son, since the beginning of the century. A stoical lot they were; the older generations worked themselves to the bone, and the children prepared to take their place. The men were out in the fields all day, alone with the beasts of burden and akin to them by their silence and grim resignation to their fate; at nightfall, having no strength left with which to produce words, they'd toss back a few glasses of pastis, shovel a plateful of stew into their mouths and lurch off to bed. Thus, in this household as in countless others like it, the women controlled not only the purse strings but the conversation.

As Elke was soon to learn, the tenets by which they lived were few and unshakeable: God and church are twaddle, there's no such thing as life after death, life on Earth is all there is and the meaning and essence of that life is work. You have to earn your living by the sweat of your brow, every penny counts, that's all there is to it. (A good half of their sentences ended with *that's all there is to it*.) Thus, the young orphan from Paris rolled up her sleeves and set to work. She learned to kill and pluck chickens, milk cows, stitch quilts and stuff them with goose feathers; when July came around, she even lent a hand with the haying. She wasn't miserable — nonplussed, rather, by the pragmatic taciturnity of these people. As the Lebanese cedar pointed out a while ago, peasants rarely have the luxury of being moved by a landscape. Having been raised in the capital, Elke had a true passion for nature, inherited from her mother and enhanced by her readings in nineteenth-century literature.

Yes, Your Honour: our mother loved this countryside as thoroughly as our father detested it. She loved everything about it. The swooping swallows in June, the great leaps of fish in the ponds, the barnyard buzzing with insects and slithering with lizards, the repetitive night music of frogs and crickets, the full, sensuous evenings of late summer, the shimmering of silver poplars in the wind, the great conferences of crows in November, the ice which, every four or five years in mid-winter, would coat each tiniest twig, each blade of grass, and turn the world into a glistening fairyland. More than anything else, she loved the acceleration of change in late October: the cranes winging southward, the sudden yellowing of ferns and reddening of sorbs, the distinctive knock of chestnuts as they fell and hit the ground, the smell of ripening pears, the taste of freshly pressed apple juice, the artistic patterns of orange and green on a dozen varieties of squash, the satisfying squelch of rubber boots in the mud...

The little girl was troubled by the aesthetic indifference of her foster family. The Marceaus *saw* the same things as she did, of course, but somehow these things had no impact on their souls. Worse, they couldn't hear *words*. In their view, just as the land was something to be used for eking out a subsistence, language was for the communication of facts, *that's all there was to it*. One day Elke tried to convince them that lilypad was a beautiful word, and they shrugged her off impatiently — Lilypads are a nuisance, they told her; in the first place they attract frogs; in the second place they clog up the surface of the ponds and prevent the fish from getting enough oxygen; therefore they must be gotten rid of.

They had this frightening way of sticking to facts... Elke couldn't understand it. Everything her whimsical young mother had taught her to love at the beginning of her life — contemplation, reverie, meditation — was dismissed by them as religion in disguise. The same went for reading: novels were a waste of time because they described a world that didn't exist and took your mind off your *real problems*. Now, to ordinary mortals, problems are the unexpected syncopation of life; but for these people who have lost God and found nothing to take his place they are its essence, its substance, its overriding theme. Problems can be major or minor, potential or real, our own or other people's; they are blows and losses, bad weather, the diseases and deaths of human beings, animals and crops; they are endlessly discussed, dreaded, and dreamed about at night, they can be held at bay temporarily but sooner or later they will hit you, and when they do, you feel something akin to relief, because they are what gives meaning to your existence.

Listening to people like this, Your Honour, you wonder what it would take for them to feel happy, to rejoice in the way things are going. But as time goes by, you come to see they don't actually wish for happiness or success; they've been identifying with their hardships for so long that were the latter suddenly to vanish, they'd be at a loss; they wouldn't know what to talk about, what to think about, *whom to be*. In a word, their lives would lose all interest for them. As much as the local climate, it was this philosophy that depressed my father and eventually drove him away, so it's only natural that I've given considerable thought to the matter. The key word of this philosophy is... *Beware.*

Elke

You yourself should beware, Your Honour. Michael's departure was a shock to the children — and ever since, being unable to embrace their father, they've chosen to embrace his prejudices and obsessions. It was all he left them — I could hardly deprive them of that, too! Thus, without actually lying, they tend to exaggerate the defects of the local population, and you should take everything they say with a grain of salt. Contrary to what Fiona claimed at the outset, the customers of *La Fontaine* do *not* spend all their time griping — and despite Frank's disparaging description of them, my foster mother and grandmother were *not* devoid of kindness and sensitivity.

Fiona

No, my brother is right — the basic principle of life in these parts is *trust no one*.

The minute a child learns to talk, its parents teach it to be apprehensive and diffident. Be on your best behaviour at all times, never draw attention to yourself, never show the slightest sign of mental or physical discomfort, never hint that you might need other people or be curious about their lives. Other people are *none of your business*. In order for no one to owe anyone anything, it's best that *nothing ever happen*, that no exchange of any kind take place among human beings. If someone gives you a gift, mutter *you shouldn't have* and stash it at once — whatever you do, don't open it in front of them, or they might see how happy it makes you and you'd be indebted to them. No one can predict the future — if you love your husband too overtly, or smother your child with kisses, or throw a party to celebrate a bounty crop, the source of your joy might suddenly dry up — and then wouldn't you look stupid?

Virtue, to these people, consists of proving that they *work much* and *earn little*. So when Elke met and fell in love with Michael, her foster family disapproved of him — not, as you might think, because he was a foreigner, but because he *worked little* and *earned much*. A photographer! They couldn't fathom such a thing. Who would be silly enough to *pay*, and *good money* at that, for *photographs* of *animals?* Each separate word of this sentence elicited their stupefaction.

At age twenty-one, Elke was still in love with Michael, but she was no longer a minor. On the very day a foster child comes of age, the Department of Health and Social Service cuts off its funds and the foster family's responsibility comes to an end. Overnight, the child becomes an adult; he has to make his own decisions and suffer the consequences, *that's all there is to it.* So from now on, the Marceaus told themselves, Elke's choices and preferences are none of our business. She wants to marry an animal photographer? Let her marry him! She'll find out soon enough what life is all about.

Frank

Naturally, in telling Cosmo about her foster family that day, our mother didn't give him as many details as we've just given you. Cosmo was a son of the land; his own grandfather was a tenant farmer; he was well acquainted with the local psychology. But I'm not sure that *you're* that familiar with it, Your Honour. Indeed, this character type is something of a rarity nowadays. Whereas local behaviour managed to eschew evolution for several hundred years, in the final decades of the twentieth century a number of factors finally succeeded in shaking it up — the massive arrival of TV sets broadcasting images from all over the world, the draining of the rural population towards the cities, the regrouping of lands, the buying up of farms by wealthy Dutchmen, Germans and Belgians, the whim of increasing numbers of Parisians to refurbish ancient farmhouses and use them as summer homes, not to mention swarms of ex-hippies returning to nature to strum their guitars and make honey or raise goats.

What about Cosmo? you must be wondering. Surely he can't

have remained silent all this time — he, too, must have conveyed some basic information about himself. Just what did he tell this woman whom he planned to seduce, and who was already staring at him with stars in her eyes? Don't worry, Your Honour — Cosmo's words, too, are indelibly engraved in my memory.

You mustn't think that I lead an exciting life, he told her. You'd be appalled at the amount of emptiness it contains. An incalculable amount. A shameful amount. Hours wasted in travelling, pacing the waiting rooms of airports between planes, or train stations between trains, watching asinine TV shows in tacky hotel rooms, lying awake at night, signing autographs for uninteresting people, answering the same stupid questions from journalists over and over again, smiling when you haven't the least inclination to smile...

Good heavens, said Mama, taken aback by this unexpectedly dark picture of the artist's life. Why do you do it, then?

Why? said Cosmo. Isn't it obvious? I do it for the rare moments when I'm onstage. And even those moments are preceded by hours of tedium with my crew — those kind, gregarious devoted talented burdensome individuals who are constantly flitting and floating around me, bending and straightening, preparing the set, sending each other signals, setting up lights and mikes, checking each last detail of my makeup and costume...

But then they glide away, melt into the darkness... Everything is ready at last... and *it's now*. Suddenly the universe closes in around me. I'm alone in the light. Nothing else exists. My every blink and twitch and murmur is saturated with meaning. I live for those moments, Elke. And, starting today, for you.

Thus spake the fornicating clown.

And then he split.

Elke

As of the very next day, the telephone rang and it was Cosmo.

The Psychiatric Expert

If I may, Your Honour, I'd like to point out the frequency with which the star witness uses the root word *tête*, far off. At first she said she knew Cosmo only through the intermediary of *television*; now she will get to know him over the *telephone* — the important thing being that their love be kept at a distance, that it virtually never undergo a reality test.

Elke

Reality, reality — the man sounds just like my foster mother and grandmother! And what, may I ask, is reality? The married life *those* women had? Or that of André and Josette — who, torn from their sleep by an alarm clock every morning for forty-four years, got up and went about their respective business without exchanging a word or a glance?

Listen to me.

The voice I heard when Cosmo spoke to me over the telephone was Cosmo's real voice. Had he been in the room with me at the time, and had I had my eyes closed... and even now, when my eyes are closed... do you understand?

So let me go on.

He was at Orly, about to take off for Lausanne, and he was calling me because he'd seen the strangest couple in the airport shuttle. The man in his fifties, the woman fortyish. Were they lovers? Husband and wife? Actress and impresario? He couldn't figure it out. Both were dressed with an ostentatious, almost aggressive elegance. As they took their seats, the man reached out a hand to prevent the woman's skirt from getting bunched up, and she said in a loud voice, as if to be sure that everyone in the bus would hear, No no, it's all right. If I leaned back in my seat it would get crushed, but this way it's all right. Fortunately, I never lean back in my seat. Those were her exact words, Elke, I swear it, said Cosmo. *Fortunately, I never lean back in my seat.* I looked at them more closely, he added, and saw that they were wearing nothing but the best suede and cashmere in shades of cream and tan... And yet there was something unrefined, almost vulgar, in their appearance. They began discussing her skirt. Yes, I know, she snarled, it *looks* nice, but the material wasn't worked on enough. Given what I paid for it, it should be better than it is. And then she added, in the same brassy tone of voice: I don't know why, but I feel like singing "Bandiera Rossa." What's that? the man asked politely. And on the spot, the woman launched into the famous refrain — *Avanti populo, tralala la la la, Bandiera rossa, Bandiera rossa!* That's all I know, she wound up ruefully. You should learn the words; it would be fun to sing it together. I don't speak Italian, said the man. Well, you should *learn* Italian, said the woman. It's not that hard! Lapsing into silence, she spent a long while scrutinizing her beige gloves; when she spoke again, it was to inform him (as well as every other passenger in the shuttle) that her chewing gum had been conceived especially for cleaning teeth after meals. It has *nothing* to do, she insisted, with the stupid, ordinary, run-of-the-mill chewing gum I used to quit smoking. The man listened and nodded, reaching out a hand every now and then to smooth the material of her coat or straighten the hem of her skirt.

The Cosmophile

Within a few months, this would become the famous *Cream and Tan* dialogue — an expanded, exaggerated version of that improbable scene in the shuttle bus — and thousands of people would be rocking in their seats, weeping with laughter as they watched Cosmo smooth his skirt, touch up his rouge, and belt out a nouveau-riche rendition of "Bandiera Rossa."

Unfortunately, there is no known audio or video recording of this number. However, I do have in my possession an amateur film shot in 1965, showing part of a rehearsal for one of the artist's first shows. It's only a few minutes long — and if you agree, Your Honour, I suggest that we view it at once. Lights, please... Thank you.

Here we go. He's twenty-two years old. As you can see, he's in clownface — his neck, face and hands thickly plastered with white makeup. His air of terrified surprise is due partly to his eyebrows — two inverted Vs painted in black on his brow — and partly to his hair, which sticks up in Brylcreemed tufts all over his head. He's talking about love. It was a number he would keep coming back to in the course of his career, revising it according to the political and social dramas of the day — a number which grew darker with every passing year.

Despite the film's technical shortcomings, Cosmo is already there in all his glory. His body is thin, wiry, almost spidery, dressed in a leotard of the same bright white as his makeup. Through the elastic material of his costume, you can see his every muscle and tendon; you can practically make out the individual veins. It's as if, somehow, he were not only nude but the very quintessence of nudity — as if you could see far inside his body, all the way to the core, to the image we each have of ourselves, before determinations of sex, class, race or age come into play — a sort of quivering, electrified body-mind.

The film being silent, we have no way of knowing what the specific content of the number was in 1965, but the general idea never varied: for half an hour or so, Cosmo desperately strove to love humanity.

I am love incarnate, he would proclaim with an appalled look on his face. *I love everyone — just everyone!* And he would go on to show us some of the people — frightening by their very diversity — who were worthy of his love.

The film begins in the middle of the number and breaks off after four minutes with the image of Cosmo trying, clumsily yet persistently, to caress an enormous Mafioso bristling with guns. When I myself saw the show in the mid-1980s, he was trying to love a young American yuppie obsessed with the intricacies of the stock exchange, a Yemenite adolescent strung out on *das*, a fat businessman who farted at meetings and had a weakness for four-hundred-dollar ties, a jittery schoolteacher who picked his nose and humiliated his pupils in class for the pleasure of watching them squirm, a psychoanalyst speechifying in an impenetrable jargon and collecting new diplomas and degrees... *Wonderful, wonderful people*, murmured Cosmo, aghast. I also recall the young guard at the Chinese-Pakistani border who, at age nineteen, had already learned never to smile, flinch or meet anybody's gaze... It was impressive, Your Honour, to watch Cosmo breathe life into this icy-eyed, lock-jawed youngster, just as he breathed life into all of his characters... Then, resuming his appalled-clown expression, he would cry out, *Ah, what an endearing species! I certainly do love mankind!*

The spectators, wary at first (yes, always preferring to start off with skepticism), gradually allowed Cosmo to pick them up and carry them away, taking them hither and thither, all over the world; by the end they were forced to acknowledge not only that these individuals existed, but that they knew them well... It was impossible not to laugh at the expression of this poor, stupefied God arriving in the midst of his creation for the first time, and running into all these atrocious samples of the species he had sworn to love...

Sandrine

That's it, exactly! I attended his thirtieth-birthday performance, and let me tell you, it was something to see, the way the audience silently left the ground ten or fifteen minutes after the curtain went up. Little by little, people relaxed; ceasing to be themselves (for as *themselves* they would have found the content of the performance reprehensible), they slid surreptitiously into the actor's skin. Once there, safe in the anonymity of the darkened theatre, they gave themselves up to Cosmo, drank in the light of his features and adhered to his every word and gesture, for he gave them a fabulous freedom — one they knew from their dreams at night but to which none of them dared lay claim in their daily lives. The town mayor, for instance... or Cottereau, the notary public (Cosmo's own grandfather)... or Tabrant, the fat journalist who prided himself on being as nasty as his colleagues from Paris... Thanks to the straw-haired little man running around up there in the spotlight, they were able to recognize that ferocious, childlike part of themselves which they repressed the rest of the time.

You hold your breath. You leave humdrum reality behind and go floating up to a higher level of existence. You yearn to go higher still. You begin to laugh. The laughter rolls across the stage like a breaker, like machine-gun fire, and is instantly effaced. Silence is total. It is good. The spectators are open now, wide open, eyes, ears, hearts, souls agape, welcoming, eager to capture Cosmo's every blink and breath — they've given themselves up to him completely. Now the actor can play on the whole gamut of their emotions — he can take them with him to extremes of violence and beauty, in the absolute certainty that they will follow. It's an extraordinary form of power, Your Honour, to thus possess a group of people and make them not only consent to this possession but *wish for it* more than anything in the world, and that it should never end. The audience abdicates its will, putting itself in the actor's hands. And the actor, breaking through one barrier after another, gives of himself to an extravagant, an almost impossible degree: after three hours, you've seen him perform so many feats and undergo so many metamorphoses that you're no longer sure he's human; his sweat blinds you; his heart pounds in your chest, his blood courses through your veins. It's a thing of violence — like a bullfight, an orgy, a primitive ritual — and when you applaud, it's because you want to hit something as hard as you can so as to go on partaking of this violence, express this thing that has been rising within you and is now about to overflow, break through and overwhelm you, Cosmo has shattered the limits of your being, saved you, plunged you into molten gold and you no longer know what is happening, it's fabulous and fearful at the same time, something unspeakably intimate has been exchanged and you feel almost ill afterwards because you've let this perfect stranger fling you into bliss, a bliss you never allow yourself in real life — so what can your real life be worth if it precludes this gorgeous intensity, if you're more authentic as a spectator than as a person? The minute you leave the theatre, the communion between you and Cosmo will vanish because it involved neither the real *you* nor the real *him*, and you'll have to return to your polite normal petty mediocre existence, it makes your stomach heave to think of it, but in the meantime you go on applauding and shouting bravo! bravo! to postpone as long as possible the moment when the actor will leave the stage for good and the banal lights of reality will come up in the theatre.

Cosmo embodied freedom, Your Honour. It was as simple

as that. It made some people love him, others worship him, and still others... hate his guts.

Vera
I cannot remain silent any longer.

Josette
Oh, no! I don't believe it! What is *she* doing here?

Vera
I have the right to testify, Your Honour, because... I was... er... well acquainted with André, Cosmo's father.

Josette
Well acquainted! I must be dreaming! Well acquainted!

Vera
I have some important things to say, Josette, whether you like it or not. And since we've finally broached the most important topic, namely the character of the victim, it's important that one thing be made clear: *Cosmo inherited his vocation from his father.* Yes. André passed down to him the aching, imperious need to communicate with other people, shake them up, wake them up... A little while ago, the Lebanese cedar described André's religious fervour for trees, the discovery of his sacred mission in the forests of Chantilly and Fontainebleau... We have yet to learn, however, what brought his stay in Paris to an end.

André was desperately lonely. In the various hotels and

restaurants where he was employed, none of his co-workers seemed interested in his message of universal beauty and harmony. More and more frequently — even in full daylight sometimes, during working hours — he would be overcome with emotion and begin to rave and gesticulate, eventually falling into a faint. He explained to me later that he never actually lost his reason during these crises, but was temporarily unable to use it. A lengthy prostration would ensue, accompanied by violent headaches. The attacks worsened until he could no longer hold down a job. Eventually, unable even to pay the rent on his miserable attic room near the Saint-Lazare train station, he was forced to admit defeat. He went home in despair — a prodigal son received without a word, without a smile.

His failure to live up to his calling was a torture to him. He was devoured by guilt... And then one day he met Josette, the notary public's daughter, and fell in love with her. You might find it hard to believe looking at her now, Your Honour, but Josette was a lovely girl back then. And... in his innocence, you understand, André felt certain that the young woman's outward beauty, like that of the trees, denoted spiritual profundity.

Josette
How *dare* you...?

Vera
He spoke to me of this, Your Honour, on many occasions and at length.

When I first set eyes on Josette, he told me, I felt I had

always known her. I thought she would be for me what the forests had once been. A tiny flame in her pupils reminded me of the full moon at Fontainebleau, and it was like a sign between us. Dear God, I thought, she's *one of us!* The spiritual partner I've been waiting for all these years! With a companion like that at my side, I'll be able to carry out my mission at long last — she'll give me the strength and support I so sorely lacked in Paris.

His illusions didn't last long. Josette was blind and deaf to the cosmic messages that stirred her husband; her inner life was of much less importance to her than her interior.

Josette

Talk, you gypsy! Go ahead and talk! Everyone knows what a pigsty *you* live in!

Vera

I'm under oath like everyone else, Josette. I'm simply repeating, word for word, what my lover told me.

When I talk to her, he said, my words remain on the surface. I can see them sliding down her face and dripping to the ground. She doesn't know how to take them inside of her as the Lebanese cedar used to do. She tries to fool me by smiling, but I can tell she has understood nothing of my ideas...

It hurt him, Your Honour. But André was a good man. He was also — at least at the time, before the dreadful, criminal thing Josette did to him — the gentlest man in the world. Other people's pettiness always disconcerted him; he couldn't get used to it... Nor could he fathom that eyes as beautiful as

Josette's, hazel flecked with gold, could be the reflection of a narrow, materialistic mind... His marriage was a cruel disappointment to him.

Josette

For Heaven's sake, Your Honour, tell her to sit down! Her testimony is utterly *worthless!*

Vera

Still, he almost never complained. It was beneath him to criticize the woman he'd married. She's a good woman, he would say to me over and over again. She keeps the house as bright and clean as a new penny, she does everything a wife is supposed to do, I've got no reason to complain... It's not her fault if she isn't like the trees. I'm the one who misread the signs...

He couldn't forgive himself for having made this mistake. He felt even lonelier in his marriage than he had in his garret room in Paris.

But Charles Philippe. But Charles. Their only son. Perhaps little Charles would be able to decipher and transmit his precious message?

Yes of course I knew him, too. He came to my place with his father on several occasions... And as the years went by, hope was rekindled in André's heart.

Cosmo's career, Your Honour, can only be understood as homage to his father. Directly or indirectly, overtly or covertly, every one of his numbers was an attempt to redeem, rectify and repair the dreadful rent in André's soul.

Elke

Who can claim to know the origins of genius?

It's true that André had told Cosmo about his exalted nights at Fontainebleau and in the Botanical Gardens; he'd also told him about his migraine headaches and auras. To Cosmo as a child, these things were suffused with beauty and mystery... but also with danger. The air of urgency in my father's eyes, he told me once, impressed me at least as much as his words...

Now we can return to the story.

After Cosmo's Sunday visit to our home, more than three months went by before I saw him again. But he called often...

Frank

Mama didn't even seem to notice the incredible banality of the set-up: the man is active, the woman passive; the man is mobile, the woman inert; the man decides when and where they will meet; the woman is perpetually available... We were shocked, Your Honour — well, Fiona was still too little but *I* was shocked — to see our mother, who had always been a non-conformist, turn into a walking cliché.

Elke

Like André, Your Honour, I did everything in my power to pass my values on to my children; I have to admit that he did a better job of it than I did. But just now my children are beside the point — *you*'re the only one I care about convincing. Believe me, not for a single second did I suffer from Cosmo's absence — for the simple reason that *I never felt it.*

When we spoke over the phone, he was neither more nor less present than usual, and his voice heaped newness upon me. He described everything to me with great generosity — and, far from being inert, I travelled with him wherever he went. Staring out the windows of his hotel room in Marseille, I could see the blue and white boats in the harbour, and beyond that, orange-tiled roofs going up the hillside in a triangle and culminating in a baroque basilica. In Besançon, I accompanied him through a rainy, rushed, metallic day, a day of hitches and traffic jams, a day so awful that it became the very epitome of awfulness — and as such, he told me, almost pleasurable.

Once he called me at 9 a.m. from the airport waiting room in Geneva to tell me about a scene he'd just witnessed. At a table near his own, two men and a woman were drinking Coca-Cola and chain-smoking. The men were dressed in cheap black leather; the woman had bleach-blond hair and a leopard-patterned scarf; all three were under thirty, but there was something sleazy and depressing about them. They were travelling with two little boys, who tried to stave off boredom by running around the waiting room inventing games and contests, but the noise they made got on the grown-ups' nerves: Hey, will you guys siddown, for chrissake! Shuddup! How many times do we have to tell you?

Finally, said Cosmo, the woman strode across the waiting room, cigarette in hand, and without a word, slapped them across their heads as hard as she could. Then she went back and sat down with the men. So now the little boys are lying on the floor, screaming their heads off...

Thanks to Cosmo's ears, I could hear the wailing of the tiny martyrs of Geneva, victims of arbitrary maternal law; thanks to his eyes, I could see them reddening with rage, overcome by a sense of injustice, and feel a bitterness rising in their souls that might later incite them to torture a prostitute or batter their wives and children — and now you, too, can visualize the scene, can't you, Your Honour? You can see the young bleach-blond with her leopard-patterned scarf, her skinny legs coated in black leather, her cheap high-heeled boots... Wasted by the excesses of the previous night, her nerves frayed by the children's shouts and squeals, she gets up, stalks across the waiting room, and delivers a blow to each of their heads with the palm of her hand — purposely striking them on the ear. You can feel the shock of it in your own head, the waves of pain reverberating... That's all I'm trying to convey — this miracle which, because it forms the very warp and woof of our existence, generally goes unnoticed — *images that were in Cosmo's head are now in mine; part of his life has become part of my own...* and, now, of yours as well.

Throughout the summer he called me irregularly, unpredictably, sometimes in the middle of the night. It was never the wrong time to hear his voice. When Cosmo was on the line, I cradled the receiver as gently as if it were the curve of his head... For long minutes, I'd let his voice flow into me — soft, cracked, already so familiar. He bombarded me with questions, and grew impatient if my answers were too vague: he wanted *details*, as many details as possible. He wanted to know precisely where I was standing, what I could see of the garden and

the sky looking out the window, what Frank was up to, what
Fiona had said that morning, what the latest gossip was at *La
Fontaine*, how my friend Sandrine's pregnancy was going...

And so I searched for words, Your Honour, and found
them. Unstintingly, I offered up to Cosmo the sentences that
reflected my life of the moment. Our conversations could last
anywhere from thirty seconds to an hour. The long ones cost
him money — the equivalence of my day's earnings — but
when I expressed concern about this, Cosmo chided me. My
phone bills are none of your business, he said, and I felt a rush
of gratitude. Michael had been a frugal man; even around the
house, he'd treated language as if it were money, never to be
wasted or splurged, and over the phone he was terse to the
point of rudeness. Since our divorce, he'd called each of the
children only once, on their birthdays. The idea of spending a
whole hour on the phone to chatter about trifles... or, worse,
nothing at all... *Long distance silence...!* To be connected in the
air by an invisible network of wires and then sit there simply
listening to each other breathe... what a scandal!

Sometimes Cosmo would tell me that he was stroking my
cheek, or my back, or kissing my throat, or gently pushing
my hair away from my face and brushing my forehead with
his lips — and, listening to him, I would shiver and moan...
Other times, he'd ask me what I was wearing. I'd tell him the
truth, however unflattering — red wool sweater, blue jeans,
barmaid's uniform, old housecoat — and then his words
would come and fondle me through my clothes... Once, as I
lay curled up in bed at two in the morning with the receiver

delicately cradled between ear and shoulder, he asked if he might touch my breasts through the blue material of my nightgown and I answered, stifling a yawn, All right, but only for ten seconds.

My hands were his hands. His touch made me swoon.

Third Day

Elke

Did Frank and Fiona notice the change that came over me that summer? I was more attentive to them than I'd been in recent years...

Fiona

Attentive, she was. Attentive. Ha! Forgive me for laughing.

We missed our father, Your Honour. It was our first summer without him. The minute we woke up in the morning, we felt annihilated by his absence. He'd written in June promising to send us train fare to come and visit him, so we were jumpy. Every day we waited for the mailman; the weeks went by and there was never an envelope from our father. But he loved us, *I know he did*, I'll kill anyone who dares to say our father didn't love us.

Our exercises in pain grew more intense. We found some mousetraps and a fox trap in the basement and started playing with those, while Mama was off at *La Fontaine*. When the mousetrap first snaps shut on your index finger the pain is spectacular, it lights up your whole brain; I had to breathe hard through my nose to keep myself from moving; the impulse to shake it off your hand is almost overpowering. Then, in a soft, loving voice, Frank would describe the doe in papa's photograph and I'd do my best to imitate her, gazing up at him with a look of mute entreaty in my eyes.

Sometimes we'd ask Frank's friends from school to join us; we'd go down to the Arnon River after lunch and stay there till it got dark. Mama would leave sandwiches for us. Attentive, she was, ha ha. I was the only girl in the gang. I was six years old and they were ten, twelve, thirteen, but when push came to shove they were the ones who trembled in their boots. Inwardly, I was stronger than they were and they knew it; I was the strongest girl on Earth, a real Fury, I loved to feel the rage boiling up inside my chest and look at them and see how impressed they were. Nothing could stop me. Nothing. When we wrestled, I'd bite and scratch and pull their hair, it drove them wild, three or four of them would grab me and start banging my head against the rocks, I didn't care if they killed me, it was fine with me, nothing could have made me cry uncle. Then Frank would tell me to take off my clothes and I'd obey because I always obey my brother's orders; if he told me to kill myself I'd do that, too. So I'd be standing there naked in front of the boys but they didn't dare take off *their* clothes because they were ashamed of what they had between their legs, it was all puny and dangly and even on the rare occasions when it stiffened it didn't last, it wasn't a valid weapon yet, so usually they just took off their belts and tied me to a tree, and when I struggled to get away the leather would burn my skin and the buckles would dig into my flesh; *that* I loved, the idea that I was completely helpless because no matter what I did the boys would overcome me, their muscles were made of steel, their cruelty was without reason, without limit, without recourse. Then Frank would take out his pocket knife and let each of the boys threaten me with it; they'd come up to me one after the other, the blade flashing in the sun, and slide the sharp point slowly down my stomach, chest or throat, but in the end they gouged their initials into the bark of the tree I was tied to, right next to my eyes, and when at last they set me free I'd be panting, spent, ecstatic.

The Knife

It was like cutting into butter, Your Honour.

Oh, I'm sorry — it's not my turn yet? Ah, it must be because I heard the word *knife*, and I thought...

Do forgive me.

Fiona

One day when Frank and I were both feeling down because the mailman had come by again without a letter from Papa, Mama said, Hey, I've got an idea, it's a beautiful day, why don't we all go fishing?

We just sort of shrugged; before the divorce, it was always Papa who took Frank out fishing.

How about it? she said. Who says fishing is only for men? It can't be *that* hard. Come on, Frank, you can show us how! We've still got the gear; all we have to do is buy some worms.

She probably thought I'd be squeamish, make a face and take to my heels the minute it came to impaling the worms on a hook, so she tried to reassure me by telling me they didn't suffer at all, they didn't even have real brains to register pain with — but I calmly picked up the hook and got on with it; I was hauling in gudgeon within minutes. They jerked and flopped at the end of my line and I took great relish in the idea that I was going to eat them whether they liked it or not, they no longer had the right to swim freely and happily down the river because I had decided otherwise, I'd taken them out of the water and they were choking to death because they didn't have lungs for breathing air, and now I was going to rip their mouths apart by yanking out the fish-hook and then I'd toss them into the pail, where they'd all die together in a heap, just like the heap of dead Jews at Auschwitz we saw in a TV documentary once, I'd be as cold and pitiless as a Nazi officer, and then I'd fling them into boiling oil and grind them to mush with my teeth and gulp them down and turn them into me, me, *me!*

At noon, as we trekked homewards with our pail half full of dead gudgeon, we saw from a distance that there was someone on our front doorstep, and as we got closer it turned out to be Cosmo. He was sitting there with a bottle of wine between his feet, waiting for us.

It's that same man, I whispered to Mama.

She tripped on some invisible object in the road and all but fell flat on her face.

Well *that's* a surprise! she said, laughing, to make fun of herself.

Frank maintained a tight-lipped silence.

Catch any whales? asked Cosmo when we got close enough to hear him. Mama laughed again, but I don't like it when grown-ups try to get on my good side by making wise-cracks.

Share our lunch? asked Mama.

He eyed the pail and made a face.

Thanks. I just got up.

That I found interesting, because nobody gets up at twelve noon around here. Everyone takes pride in rising at the crack of dawn, I've never been able to figure out why.

Come on in, said Mama, and we all went in.

Cosmo sat down at the kitchen table and proceeded to do nothing. This, too, was unusual. He didn't say silly things like can I give you a hand; he didn't take out a pack of cigarettes; he didn't drum his fingers on the table; he didn't glance around for a newspaper — nothing. He just sat there. Meanwhile, Mama was running around getting lunch ready. Her eyes were as glittery as the silvery skins of the gudgeons she'd just slid into the sink and was now rinsing copiously with tap water. You could tell she was happy because she was humming under her breath and she didn't even tell me to set the table. Then she put the frying pan on to heat and went down to the garden to fetch a head of lettuce — not just any head of lettuce, the very biggest one...

Elke

Yes, I chose the loveliest of all my lettuces — pale green ruffles as perfect as the Pompadour's petticoat, I remember thinking, and when I plunged it into cool water and ripped it apart, it was like Casanova tearing his mistress's petticoats to shreds...

Fiona

And when she went back out to the porch to dry the lettuce, she swung the metal mesh basket through the air in circles with her whole arm, instead of just back and forth the way she usually does...

Elke

The sun caught the droplets as they flew and turned them into a shower of diamonds...

Fiona

We had lunch. Cosmo didn't eat anything, but he drank two glasses of the wine he'd brought with him and told us some tall tales about his own fishing trips as a child. I didn't think he was overdoing it, but Frank was clenched up tight as a fist, he ate with his eyes on his plate and asked to be excused the minute he was finished.

I felt torn. Loyalty towards my brother; curiosity about this guy who made my mother's eyes gleam and was like no one else I knew. I decided to hang around a bit, just to see. That way, I told myself, wanting to have my cake and eat it too, I can be Frank's spy — I'll tell him all the stupid things Cosmo says. But instead of saying stupid things, Cosmo started doing magic. Not like someone who whisks out a pack of cards to show you all the tricks he's learned — no, I mean *real* magic, with no props or anything, while Mama was clearing the table. Like first of all he smiled at me, and then he lost his smile and looked for it everywhere and then he found it under my left foot and apologized and picked it up and put it back on his face — only the wrong way up at first, which made him look glum, and then the right way up. Stuff like that. I laughed in spite of myself. Just because I have a penchant for torture doesn't mean I'm not an ordinary little girl who appreciates enchantment.

Next, taking an apple from the fruit bowl, he rubbed it on his sleeve until it shined, then held it out to me and said: Who do you see reflected in there?

Fiona, I said.

Well, he said, we'd better not eat from that side then; we wouldn't want to eat Fiona, would we?

He rubbed the apple again and held it out to me. And who do you see in *that* side?

Fiona, I said.

Come, come, he said, you can't be *everywhere* in the apple.

Yes, I am! I said. I'm *everywhere* in the apple!

Let me have a look, said Cosmo — and, scrunching up his features like he was a hundred years old, he squinted at the fruit. What are you talking about? he said. That's not Fiona at all, that's an ugly old *witch* in there!

I snorted with laughter.

Then he turned the apple around to check the other side. Good heavens! he exclaimed. *Another* ugly old witch! I'm sorry, young lady, I don't see you *any*where in this apple...

He stayed the whole afternoon and for me it was fun because when we played together I could be myself, I didn't have to be good. A while later Mama went out to pick string beans and Cosmo suggested we play *Jack and the Beanstalk*; he was Jack and at first I was the giant's wife and then I was the giant himself in all his gory glory. *Fee, Fi, Fo, Fum,* I cried, stamping my feet in slow menace and suddenly it all became real and it was just fantastic. I thumped my fist on the table and it split in two; I stamped on the floor and mice went scurrying into every corner of the room; I let out a holler bellow gale of fury, and windows swang and banged in their frames; faint-hearted females gasped in fear and buried their faces in their hands. *I smell the blood of an Englishman!* I fumed, eyes flashing with the threat of murder — and meanwhile Cosmo cowered and trembled in the linen chest where the giant's wife had hidden him, stuttering incoherent prayers — but instead of bursting into laughter, I only grew increasingly grim and determined, increasingly furious and red in the face, shouting at the top of my lungs, *Be he alive or be he dead, I'll grind his bones to make my bread!* I meant it, too, and Cosmo believed me: quaking, white and faint, he made himself small as a mouse, squished up against the wooden walls of the chest, trying to melt into them, for he knew what my furor was about — it was about my father, who might come home at any moment and find another man sitting at my mother's table.

The Psychiatric Expert
Yes, of course. To a child of five, there is nothing final about divorce. The real, irreversible separation of one's parents is of the order of the impossible.

An Adoration

Fiona

My father had just stepped out for a minute to check on his traps and see which animals he'd caught and capture their death throes on film, but he'd soon be back, and when he got here, his tread would cause the house to shake, and when he saw Cosmo — *Fee, fi, fo, fum* — his body would become tumescent with rage, his biceps would ripple and swell, his chest would puff up, his eyes would bulge as if to pop from his head, his voice would be a thunderclap echoing from the mountaintops...

Sandrine

Elke was delighted to see Cosmo and her daughter hitting it off so well. And she told herself that where Frank was concerned, things would improve with time. That's what we always tell ourselves, isn't it, Your Honour? It's just as well to be optimistic, for pessimists suffer twice: first in advance, and then when bad luck strikes.

Later that afternoon, Cosmo walked Elke to work and I ran into them in the street. I was on my way to the drugstore and, as usual in the summertime (to say nothing of the winter, spring or fall), the town looked dead, sad, silent; people were locked up in their homes, the streets were all but empty. The tightly closed window shutters — white, grey, pale blue — looked like the eyelids of corpses. I was pregnant at the time and, like all pregnant women, I couldn't help wondering about the world I was bringing my child into... Suddenly I saw Elke and Cosmo coming down the street side by side, same height, same stride, in unison — like twins, I said to myself, or like lovers... And whereas they weren't holding hands or even touching, I could tell they were together. In the deepest sense of the word, I mean.

It made me feel weird.

You see, Your Honour, Elke was my best friend, and as for Cosmo... well, without wanting to disturb Don Juan again, Cosmo, as I told you, was Cosmo.

Elke

Cosmo came into *La Fontaine* with me and stayed to have a drink at the bar. Did we want the villagers to start gossiping about us? As Frank said a while ago, people in these parts like to pretend they take no interest in the affairs of others. But women on doorsteps and men in bars need *something* to talk about, and speculations about who's sleeping with whom come right after money problems as the preferred topic of chit-chat.

Pouring Cosmo his glass of rosé wine, I murmured, Aren't you afraid people will talk?

He grinned and answered me, We wouldn't want to deprive them of this chance to use their imaginations, would we?

Then he added, Come here, Elke.

I leaned towards him over the bar and he whispered in my ear, Can't you just see them lying in bed at night, making up hot porno movies with us in the star roles? Oh, they'll be grateful to us, I promise you...

You're right, I said, straightening up. What a godsend!

Glancing about the room at the aging failing bodies of the

customers, I couldn't help but laugh at the idea of the two of us fornicating furiously in their brains.

But then I felt sad — because, deep down, I suspected these men didn't know *how* to dream anymore. I thought back to Frank and Fiona that morning at the water's edge: as they plunged their bait into the river and waited for the fish to bite, dreams were buzzing in their heads, so loudly I could almost hear them... All children dream... And then what happens? What becomes of unfulfilled dreams? The women around here stay home from morning to night and exhaust themselves with tiny chores, never daring to either relax or explode. The men go out into the fields every morning, work hard, sweat, swear, then come into the café to drink, play cards, make gruff conversation and smoke yellow cigarettes; after ten or fifteen years of this regimen their bodies go lumpy, their eyes fog over and red blotches appear on their cheeks, while their minds... *Oh Cosmo, is it possible that their minds are devoid of dreams?*

Have you met Vera? he asked me out of the blue, interrupting the question I was asking him in my brain.

Vera? I said, taken unawares. Sure.

The fact was that I knew her only by sight. She owned the newspaper shop on the town square and came into *La Fontaine* every day at around eleven to do crossword puzzles and drink a *café crème*. It was unusual in those days for a woman to enter a café alone. In fact, it was virtually unheard of. Even a Parisienne would have felt uncomfortable. But Vera was an exception — the male customers greeted her warmly and she had a smile for every one of them.

Josette
Ha! Not only a smile...

Elke
Naturally, the village women thought of her as a hussy —
because, though already in her mid-fifties, she used henna on
her hair, embellished her lips with lipstick and wore brightly
coloured clothes... At the time, this was the full extent of my
knowledge about Vera.

Over the next few days, however, Cosmo told me bits and
pieces of her story...

She's an *outsider*, he told me. Born in the medium-sized city
some forty miles away, she'd come here with her husband
during the war — a young couple, Communists both, and
ardent Resistance fighters. From the start, Vera was resented by
the village women for her flamboyant beauty and her political
outspokenness; but when the Germans shot her husband in
July of '44 and she found herself widowed at the age of twenty-
five, she was not only resented but feared.

She decided to stay in town out of sheer defiance. Single-
handedly, she took the initiative of setting up a newspaper
outlet, and within a few months she'd attracted a large, faithful
and wholly male clientele. Men enjoyed her company — she
had a ready tongue and a bright, pealing laugh, and without
being a pretentious bluestocking she could hold her own in a
conversation on any subject, from the Algerian war to the
price of string.

Latifa

Speaking of the Algerian war, I wanted to say, since my husband Hassan won't be able to take the stand, his French not being good enough, besides which, even in Arabic, he stopped speaking a long time ago, and in my opinion it's partly your fault, when I say you, I mean the French in general, of course I can't be sure that you yourself are French, Your Honour, but I assume you are, I'm not asking to see your pedigree or anything but in all likelihood your skin is as white as the novelist's, I'd be surprised if it was brown or black, it's not impossible of course, in our day and age you see all sorts in the magistracy but as I say, I'd be surprised, where was I, oh yes, in my opinion it's partly your fault...

What? I'm still not allowed to talk? Well, all right then, I'll go on waiting patiently but don't forget to tell me when my turn comes round because I'm very upset — I'm warning you, I've got a lot on my chest...

Elke

So the years went by and Vera's presence was a continual thorn in the village women's side; she infuriated them by flirting openly with their men, while at the same time proving by her own example that it was possible for a woman to be independent.

André, too, started buying the newspaper every day. Disappointed by Josette, starved for spiritual companionship, anguished by the passage of time, he was irresistibly drawn to the beautiful redhead. And Cosmo, though only a preschooler at the time, sensed that there was a special connection between Vera and his father.

It's so long ago, he told me once, that my memories are like dreams, and I've never dared to broach the subject with my father. But I have the distinct image of Vera's hands coming up to frame my face. I can still feel how gentle they were, smell the perfume at their wrists and see their ruby-painted finger-nails... So different from my mother's hands, forever involved in doing something *useful*. Not once in her life, I think, did my mother make a gesture to *express* herself...

We were walking down the street together and, even as he walked, Cosmo's hands made a series of swift movements in the air — I caught glimpses of a flamingo, a lick of flame, a harp arpeggio.

Taking my face in her hands, he went on, Vera would plunge her sapphire eyes into my own. There was something disturbing in the way she looked at me. Even now, when we pass each other in the street...

I have only one clear memory of her — and even that one is not so much of *her* as of her house. I must have been four or five years old. My father had taken me over to her place... I can see myself sitting in the front room, watching a cigarette burn itself out in an ashtray. Vera must have lit it and aban-doned it at once, she and my father must have gone into the next room and closed the door behind them... There was a trace of lipstick on the golden filter, and it seemed to me the most sophisticated, desirable thing in the world, this smudge of red on the white-flecked golden filter of a burning cigarette.

As I sat there waiting for my father, it slowly consumed itself, the tobacco turned to ash and the ash preserved a cylindrical shape — as if the cigarette were becoming its own ghost... Was there some sound coming from the next room that forced me to stare so fixedly at the cigarette? Was my father using me as an alibi to see Vera? I wonder about that now, I didn't then... Had he told Josette he was taking me out to buy a pair of shoes, and were he and Vera now passionately embracing or even making love in the next room, as I sat there, motionless, staring at the cigarette's slow and perfect consuming of itself and wondering at what point, defeated by its own weight, the cylinder of ash would crumble at last and fall into the ashtray? The memory ends there.

Josette

All this is nothing but digression and diversion. It doesn't have the slightest bearing on the matter at hand! We're here to under-stand my son's death, not to dig up all the old village tittle-tattle.

I insist that every mention of Vera be deleted from the record.

Elke

Nothing can be deleted, Josette, you know that as well as I do. *Vera is here;* there's no getting around it. She's a part of this story, and at some future point she'll bring in testimony of great importance. You see, Your Honour, something dreadful happened... but at the time we're talking about now, Cosmo didn't yet know about... this event. He didn't learn of it until much later, after his father's death...

Anyway, for the time being, here's the other episode of Vera's life which Cosmo shared with me that summer: at the age of forty-two, she'd had a baby. A little boy named Jonas. Ah, that was a scandal! The scandal was twofold: firstly, the child's father was a gypsy; secondly, and still more shockingly... Vera handed her son over to him!

At this, the village women literally choked with indignation. Their fear and resentment of Vera turned into outright hatred. Not content with having enticed their husbands away from them, she had now chosen to shirk her responsibilities as a mother! She could scarcely be oblivious to the implications of her choice — it meant that her son would not attend school, that he would be raised in filth and promiscuity like a little savage. Being unbelievers, the village women couldn't even console themselves with the idea that later on, as the red-head roasted in hell, they'd be up in heaven reaping their rewards for the years of sterile sacrifice to which they'd consented with clenched teeth. No! Their narrow-minded virtues would never be recompensed — any more than Vera's sexy sins would be punished! Nothing is bitterer, Your Honour, than the bitterness of miscreants.

Vera went on just as before, selling her newspapers and stopping off mornings to do her crossword puzzles at *La Fontaine*; several times a week she'd drive out to visit her son at the gypsy camp beyond the town limits... When Jonas, at the age of three or four, showed signs of promise on the violin, she started setting money aside...

Jonas

My mother and Cosmo's father had been lovers, Your Honour, and... Cosmo and I were lovers.

There was something ineffable about our love due to the fact that we were almost as brothers — our flesh having mingled in our parents' embraces, so to speak, long before we'd even met.

The Knife

It was like cutting into butter, Your Honour. I entered Cosmo's body, slicing through the skin of his abdomen without encountering the least resistance — I mean, the skin itself resisted, naturally, as did the muscles and the viscera, but not the *man*, not the person to whom these organs belonged. True, I'd been meticulously readied for the task at hand — whetted, filed, honed to a point. But Cosmo put up no struggle whatsoever — I swear, he succumbed to me as rapturously as a woman to her lover. So I advanced through his body with consummate ease, alacrity and, if I may say so, even jubilation; in no time at all I arrived at the deepest, darkest, most secret part of him, at which point I came to a halt...

It's an extraordinary memory, Your Honour. Never have I known anything like it, I assure you, and I'm a very old knife — I come from the High Plateaux in Algeria and I've been passed down within the same tribe, from father to son, for over a century; naturally this was not the first time I'd been entrusted with sending a man to meet his Maker — but never, *never* I repeat, have I taken part in so sensual, not to say consensual, a murder!

Yes, in all honesty, I had the feeling that the victim had given his *consent* — that it was not without his knowledge, and even his approval, that he felt life ebbing away from him, as scarlet blood pulsed from the ravine I had dug...

When Jonas came upon us, I was still deeply immersed in his lover's body... Do forgive me, Your Honour. I find it hard to restrain myself, and since everyone else has been stretching the rules of chronology...

The Wisteria

You've probably been wondering for some time now, Your Honour, about the... how shall I put it... the physical relationship between Elke and Cosmo.

He grazes her breasts over the telephone — right.

He walks her to work — okay.

They look like a couple — fine.

The peasants fantasize about their lovemaking — no problem.

But when you come right down to it, apart from Elke having laid her hand on Cosmo's hair some three months ago, so far the two of them have exchanged nothing but words. Notwithstanding her panegyrics on the theme of *melting* (a fairly hackneyed image for female pleasure, if I may say), Elke is clearly reluctant to broach the topic; thus I see no alternative but to take the stand myself.

Unless I'm mistaken, I was the sole witness of their first night in bed together. This was due to my strategic location: the pergola over which I'm draped stands directly in front of

Elke's bedroom window — which, I hasten to add, was wide open that night because of the summer heat. I may be delicate, mauve, sweet-smelling and romantic, Your Honour, but even I cannot perform miracles.

It was the night before Cosmo was to return to the capital. That evening, at long last, he asked Elke if he could walk her home *after* work, and she agreed unhesitatingly. Arms entwined, they glided through the village, carrying their silence amidst that of the sleeping streets — and having skirted the house so as to pass through the garden, they sat down for a moment under the pergola, directly beneath me. If not a word crossed their lips, it was because their lips were finally otherwise occupied. They were kissing. They began with light, exploratory, spitless kisses — we flowers recognize the gestures and odours of sex at once — pistils lifting, sap flowing, organs swelling and throbbing and growing congested, you mustn't forget that we ourselves are neither more nor less than reproductive organs, the androecium contains a stamen that looks exactly like a glans penis, the gynaeceum includes an ovary fairly bursting with ovules — which is why, as of their first evening in the barn, Elke told Cosmo a story about flowers, *All you need to do is think about a flower for it to appear before you...* Thus, it was with considerable relief that I saw Elke's lips part and Cosmo's tongue begin to flicker between them. Elke fairly reeled — the flood of emotions that can be set off in humans by the mute, wet contact of mucous membranes is rather amazing when you think about it: his tongue inside her was like his sex inside her, and his sex inside

her would be like something else, but what? No one knows.
What is human desire the metaphor of? No one knows. Shortly
after this, Cosmo's hands moved onto Elke's breasts — not to
graze them, as they had once done over the telephone, but to
discover their precise shape — and, overcome with dizziness,
Elke was forced to open her eyes; she looked straight up at me,
and I corresponded so precisely to what was going on in her
soul that she recovered her balance at once. Moving slightly
away from Cosmo, she took his hand in hers and licked its
palm, then undid the top buttons of his shirt with trembling
fingers — revealing, at the level of his breastbone, a small tri-
angular hollow into which, bending her head, she slid her
tongue. Cosmo let out a low, almost feminine moan, he uttered
her name several times, she uttered his, and although these
were not their real names, they undeniably produced an effect,
I saw it with my own eyes, their bodies were now taut and
fairly vibrating with desire, sweet erotic sweat exuded from
their every pore as they moved out from under the pergola and
towards the stone staircase that goes up to the kitchen — he
leading the way, she close behind. I did lose sight of them for a
few seconds when they entered the house, just the time it took
to go down the hallway to Elke's room, but then the bedroom
door was flung open and there they were in front of me. Cosmo
turned the key in the lock, sank to his knees at Elke's feet,
removed her sandals and pressed his lips to her toes; though
they hadn't turned on any lamps, I could see quite clearly
thanks to the moonlight, I saw them remove each other's
clothes, this was beautiful, desire made their movements swift

and graceful and there was no false modesty between them, Elke wasn't giggling nervously the way women so often do when it comes to taking off their clothes, suddenly seeing themselves from the outside and growing embarrassed at what they're about to do, perceiving it as bestial, incongruous and therefore comical — but here, no, not at all, their disrobing seemed to form a part of some timeless, inexorable choreography, and when they were naked at last, pressed up to one another, slippery with sweat, they tore the blankets from the bed, dropped down onto the sheets and began to roll upon one another, gasping, panting, biting, clutching, and then, imperceptibly, their movements slowed down, their gasps grew intermittent and Elke realized that Cosmo had fallen asleep in her arms.

She pulled the sheet up over their two bodies. Her gaze floated out the window, through me, towards the moon, through the moon, towards I know not what. After a while, she, too, fell asleep.

The next morning, Cosmo awoke with a start. It took him several seconds to remember where he was. Then, burying his head in Elke's chest, he told her about the dream he'd just had.

We were at the morgue together, he said. The two of us. And the police were showing us the bodies of the dead. There were dozens and dozens of them, lined up in long rows of beds, young men with ghastly bullet wounds in their temples, women with their guts ripped out, old men who had clearly been clubbed to death... Gradually, we realized that all of them had been murdered by *the police themselves*, they were proud of their night's pickings, they kept taking us up and down the rows and encouraging us to admire their work... The corpses were grey and still — shockingly still, as if they had been turned to stone. Even death can't be *that* still, I said to myself; they must have endured a fate *worse* than death... And in the dream, Elke, you and I weren't merely together... We were *a single person*, do you understand? Our gaze upon the scene was a single gaze.

That's all I can tell you, Your Honour, about the first night Elke and Cosmo spent together.

Frank

This is abject. This is absolutely revolting. It's *my mother* we're talking about!

I mean, the woman had *kids* to look after, and that bastard could find nothing better to do than to go visiting stiffs with her in the middle of the night.

The guy was morbid. You know? *He's* the one who's morbid — not our father Michael with his trapped animals. Papa was fascinated by to the flickering flame, whereas Cosmo — to put it bluntly — was disgusting. He did disgusting things — to my mother, my sister, his audience... He was drawn to suffering like a fly to dogshit.

All right, all right. I'll calm down.

Let me tell you what he did.

Let me tell you what he did.

I heard him... All right. For instance.

One day he came over to our place... it must have been a few months later, because Fiona had just started school. She had this new atlas and she was so proud of it, she was dying to show it to Cosmo. Less then five minutes after he walked in the door, they were sitting side by side on the living-room rug, leaned up against the couch, with the atlas on their laps; Fiona was turning the pages and Cosmo was reading out loud to her. I went into my room and closed the door, but I could still hear snatches of what Cosmo was saying; it makes my stomach heave just to think of it.

Look, he said. This is a volcano in southern Italy, volcanoes are formed when... and this is a fishing village in Portugal... Chinese people spinning silk... the Tutsis of Rwanda sometimes grow to be... polar bears who live and lumber in the Great North... dromedaries have one hump and camels have two, they store water in their humps and this enables them... Of the Seven Wonders of the ancient world, only Cheops's pyramid in Egypt has... a mausoleum built by Shah Jahan for his beloved wife... the weird baboons and baobabs of South Africa... church founded in Constantinople in the fourth century A.D.

Well, Your Honour. Do you know what became of this hour of intimacy Cosmo shared with my little sister? Do you know what he turned it into? A number! A number called *Explanation of the World to a Little Girl*. I saw it on TV once and it made my blood run cold. Pure pornography was what it was.

He'd sit down alone in the spotlight, smack in the middle of the stage, in exactly the same position as he was that day with Fiona — cross-legged on the floor, one arm gently, protectively curved in the air as if to encircle the shoulders of a small child. He was a daddy showing his little girl the world atlas, and his face glowed with the pleasure of knowledge imparted.

Look, dear, he would say, in the warm, singsong voice of parental pedagogy. *These are dromedaries, and these are camels...*

He'd run through a number of examples taken from Fiona's atlas. Shah Jahan, Cheops's pyramid... But then the images would gradually darken. As they darkened, his voice remained the same.

Now let's see, my dear, he said. *Ah, yes... this... Yes, well, you see, these are sheep who have been purposely inoculated with a disease, to find out if it will work for killing human beings... Sure looks as if it works for killing sheep, doesn't it?*

He played the little girl as well. Eager to impress her father with her intelligence and maturity, she did her best not to seem shocked by what she was learning. But despite all her efforts, as the explanation proceeded, her chin began to tremble, her brows to work, and finally her eyes filled up with tears...

The man you see here is the president of a country called Chile — yes, that's right, he's just been shot to death...

This is a factory in Indonesia where little girls your age weave carpets from morning to night... Yes, of course their hands are bleeding, dear. Wouldn't your hands bleed if...

What, you ask, is a death camp? Well, it's a place where...

Now, this is Nairobi, these men are soldiers in their thirties, and they give little girls a few pennies or a pack of cigarettes you see, and in exchange they get to...

Why, you ask, do the Palestinians live there if they don't want to? Well, it's because...

Always in the same loving, lilting tone of voice, the voice all parents use to initiate their children into the wonders of the world, Cosmo taught horror to my invisible little sister. It went on and on and on. The atomic bombs dropped on Hiroshima and Nagasaki. Napalm in Vietnam. Drug traffic, weapons traffic...

Had he been thinking about all these tortures and turpitudes even as he sat in our living room reading aloud to Fiona? The man's a pervert, Your Honour. A dangerous pervert. All things considered, I would rather he had raped my little sister than exploited her so abjectly...

The Cosmophile

Yes — in *Explanation of the World to a Little Girl*, as much as the actual content of the number, it was Cosmo's tone of voice that made people weep. They wept because the father's voice was so soft and loving, and because he tried to break the news to his young daughter as gently as he could...

But the word *exploit* is inaccurate, Your Honour — inaccurate and trite. For Cosmo, there was no clear-cut distinction, as there is for most people, even artists and movie stars, between life and work; there was his *worklife*, his *lifework*, no distance and no difference between the two. When people suggested it was egotistical of him to perform exclusively in solo, he would reply that, on the contrary, he was *not* alone onstage, that thousands of other people lived with and through him, whereas most actors are stuck with playing a single character at a time, repeating the same lines in the same order night after night. When people accused him (as Frank has just done) of cannibalizing his loved ones, he'd insist that just the opposite was true.

Let me read to you this excerpt from one of Cosmo's radio interviews: *As a rule, people don't listen to each other. Words they would deem boring if pronounced by a friend or neighbour become poignant and memorable when I pronounce them onstage. Far from devouring the people whose words I use, I immortalize them.*

Clementine

Little Charlie couldn't stand to see people suffer — that's what you've got to keep in mind, Your Honour, if you want to understand a show like *Explanation*. Not just people — animals, too. He was always that way, even as a little boy. If he saw a fly go banging into a windowpane, he'd put himself in the fly's place and get a headache. I remember once he came to me in tears because one of his Grandpa Cottereau's clerks had grabbed a rifle and shot a magpie — just like that, for the fun of it. The bird dropped dead at Charlie's feet. Well, little Charlie picked it up — its head was practically torn off its body — and he rushed over to my place. *Look*, Titine! — I can still see him carrying that fat magpie in his arms, it must have been half as big as he was — *Look*, Titine! he sobbed. Well, you may not believe it, Your Honour, but seeing how het up he was, I fetched my needle and thread, put on my sewing glasses, laid an old apron on my knees and sewed that magpie's head back on. Yes, I did! Just like a surgeon. And I can tell you I made one boy happy that day! Here you are, dear, I said. The bird's head is back on its body again, good as new!

I was their closest neighbour and Charlie used to drop by to see me pretty often. I kept a cookie tin in my pantry; there were always cookies in it and he knew he could help himself, he didn't even have to ask. I didn't have kids of my own. Like lots of other brides, I lost my husband in Verdun and that was it as far as marriage and motherhood were concerned, so I appreciated it when the neighbours' boy dropped by. Sometimes it was just to say hello — but other times, if he was upset about something, he'd come and snuggle up in my lap because his mother never sat down and if you don't sit down you don't have a lap for your kid to snuggle up in. Josette was busy from morning to night, forever cleaning and dusting and polishing things around the house. I think her TV set must have gotten more coddling than her son did. Oh, that woman sure kept a clean house — you have to give her that! You would have thought they were expecting God In Person to drop by, but He never did! All the furniture was protected by dust covers, the dining-room table was so shiny you were scared to leave fingerprints on it, and you had to slide around the kitchen floor on cloth pads so you wouldn't muddy the tiles...

I wasn't as fussy about cleanliness as Josette, a bit of dust here and a cobweb there didn't bother me — not only that, but I had a chicken coop and a rabbit hutch back in the back and little Charlie knew he could come and play with the rabbits whenever he felt like it, plus he helped me gather the eggs every now and then. Boy, did the two of us have some good times together! I used to sing to him — all the songs I could remember from my youth! I remember once, for Saint Blaise's Day, I taught him to sing *Swish-swish*. I dressed him up in one of my old lace headdresses and a pair of white cotton knickers

— the very ones I'd worn on my wedding day in 1912, with a flap over the opening you-know-where, and I showed him how to mince and simper, lifting his long skirts just high enough to reveal the embroidered edges, and how to roll his eyes coyly left and right, and when he got up onstage in the village hall that day, boy was he a sensation!

It's the woman who often
wears the pants in the house
At least, so I have heard tell
As of the wedding bell
Her petticoats go swish-swish
The man gets a powerful wish
Suddenly he's so glad
He's electrified, he goes mad...

Ha ha ha ha! Oh, it was really something! Little Charlie sang off-key but that just made it all the funnier, people were falling off their chairs laughing, especially the women my age, who'd worn knickers like that when they were young... Ha! ha! ha! ha! I'm not saying that's what made little Charlie decide to become an actor, but it certainly didn't hurt!

I was already well into my sixties by that time. I died in 1970, aged eighty, and Charlie couldn't attend my funeral because he was on tour at the time, but he put flowers on my grave the next time he came home, and then at least once a year until his own death — it's true, I swear it! Not just *my* grave, lots of other people's, too... He was a good boy, Your Honour — he never let success go to his head.

Speaking of putting flowers on my grave... One year on All

Saints' Day, not long after I died, there was a painful scene in the cemetery between Charles and his father. I thought I should tell you about it. You never know, it might be important... Well, here's what happened.

It wasn't exactly what you could call a nice day. The sky was all drizzle and drip, and there was a stiff little wind blowing... Typical early November weather... Father and son had donned their oilskins and come out to the cemetery on foot to visit their dead, swinging a basket of red, purple and orange chrysanthemums between them. As they dug little holes in the soggy soil around the tombstones, they chatted together — or rather, Charlie kept going on about his career (he was twenty-seven at the time, and eager to make his father proud) and Dédé listened.

I fill houses now, said Charlie. I'm under contract with the best theatre agent in the country. I've got twenty-five performances scheduled in a dozen different cities between now and Christmas. Last September the prime minister in person attended one of my shows — I was introduced to him afterwards, I shook hands with him.

Charlie noticed that André wasn't responding, but this only made him more effusive; he was doing his best to distract his father, make him laugh. André's silences had scared him ever since he was child, I know that. His hope now, in the course of this hour or two they'd be spending alone together in the cemetery, was to fill his father's mind with a series of precise, colourful images of himself onstage — images to which André could return later on when Cosmo was gone, and in which he could take comfort.

Elke

It's true, Your Honour... More than anything in the world, Cosmo longed for his father to be happy, relax, forgive himself, treat himself more kindly. Why couldn't he derive any pleasure from the life he'd led, even if it was radically different from the one he'd dreamed of leading?

Clementine

So he kept talking.

It's such an incredible feeling, he said, when you hear the first chuckles in the theatre... when the spectators begin to trust you and let you into their minds. No kidding, Papa! Sometimes I feel as if I were prancing around not onstage but in their very brains — tickling their memories, prodding their consciences, reminding them of when they were little kids, mocking the airs they put on, forcing them to see themselves from a distance and shrug off the shackles they've gotten used to wearing. It's the most amazing thing...

By this time they were patting the rooty clods of the flowers into the little holes they'd dug in the ground. I appreciated the trouble they were taking for me and my neighbours (it's pretty comical when you think about it — you get a whole new set of neighbours when you die; you can end up right next to your worst enemy for all eternity!), but I was starting to feel sorry for them. The icy rain was blowing in their faces and they'd been trudging around in the mud for so long that their shoes were soaked through. I could hear Dédé's old shoes wheezing, but he himself still hadn't said a word. The longer his silence lasted, the more talkative Charlie became, terrified by the gloom that seemed to be oozing from his father like black mud — *Come to my light*, he pleaded with him inwardly, *don't drag me into your darkness, come to my light* — and the sky itself was neither dark nor light but a disquieting mixture of the two, like a sickly twilight.

Once the mums had all been planted, they stood wordlessly with their hands in their pockets at the foot of each grave in turn. The tension between them kept rising. Cosmo desperately tried to figure out what he could have said to alienate his father so badly. He was on the verge of panic.

And then it came. Wheeling on his son, Dédé began spitting words in his face.

You... you... he began — and Cosmo to his dismay saw that his father was weeping, hot tears were mixing with the cold rain on his cheeks. You... you can come home and — do *this* to me, when — when — when *you*, you of all people, know... when I've told you... I told you what my dreams were — how I longed — for the *right* — the *ability* — to say something to others, and you, who know what my life has been like — you may not know everything but you've *seen* it, here — how — how I'm treated — by — Josette's family — the people in town — treated with pity — with contempt — as if I were handicapped — a cripple — an idiot — whereas I had *so much to give...*

Papa, said Cosmo, aghast.

Don't Papa me! shouted André. The two men were now standing face to face, dripping hood to dripping hood, scarcely a foot apart. *Don't Papa me!* he repeated, his voice a tight knot of pain, his eyes dark whirlpools dragging Cosmo's eyes into their depths and drowning them there... All at once Charlie became acutely aware of everything around him; he noticed that brown and dun and wet green were not the only colours of the landscape, that there were sweet purple clumps of heather along the roadside, bright red leaves clinging to the bramble bushes in the ditch where they'd floated down from nearby sorbs, yellow leaves still dangling in twos and threes from the naked branches of the oaks overhead, and he realized (the novelist is lending me the words to say this, but the idea is my own) that all these things had the clear-cut simplicity of nature whose decline includes the promise of rebirth, whereas his father's eyes were a bottomless hell, the hell of time irreversible, loss irremediable, hope annulled.

And you can just breeze into town like this, André went on, as Cosmo's eyes dropped to the ground, unable to bear the overdose of pain his father's eyes were pumping into them — between performances, and calmly boast to me — *oh Papa, I'm so famous I'm so fucking famous — I shook hands with the prime minister and forgive me — do forgive me if I don't have much time to spend with you — between engagements with the King of Prick and the Queen of Cunt — yes my poor little father, my poor little miserable nothing of a father — you can stay here with your migraine headaches and your nagging wife and your nightmares — the cackling geese and geezers — please excuse me, I must fly off to Paris, or Montreal, or Geneva, or some such fucking place — just wanted to make sure you still had your face in the manure heap*

— really rubbed into it — Just wanted to make sure you — didn't
have any plans to — climb back out of the mud and dung —

Don't Papa me!

This last sentence a scream — the more heart-rending to
Charlie, I think, for being all but inaudible.

Elke

Thank you, Clementine, for your deeply moving statement.
Cosmo took me with him to visit the cemetery on several occasions, and I knew you were one of his dearest departed, but he
never told me about the scene at the foot of your grave. I'm sure
it will clarify a number of things, later on in the hearing.

Fourth Day

Elke

What should I tell you next, Your Honour?

In order to tell a story, you have to exclude virtually all the details and make do with fragments and approximations. Even the word *I* is an approximation — what I call *I*, evoking this distant past, is not the same person as the *I* who is standing in front of you today — anymore than *you*, Your Honour, are the same *you* now as then. It would be impossible for me to give you an exhaustive account of the events, large and small, which helped to consolidate the love between Cosmo and myself. Partly because — as the novelist herself pointed out a while ago in a burst of impatience — it would take forever, but also because people forget. And fortunately so. Without our precious ability to forget, we should drown in an inextricable mass of old and new impressions which, being deprived of all order and hierarchy, would also be deprived of meaning.

So what shall I tell you...? In the course of that first summer and fall, I became not only Cosmo's lover but his confidante, his sister, his other self. He spoke to me at length of his profession. Its enormous rewards; its equally enormous risks. Sometimes, he told me, he got so carried away by his communion with the public that he fell into a sort of trance. For the space of a few seconds, he knew neither who or where he was. Black hole. Heart-stopping silence. The words, sentences and ideas of a performance do have to be strung along in a certain order, he told me, laughing, so it's important to keep at least one foot in reality...

Another time, I remember, he described to me what he called *detumescence* — how, walking off stage at the end of a show, he'd feel himself deflating like a punctured balloon...

The Psychiatric Expert
I assume there's no need to comment on the witness's choice of vocabulary.

Elke
Onstage, you understand, he would swell up with being (and this was true quite literally: though he perspired abundantly and burned thousands of calories, he actually *gained weight* in the course of a performance); then suddenly all his characters left him and he was only himself again — a single, arbitrary combination of traits among the millions of possible combinations... He was condemned to using his own voice, bearing and personality — using them, moreover, to shake hands, smile and pronounce inanities such as *Thank you, Good to see you, Thank you so much, Glad you liked it,* over and over again. As if *that* were the real Cosmo! As if the real Cosmo were not the transcendent, polymorphous giant who had just appeared to them onstage, wreathed in shining light!

Those conversations I remember; others I've forgotten — but even the forgotten ones haven't been lost completely; they've gone melting into the air in a gentle swirl of molecules that has made some small difference in the lives of glow-worms, blackbirds, moles... You do know this, don't you, Your Honour? — that the world is perpetually, if faintly, shimmering and shifting in response to all the events that ever happened there, from ancient bloody wars and cataclysms to the most softly whispered promises of love... *Everything is present*, do you understand? All the dead children are amongst us at this hearing — here, now, diffuse and intangible, but *present!*

The Psychiatric Expert
The woman is deranged.

Elke
All right. I'll return to the facts.

To what happened that year at Christmas.

A freezing, snowless Christmas, I remember.

This, too was a *first* — our first Christmas without Michael. I was impatient to get beyond the *firsts*, move on to the *seconds* and then the *thirds*, establish a new routine and at last, one day, be able to stop counting.

The previous year, through our divorce was imminent, Michael and I had tried to celebrate Christmas together one last time for the children's sake — a mistake, of course. A sinister joke. This year, Michael had sent a plastic Batman clock for Frank and a Barbie doll for Fiona — cheap gifts which had fulfilled their double purpose of thrilling the children and infuriating me.

Then — mad, enormous, unbelievable, special delivery

from Paris — Cosmo's gift arrived, an entire hi-fi system, along with a splendid selection of records and tapes. I'd spent the better part of Christmas Day learning the ins and outs of amplifiers, tuners and turntables — and now, for hours every day, Cosmo's music flowed through my veins like a drug. It was the miracle of sharing, as with the scenes he described to me over the phone — *what had been in his head was now in mine...*

One evening a few days after Christmas, Frank and I were watching an old Hitchcock movie on TV together, he was sitting on the floor next to me on the couch; Fiona had already trundled off to bed. In the film, there is a close-up of a large round wall clock ticking loudly; as I watched the second hand jump forward, I said to myself: *this is real time*: that clock could be in this very room, in fact it *is* in this room, ticking more loudly than my own, real clock. A bit later in the film, there's a close-up of a man's hand dialing a phone number. Again, staring at it, I thought, *real time*: the dialing of those seven digits has taken up seven seconds of my life, just as it would have if I myself had dialed the number. Isn't it strange, Your Honour, how the modern world encourages us to live with ghosts? The actor who played in Hitchcock's film is dead and buried — yet here he is in the room with me; I'm watching him intently and the result of his phone call matters to me.

Even as I mulled these things over in my mind, I was absently stroking my son's hair, winding his black curls around my fingers. But suddenly Frank twisted away from me with an angry toss of his head. I snatched my hand back as swiftly as if I'd burned it on an iron.

I found it hard to concentrate on the film after that. Staring at the jittery black-and-white images on the screen, I wondered how I could know so little about this person whom I had not only brought into the world, but seen and spoken to every day of his life. We tend to believe, Your Honour, that the closer the quarters at which we live with people, the better we know them. This is sheer nonsense. At the moment, Hitchcock's hero seemed more comprehensible to me than my own son.

The screen eventually told the film was over but Frank didn't budge and I saw he'd fallen asleep. I bent down to gather him in my arms and carry him off to bed... but no, I couldn't manage it; he'd grown too heavy; I was forced to wake him up and let him growl and snarl at me as I led him to his room.

Fiona

Since my mother seems to be having a hard time pulling herself together, I suggest we let her blubber to her heart's content, and I myself will tell you the next episode of that particular merry Christmas.

Here's what happened: Frank savaged the hi-fi.

I didn't take part in the destruction. Not directly, that is. Except for the LPs — there I did give him a hand because it was tedious, you had to take them out of their covers and break them one by one; there were dozens of them and Frank was afraid he might not have time to break them all before Mama got home from shopping, so I pitched in. Then we yanked the brown ribbons of magnetic tape out of the cassettes, to me they looked like brown spaghetti but Frank found an even better comparison, he said it reminded him of the intestines of World War I soldiers, we'd never actually seen that on TV but we'd read about it somewhere, how young soldiers disemboweled by their enemies would lie there with their tangled guts in a heap next to them in the snow — that really fired our imaginations!

The rest of the time I just watched, but I know my approving gaze helped Frank go through with his plan. And it was something, let me tell you! When we play our pain games, the idea is to treat each other like objects: I bang the rock against his head as if his head were a rock; he twists my arm as if it were a tree branch. Here it was just the other way around: he attacked the record player as if it were Cosmo in person, as if every blow of the hammer could elicit a scream, a groan or a whimper from the man he called the fornicating clown. I myself had nothing against Cosmo — but to me what Frank says is sacred, there's no getting around it; if he says Hey, come take a look, I go take a look; if he says Brilliant, eh? I say Brilliant.

The amplifier was easy to destroy; so were the loud-speakers.

Then Frank went and hid down in the basement. He could have found a better hiding place — in fact he could have just split completely, left the house till nightfall — but he wanted to hear Mama yell when she got back from shopping and saw the havoc he had wreaked.

She didn't yell at all. Our mother is unpredictable, Your Honour. What she did was drop the groceries she was carrying, so there was a fair amount of damage to the fruits and vegetables and eggs. A long silence ensued — so long, in fact, that I thought she must have fainted, but I didn't dare go check. After several minutes, I heard her go into the kitchen and sit down. Another bad silence. I could hear the kitchen clock ticking and nothing else, nothing at all. Was she crying, you want to know? No, she wasn't. Right *now* she's crying, but that's unusual — and that day, I remember, when she finally came to look for me in my room, her cheeks were completely dry. It wasn't easy for me to act as if nothing had happened, but that's what I'd promised Frank I'd do, so I sat there humming a little tune and playing with my new Barbie doll, making clothes for her out of Kleenex tissues, and when Mama walked in I jumped as if I'd just that minute noticed she was home. Usually I'm a pretty good actress, but that day I doubt my mother was fooled. Besides, she wasn't paying attention to me — there was only one thing on her mind, and that was finding Frank.

I'd promised not to betray his hiding place. I didn't break my promise but she found him anyway; it took her no time at all. Mothers do have a sixth sense somehow. Frank told me about the time a little fox cub got caught in one of Papa's traps, and by the time Papa arrived, its mother was sitting there right next to it and refused to go away; he had to give up trying to photograph the dying cub — because with the vixen in the picture, it would have looked sentimental.

Mama went straight down to the basement and found Frank hiding behind some old cardboard boxes — you would have thought it was the only hiding place in the world. Even then she didn't yell at him, it's not her style; all she did was make him clean up the mess upstairs, stuff it into an enormous garbage bag and vacuum up the living-room rug. Meanwhile, I had to pick up the groceries that had rolled all over the floor in the entryway and bring them to her in the kitchen.

Then, using the eggs that had cracked open in their box, she made us an omelette.

No one breathed a word during the meal but, oddly enough, we were happier than usual. A strange calm seemed to float above the table. We were hungry as wolves, the omelette was scrumptious, we passed the breadbasket back and forth and sopped up every speck of egg and butter in our plates.

When the washing-up was done, Mama said to Frank: Let's go down to the pond — I hear it's frozen over.

The Pond

I was frozen over. It doesn't happen often — since the end of World War II, you can count the years of real cold on the fingers of one hand; that day, however, I had a good layer of ice on me, two or three inches thick. It was excellent protection for my fish — and it made me rather beautiful, if I do say so myself. I'm always beautiful, for those who know how to look at me, but the unfortunate truth is that not many people do. This part of the country is scarcely famous for its winter sports — the local population tends to stay indoors when the thermometer goes down. When it goes up, too. I'm not the Mediterranean Sea, my shores do not draw crowds. Murky in the summertime (so murky I don't even reflect the great buzzards that soar over me, wings flapping slowly), my edges spoked with reeds and rushes, my banks studded with minuscule pink daisies, my surface stippled with lilypads and continually amove with bubbles, skating insects and leaping fish — I was, that winter's day, breathtaking in my whiteness, flatness and stillness. Like the stage of a theatre — with the delicate black branchings of leafless birch trees as my entranced audience.

So you can imagine my surprise when I saw two human beings headed straight for me! Evidently mother and son. Within minutes they were on top of me. I recognized them from another visit, long ago — but there had been three of them back then; the boy was smaller and the woman was walking arm in arm with a tall, craggy-faced man; all of them seemed to be in excellent spirits — they went dashing about, skidding and sliding on my frozen surface as if on skates, pushing and pulling at each other, falling on their rear ends, going into gales of laughter and getting up again... At one point, the man began to growl and roar as if he were a dragon; great fumes of smoke poured from his mouth and nostrils and the child squealed with delight... Ah yes, the little family certainly had a good time that day, but today was a different matter — the son had grown, the father was nowhere to be seen — and the mother, far from frolicking, looked like she meant business. I couldn't help overhearing their conversation.

All the kids at school, began the boy, say you're his...

His mistress?

Silence.

Cosmo's mistress, is that it?

Yeah, sort of.

Well, that's okay with me. I don't mind them saying that.

I do!

Why?

It makes me ashamed, that's why. It's like he was... I don't know... your sugar daddy.

My *sugar daddy?* Where on earth did you get an expression like that?

That's what they say at school. He's rich and we're poor and he gives us stuff we could never afford for ourselves.

We're not so poor, really.

Well, we can't buy fancy record players.

No, we can't. But wasn't it nice to have music in the house?

Not if it comes from him.

But *why*, Frank? Please tell me why.

Because he's a phoney, that's why. He doesn't want to live with us, he just wants to sleep with you and impress every-body with his expensive presents.

He *lives with us*, Frank. Whether you like it or not, he lives with us. Besides, Cosmo is *my* problem. *Your* problem is, you can't go through life taking a hammer to every little thing that bothers you.

There was another silence. On my surface, the young boy buried his face in his mother's coat. I thought I could make out muffled sobs, but I wouldn't swear to it. Finally, still without speaking, they moved off.

And shortly afterwards, night fell.

Jonas

The hi-fi incident upset Cosmo terribly, Your Honour, when Elke told him about it over the phone. It rankled with him for years. It wasn't a matter of money — he had plenty of money; he could easily have bought Elke another record player — no, it was because of the music. It was as if, by smashing his carefully chosen records to smithereens, Frank had divined his secret weakness and was telling him: *Music isn't yours to give.* Naturally, this was absurd — Frank had intended nothing of the sort; he was incapable of so subtle a motivation — but that was how Cosmo interpreted it. In his shows he displayed a startling variety of talents — he was a writer, thinker, actor, dancer, acrobat and clown — but he was *not* a musician. He knew this, and for whatever reason, it bothered him.

When he met me, music was what he found at last. What he fell in love with.

Sandrine

Not yet, Jonas — we'll get around to that later, if you don't mind. I know you must be getting impatient, but we wouldn't want the judge to lose his bearings...

At the time we're discussing now, Your Honour, Jonas had just turned fourteen and was already a phenomenal violinist... Twice weekly, Vera drove him to the middle-sized city for lessons at the conservatory, paying for them with the money she'd been setting aside for the past ten years. She was proud to bursting of her son. Sometimes, if he was spending the evening at her place, she'd bring him over to *La Fontaine* to play for the customers. Whenever that happened Elke would ring me up, and if I had no more calls to make I'd rush over to hear him play. It's not often life gives you such a treat! Try to imagine the scene, Your Honour: Jonas — an androgynous boy of almost shocking beauty, with his smooth cheeks, wavy hair, aquiline nose, high cheekbones, sharply slanted jaw and large dark eyes — standing there like an apparition amidst ten or fifteen tipsy peasants and playing "The Lark" or "The Dance of the Sabres" at lightning speed. The men's eyes would cloud over as they watched the boy plunged into rapture by the music — never in their lives, perhaps, had they known a similar abandon...

If you don't mind, we can now take advantage of Jonas's music to allow a little time to pass.

In a dark closet somewhere, on reels of silent celluloid, the hands on Hitchcock's wall clock keep turning, turning. The ice thaws on the pond, borages and violets, daffodils and crocuses come out to salute the end of winter, the president of France dies, I give birth to my first son Eugene, buds swell moistly and greenly on the branches of apple and cherry trees, then burst into pink-and-white flower. In *La Fontaine*, Elke listens to her customers' gruff comments on the electoral campaign, serves them plum brandy in tiny glasses, daydreams about Cosmo and, smiling, wipes the counter for the thousandth time; when the candidate Vera was rooting for loses the elections, she comes into the café to drown her sorrow; Jonas draws his violin from its case and launches into a dirgelike rendition of "*La Marseillaise*," followed by an improvisation that zigzags between peasant jig and gypsy dance; her blood stirred by the music and a few whiskies, Vera begins to dance in front of the fireplace; the customers, without leaving their seats, urge her on by clapping in time with the music; Jonas plays so ecstatically that his hair falls over his eyes, but this matters little as his eyes are closed — he's far away, utterly absorbed in the music of Monti or Brahms, and can thus remain oblivious to the winks the men are exchanging as they watch the sway and jiggle of his mother's not-young buttocks and breasts.

Jonas

She's right, Your Honour — I never notice that sort of thing. I know nothing about men's desire for women; desire among men is all I've ever known — ever since age six or so, when my father's brother Armand first raped me. I didn't know it was called rape at the time, there were no words for it, either before, during or after, there was only the act itself, incredible, and though I was hardly what you would call innocent (no one who grows up in a gypsy camp is innocent, you witness people and animals coupling from the day you're born), nothing had prepared me for this — the surprise of seeing my handsome young black mustachioed uncle, one day when we happened to find ourselves alone together in the trailer, suddenly turn into someone else, get an urgent look on his face, start talking to me in a louder, deeper voice than usual, a voice that vibrated like the open string on my violin, and, turning me round, tug down my pants and enter me brutally, setting off an explosion of light in my brain. Afterwards, when he was himself again,

Armand made me swear not to tell my father — and despite the burning pain in my body, I was secretly moved and flattered that he should have chosen *me* for this event, an event so powerful and mysterious as to have made him unrecognizable for the space of a few moments.

After that, it became a routine. He'd come over to our place to visit, find some pretext for taking me aside, and rape me — now I call it rape. It went on, year after year, until I was fourteen, and the whole time I held my tongue. There were two reasons for this, Your Honour — reasons which, though mutually contradictory, had no problem coexisting in my brain. On the one hand, I felt that my uncle's behaviour had to be *natural*, since he was an adult, a loved and trusted member of the family; and on the other hand, given the precautions he took to keep it secret, it was clearly *unnatural* — dangerous, taboo, and therefore exciting.

The whole thing fell apart when I discovered, upon reaching adolescence, that Armand was doing the same thing with my cousin Marie. Within the instant, the spell was broken. I saw that his desire did not concern me personally — that it was random — and I decided to put a stop to it. If you so much as lay a finger on me again, I warned him, I'll tell Papa everything. He knew my father would have murdered him. Gypsies are the worst male chauvinists, even more homophobic than citydwellers. Armand had no choice but to leave me alone.

As of that day, I went far away, as Sandrine has said — both musically and sexually. To me, loving men was like playing the violin — it was all I'd ever known; it would have been as

strange for me to go out with girls as to start taking piano lessons. Unlike Armand, however, I didn't want things to be
random. My goal was to love men in *the same way* as I loved
my instrument — and to achieve sublimity with both.

Frank

Had I known that in coming to this hearing I'd have to listen
to such obscenity, I would have brought earplugs along.

Where was Jonas's mother? What was Vera up to, Your
Honour, while her sweet angel musician was being incestu-
ously sodomized by his lecherous uncle? Oh, yes of course —
she was at *La Fontaine*, doing crossword puzzles! What else?!
Ah, we're getting quite a portrait of rural France... I must say I
can see why my father preferred to split for the Alps, once and
for all.

Sandrine

Petals fell from fruit trees, female birds laid their eggs, Jonas continued to make spectacular progress on the violin, the months
glided by, I discovered the splendours and miseries of motherhood but I doubt I'll be able to interest you with *that*, Your
Honour; odd how everyone finds sex riveting, whereas its consequences bore them stiff — anyway, when my son Eugene was
just two months old I found myself pregnant again; giving up
my job was out of the question because my husband's salary was
woefully inadequate, Jean-Baptiste worked as a gutter in the
chicken factory and hadn't had a raise in four years, so I kept
chugging around the district in my old 2 CV, parking in front of

pathologically closed houses and ringing their doorbells and waiting for the successive openings of doors, shutters, curtains — finding people locked away in their own homes like prisoners, even on the most radiant of summer afternoons, stiff little boys lying watching TV on couches in darkened living rooms, senile great-grandmothers tied to their chairs and left alone to stare at their bedroom walls... Day after day, I gave them shots, medication and advice, changed their bandages, breathed cool air onto their burning foreheads, it was exhausting, going from house to house with one baby in a basket and another in my stomach, my legs puffed up, edema is a common phenomenon in pregnant women but of course that's not worth mentioning here, Your Honour, you're impatient to get back to Cosmo and there's no way I can interest you with my hydropic legs, a thirty-five-year-old nurse with water on the ankles arouses neither curiosity nor concupiscence; fine, then let us return to the story at hand.

One afternoon in May, Fiona was ill. I dropped by to see her at about five, then stopped off at *La Fontaine* to report to Elke... and Cosmo was there.

Ah, at last!

She's still at a hundred and two, I told Elke. I gave her some aspirin and told her to drink lots of water. Hi, Cosmo.

I'm going home, said Elke. I'll ask Suzon to replace me; I hate the idea of Fiona being at home alone with a fever.

She's not alone, I pointed out. Frank is keeping her company by reading comic books out loud to her.

Yes, but still, said Elke.

Elke

And then, I remember, Cosmo said: I'll take you home — and I laughed. I laughed because Cosmo had never learned to drive; the only way he could take people home was on foot. He, on the other hand, loved to have other people drive him around, do him favours, wait on him hand and foot. He was severely handicapped where material existence was concerned — Josette having anticipated his every need as a child and André having taught him nothing but anguish, he'd acquired neither male nor female skills for daily life. So when he took me home that day, it was with me at the wheel of my own car. And in fact, just as he was settling into the passenger seat, he asked if we could make a detour on the way home.

I'd like to introduce you to some friends of mine, he said.

I glanced at him to see if he was joking, but he wasn't.

You can't be serious, I said. How can you even suggest such a thing? Didn't you hear what Sandrine just said? Fiona has a temperature of a hundred and two! I'm sorry, I really don't feel like making any social visits...

I'm not talking about social visits, said Cosmo. I'm talking about real encounters. Your daughter has just taken aspirin. And she doesn't even know you've decided to come home early — she's not expecting you until nine. Even with the little detour I'm suggesting, you'll be home long before seven. All right? Quick, turn left — right here.

He'd put a hand on my knee.

I obeyed, of course.

Following his instructions, I turned left, then right, then

left again, drove the length of a high stone wall and parked in front of a portal. We got out of the car...

Look, Elke, said Cosmo, flinging his arms wide to embrace the scene in front of us. These are my friends.

I was brought up short, overcome with dizziness.

Of course I'd seen cemeteries before, Your Honour, both in Paris and down here, but never a cemetery like this one. An overpopulated city in a state of spectacular neglect. Crosses made of chipped stone or rusted iron, a dense forest of crosses extending as far as the eye could see and seemingly in motion, for the soil had buckled beneath them as under the effect of seatide or ocean swell, so that virtually all the crosses were askew, tipped to the right, left, forwards, backwards, or knocked right over, broken, mutilated...

Look, Elke!

Not a single blade of grass. But dusty ceramic peonies, plastic pansies, black moss and yellow lichen on the jumbled, crumbled, topsy-turvy tombstones...

Look, Elke!

Many of the crosses marking the graves of humble folk were nothing but two lengths of drainpipe soldered at a right angle... Their surface had been meticulously covered with strings of tiny beads but most of the beads had fallen off and the drainpipes now sat there, naked and incongruous, while the Christs which had graced them, aggressed by frost, had swung upside-down or plummeted to the ground, where the wind had gleefully scattered their broken arms and legs...

Oh, time had had a ball with this cemetery, that much was

clear! No matter where you looked, the words engraved in stone were all but effaced, like faint whispers. Most of the names of the deceased were illegible, but here and there you could still make out a syllable evoking someone's patronym or Christian name — or else *ne, lwa, rnal, etual,* sad reminders and remainders of the solemn promises made to the dead by the living: *never, always, eternal, perpetual,* people had promised, and, decade after decade, the weather had come to pulverize first the promises, then those who had made them — whisking *them,* too, out of existence, one after the other, and mixing them tranquilly with their dear departed beneath the stones, until the earth itself began to buckle.

Oh! What are the living made of, if not the dead?

That was the day Cosmo first introduced me to Clementine, and described the thunder of applause that had followed his performance of *Swish-swish* in the town hall, that long-ago Saint Blaise's Day of 1948.

I also met his cousin Antoine — who, Cosmo told me, had had the most beautiful laugh in the world, and who'd shown him his first pornographic magazines, and with whom, of a summer's day, he would climb up into the hayloft to masturbate over glossy photographs of breasts. The two boys would rub each other's penises, laughing, competing to see who could spurt the farthest. But at age seventeen, having fallen asleep working the fields late at night, Antoine had slipped off the combine harvester. The machine had threshed his right arm, and by the time help arrived his blood had been irrigating the furrows for hours...

Look, Elke!

A long row of tiny gravestones decorated with seashells, vases, lovely porcelain plates bearing the painted images of Jesus and the Virgin Mary...

Gypsy children, Cosmo explained. All lined up in a row as if they were still in school, whereas in fact they probably never went to school...

And, a little farther on: I'd like you to meet my aunt.

The inscription was vague and greenish, eaten away by lichen, but I managed to decipher it: Marie-Louise Cottereau, 3 November 1917...

She was my mother's little sister, Cosmo told me. Born at home during the Great War, and strangled by her umbilical cord. The family was probably relieved, given the food shortages of the day! But personally, I've always regretted the fact that Marie-Louise didn't survive... Ever since my mother first brought me to visit her grave at the age of seven or eight, I've been intrigued by the idea that this aunt was at once much older and much younger than myself... Over the years, I concocted a whole personality for her — she was a charming young woman with a wry sense of humour... Often I'd come here to pour out my heart to her, and she'd listen — ah, what a wonderful listener she was! No one could listen to me as well as Marie-Louise!

I remember every single friend he introduced me to that day.

Marinette. Poor Marinette — a lovely young bride whose husband, Jean Aleonard, died of an infarct when she was six months pregnant — fell over just like that, at the dinner table! Blam! His face in the soup! Such a shock for his wife. She didn't lose the baby, but it stopped growing in her womb and when she gave birth three months later it was the size and shape of a six-month-old fetus — a dwarf. The doctors had never seen anything like it. She named it Jean, after her husband. Little Jean remained misshapen and bizarre; he never learned how to speak normally so he couldn't attend school. Marinette decided to see to his education herself. She threw herself wholeheartedly into the task — and not only did he learn to read and write, he turned out to have a real gift as an artist; his paintings began to sell, they sold well, at nineteen he had his first major show and changed his name to Aleo — yes, Your Honour, *the* Aleo! Marinette glowed with pride at his success, comparing him to another misshapen painter, Toulouse-Lautrec (whose name she pronounced Too-Loose-Latreck — you see, I have forgotten nothing)... But then, at age forty, Aleo announced to his mother that he had decided to marry — the wealthy widow of a surgeon was one of his clients in the middle-sized city — and Marinette's world collapsed. A few weeks later, she left her house in the middle of the night and drowned herself in the Cher River; a group of fishermen, setting up their lines the next morning, found her body beneath the bridge...

Last but not least: the monumental tombstone erected in honour of the local war hero, Marcel Ribeaudeau. Like Vera's husband, Ribeaudeau had been executed by the Germans in July of 1944. He had earned fame as a Resistance fighter — whereas his son Gustave, whom I knew well, was famous only for his drinking. He lived a few miles out of town with his wife Valette and a swarm of children. Their house was known far and wide for its filth and disorder. Half-wild dogs barked from the garbage-strewn front yard; toddlers mingled in the barn-yard with pigs, hens and rabbits; the older children used the rusty ruins of farm machinery as toys. Given the confusion that reigned in the Ribeaudeau household, Gustave was rumoured to be both father and grandfather to some of the children. Though he occasionally earned a few francs by lending a hand to a neighbour, alcohol had made him unfit for any permanent employment, and the family basically scraped by on his miserable military pittance.

Sandrine

The Ribeaudeaus' standard of living was indeed deplorable, Your Honour. They always called on me for their health problems because my visits cost less than the doctor's. Once, I remember, I stopped by to vaccinate their youngest child and afterwards Valette confessed they couldn't pay me anything at all. She invited me to stay for lunch — they were having potato soup, she said — and I didn't see how I could refuse. As we sat down, I gathered from the children's squeals of delight that the potatoes were not part of the usual fare but had been added to the soup in my honour. They lay, few and far between, at the bottom of a tureen filled with tepid milk and soggy white bread. When Valette leaned over to serve me, I noticed an ugly purple bruise on her chest and my blood went cold... Ah, so Gustave beat her... Had someone told me then that within a few months, my own husband... No, I'm boring you again; all right; I'll shut up.

Elke

Gustave Ribeaudeau was the laughingstock of the county — he was a brute, a real caricature of a drunk. The local police having long since revoked his drivers' licence, he drove his tractor into town every morning and parked it in front of *La Fontaine*. He was one of the pillars of the establishment — a shaky pillar, to be sure, but not one you could ignore. The minute a stranger walked in, he'd yank up his filthy T-shirt, proudly exhibit the scars on his back and chest, and offer to tell how he'd gotten them. Almost invariably the men turned away, frowning, and shook their heads.

Not Cosmo. And now, as we stood together next to Marcel's grave, he told me about the origin of Gustave's scars.

As an adolescent, Gustave had been naïve and idealistic. Eager to make his mother proud and prove himself worthy of his heroic father, he'd joined the paratroopers when troubles first broke out in Algeria, in 1954. Upon arriving in Algiers, however, he discovered to his dismay that he was expected to behave more like a member of the Gestapo than a Resistance fighter.

Latifa

This is true, Your Honour. It is true, and very important.

Yes. You see, during the Algerian war...

The Novelist

I'm sorry, Latifa — I know you've been waiting for a long time already but you'll have to be patient just a little while longer...

Latifa

Your Honour, this is the third time I've been cut off and it's beginning to get on my nerves. What kind of a novelist is this? Can't she organize her work any better? *Be patient, my heart / it will be a good thing or a constraint / Patience is the body's rest / To each his destiny.*

Elke

Thus it was, Cosmo told me, that young Gustave, horrified at first but progressively numbed by alcohol and habit, spent two long years pumping electricity into the bodies of young Muslims, then executing them whether they had talked or not. In exchange, just before he returned to France, the *fellagahs* lacerated his chest and back with their cutlasses, and even made as if to slit his throat...

There you have it, Your Honour. That was Gustave's story... And now the village children tagged after him in the streets, lifting up their T-shirts, shrieking with laughter and saying, *Look at my scars! Oh — they tortured me front and back! Yuk! Yuk!*

Fiona

Well, what of it? Of course we made fun of old Gustave, what do you expect? People who are ridiculous deserve to be made fun of...

All this time, Your Honour — while Cosmo was taking my mother around the cemetery and introducing her to all his dead friends — I was lying in bed with a raging fever.

Frank had read me comic books for a while, but then he got mad at me because I said he used the same voice for all the characters. It was true! When Mama reads to us, I can tell who's talking even without looking at the pictures... Frank got so mad he threw the comic book right in my face and ran out of the room and slammed the door. So there I was lying in bed alone, sick as a dog, and I didn't even know if he still planned to heat up the soup for my supper like he promised Mama he would. Even if he didn't I wouldn't tell on him, because the one time I told on Frank I regretted it afterwards — he'd stolen some candy at the baker's shop and I told Mama about it, just like that, because he told me, he said it was a secret but I was so little I didn't know what the word *secret* meant, I thought it was like *surprise*, so I got all excited and I said Mama! Mama! Frank stole some candies! and Mama bawled him out, and then she gave him some money and told him to go pay the baker and apologize. So the next day, the minute her back was turned, Frank just grabbed my canary and stuffed it into the toilet and flushed it down. Afterwards he told Mama it had gone flying out the window all by itself, and ever since then not only do I obey my brother but I refuse to get attached to anything because never again do I want to feel what I felt that day, when my poor canary got whooshed away by the whirlpool at the bottom of the toilet.

Anyhow, I was glad to hear Mama come home earlier than usual. She ran straight into my room and kissed me on the forehead. Wow, she said, I might as well turn off the heat for the night, you can warm up the house all by yourself! I'll make you some nice herbal tea with honey. Cosmo's here; do you want him to come and pay you a visit?

I said yes. Partly because I did, and partly to make Frank mad because I was mad at him for throwing the comic book at me and leaving me all alone when I was sick.

So Cosmo came into my room. He closed the door softly, tiptoed over to my bed and sat down on it — poised like a bird, weightless — he didn't even make a dent in the mattress. I was glad to see him but I didn't want him to know that, I wanted him to think I *wasn't* glad. That's the way I am, Your Honour. I don't like it when people make me happy because I don't want to get attached. I don't want to miss my papa. I don't want to wish he'd live with us again, if you can understand that. But maybe you're not smart enough. Who are you, anyway? What makes you so superior to everyone else that we have to call you Your Honour? Didn't you poop in your pants when you were little? Didn't you steal candy at the baker's shop? You're such a big shot, everyone's supposed to kow-tow to you, remove their hats, Your Honour this, Your Honour that — what did you do to deserve this sort of treatment? I don't even know what the word *Honour* means! Did my mother lose her honour when she let Cosmo enter her eyes and her bed and her heart? That's what people say, but I don't see why I should respect their opinion. I don't respect anything, if you want to know the truth. I think people stink, as a general rule, so from now on don't expect me to address you differently than anybody else.

Can I visit you? Cosmo asked.

You're already here.

You're not feeling well?

That I didn't even bother answering. I wanted him to feel stupid. If he wanted my attention he had to do something to deserve it.

Your left big toe hurting you?

No.

Well, that's lucky, isn't it? What about your hair?

Don't be silly. Hair can't hurt.

Hey, that's even luckier, isn't it?

I stifled a giggle.

I see you've got lots of company. (He meant the stuffed animals that were in bed with me.) Want to make some introductions?

They already know who you are.

Oh, do they? But I don't know who *they* are.

Do you have to know *every*thing?

Yes, that's exactly it. I have to know everything. I'm sick too, you know.

No, you're not.

Yes, I am.

What's your illness called?

It's called have-to-know-everything-itis.

That's not an illness, silly.

Oh, but it is, Fiona.

Where does it hurt?

In my soul.

The soles of your feet?

Ha, ha, very funny. What about you? Where does it hurt?

My throat. The doctor said I have pharyngitis. *That's* an illness. Not have-to-know-everything-itis.

Pharyngitis? Wow! That's a fancy word for a sore throat!

I happen to like fancy words.

Tell me another one.

Antidisestablishmentarianism.

Good Lord, where did *that* come from? It's so long it almost knocked me over.

It's the longest word in the language, that's all.

How did you meet it?

Don't be silly, you don't meet words.

Sure you do. I met a real nice one the other day.

Pause.

Well, what was it?

Oh, but if you don't believe you can meet words, how can I introduce you to it?... It's really a nice word, though; it's dying to meet you.

Words can't die.

Sure they can. If everyone stops using them and no one wants to meet them anymore, they just wither up and die.

Okay, so what's your word?

Idiosyncrasy.

What's that? An idiot who's crazy about sinks? Ha ha.

Not at all. Do you know what an idiot is, by the way?

Sure I do. It's like the people at Chezal-Benoît. Lunatics. Weirdos...

Vera

Chezal-Benoît, Your Honour, is the name of the nearby psychiatric hospital — where, because of Josette's unforgivable act, my André was imprisoned for nine long months. But at the time of this conversation with Fiona, Cosmo was still unaware of this episode in his father's past.

Josette

What do you mean, imprisoned? *My husband was mad!* It's written down in black and white in his files, Your Honour; you can check it out for yourself. Even as a youth in Paris, he'd been committed to a mental institution, as the Lebanese cedar told us...

Vera

Oh, yes, he was mad, all right — *about me!* And I about him! And *that's* why you had him locked away like a criminal! *That's* why you went to the town hall and denounced your own husband! Just what did you tell the mayor, Josette? The reason for confinement had to be entered in the day's ledger, along with the testimonies of friends or family members. No fewer than eight individuals marched into the mayor's office that day, at your instigation, to sign the papers. Yes, Josette — *your* friends and *your* relatives. What monstrous lie did you invent to make them do it? *A danger to himself and others!* For shame! André! My André! A danger!

Josette

In the light of the ensuing events, Your Honour, one can scarcely deny that he was a danger to himself...

Vera

You were jealous! Admit it! That's the least you can do, after all these years! It's too easy to dismiss our story by calling me a hussy! No, it *bothered* you when it turned out that your country bumpkin of a husband was a man of exceptional spiritual depth — and that *you*, the notary public's daughter, weren't worthy of tying his shoelaces. You were unable to be a spiritual companion for him, as he so ardently wished you to be. You could neither love him nor console him for his failures... So when at long last he did find a soulmate — a friend to whom he could pour his heart out, with whom he could celebrate his presence on the Earth and experience sexual and spiritual bliss, yes, I'm not afraid to say it in public — on the contrary, I'm proud of it, I've never been prouder of anything in my life, so I'll say it again, I'll shout it from the rooftops, *when he finally managed to get laid, hit the jackpot, fly to seventh heaven* — you, Josette, couldn't stand it. It rankled with you that someone like *me* should bring out the greatness in a man whom *you* treated like a doormat. The more your husband thrived in my presence, the more your own mediocrity and pettiness were brought home to you. And so you had him locked away at Chezal-Benoît.

Fiona

For us kids, anyhow, Chezal-Benoît meant crazy, just like Gustave Ribeaudeau meant drunk. I want to get back to my conversation with Cosmo; I hate being interrupted.

Do you know what an idiot is?

Sure I do. It's like the guys at Chezal-Benoît. Lunatics. Weirdos...

Who told you that?

The kids at school.

Well, the kids at school are wrong. An idiot is some-one who's totally original — like me.

It's not polite to boast.

I'm not boasting. The truth is that anyone who really wants to can be an idiot, but most people are afraid. Idiot means unique, one of a kind. Most people prefer to be like everyone else, but they all know they're idiots deep down. It's a lonely business, accepting the fact that you're an idiot. You can't even join an idiot club, because then you wouldn't be unique any-more. Still, true idiots tend to recognize each other. When I first saw you, Fiona, I said to myself, Hey, that little girl looks to me as if she just might be an idiot.

I didn't know how to answer *that.*

Are you an idiot, Fiona?

...Maybe... Did you think Frank might be one, too?

Ah, Frank is a different kettle of fish... But to get back to my word, an *idiosyncrasy* is something very peculiar indeed. So peculiar that it might characterize only one person in the world. Like, ah... putting salt in your orange juice...

Yuck!

Or saying *antidisestablishmentarianism* at the drop of a hat.

I giggled.

Or playing the piano with your toes.

Okay — pleased to meet you, idiosyncrasy.

How's your throat?

Awful.

It's awful to feel sick, but at the same time it's wonderful, isn't it?

How could it be wonderful? It hurts, you have to stay in bed all day, you get bored...

Yeah, I know, but it's fun, too — at least I remember when I was your age, I hated it and I liked it at the same time.

How can you like being sick?

It's as if you were a prisoner in a story, locked up in a deep dark dungeon of sickness with thick stone walls and clanging metal gates, you've got this thump at the nape of your neck, as if some brutish guard were clubbing you over the head all the time — you know what I mean?

Yes...

And you feel all trembly and shaky inside? Like a prisoner waiting to be guillotined at dawn?

Yes...

Yes, and then, when your mother brings you a bowl of chicken soup or some hot lemonade with honey... doesn't it taste *fantastic? Much* better than usual?

...Maybe.

I mean, doesn't the hot soup feel just *terrific* when it slides over that big raw itchy red lump in your throat?

Yes, maybe.

And what do you do when you get bored?

Nothing. That's why you get bored, silly. Because there's nothing to do.

Yeah, but it's impossible to really do *nothing*. Even if you try.

Well, I *breathe*, if you must know.

Mm-hm... And what else?

I stare at the walls.

And what do you see on the walls?

Nothing.

Come on, Fiona, there's not nothing on those walls, I don't believe you!

No, there's light and shadow, and when the sun is out I can see floaty little motes of dust in the sunrays coming through the shutters.

Ah, that's better!

And sometimes...

Yes?

Sometimes... there's, like, a little transparent bubble in there along with the dust, and it moves... it slides across the air... I don't think it's really there, I think it's, like, in my eye, you know?

Yes, I do know. I've met that bubble before. Can you control it?

Yes! It looks as if it's moving all by itself, but if you flick your eyes up to a corner of the room, next to the ceiling, you find it there, too, and then it starts sliding down again, you can look at anything you want and find the little bubble there and watch it slide.

Well, that doesn't sound so boring to me! And can you read?

I can rea-ea-ead... But when I'm sick, I can't concentrate too well. So Frank reads to me. Or else, if Mama's home, she comes and tells me a story.

Your mother's one heck of a good storyteller.

Are you in love with her?

I sure am.

Are you gonna come and live with us?

Uh-uh.

Oh, that's good, because Frank said...

But I stopped myself in time. And Cosmo didn't press me for details.

After that, we remained silent for a while. I was sort of glowing inside. It's not every day that you have such a good conversation.

Then, without a word, Cosmo took a piece of string out of his jacket pocket and taught me how to play cat's cradle. It was great — a different pattern every time. We were passing the string back and forth, going faster and faster... when suddenly Frank burst into the room without knocking. Cosmo and I jumped as if we were guilty of something. Frank's eyes were hard and stony, but all he said was, Could I have my comic book back now, Fiona? Have you finished with it?

Without another word, he picked up the comic book he'd thrown at me an hour earlier and left the room. I got the message, namely that I'd done something unforgivable. Not only had I betrayed my brother; not only had I betrayed our motto *Eyes of stone, body of stone, heart of stone* — worse yet, by playing games with the intruder (the *fornicating clown*, as Frank called him), I'd betrayed our father.

I felt like a piece of shit.

Fifth Day

Elke

I have to admit, Your Honour, that I was totally unaware of what went on between Frank and Fiona that night. And... not only that night... But we're unaware of so much that goes on, aren't we? I doubt that even *you* can claim to be up to date on the dilemmas, obsessions and miseries of your loved ones... Only fools think they know everything. To be intelligent is to acknowledge the limitless expanses of one's ignorance. Since we're here to tell the truth, the truth is that on that particular evening, because of our visit to the cemetery, I had only one thing on my mind, and that was making love with Cosmo.

Now, don't snicker. I'm not morbid — and neither, despite what Frank has said, was Cosmo. But when you see death at close range, it's only natural to clutch desperately at life — you want the fullness, the swelling and the throbbing, all those things the wisteria mentioned earlier... This is why people attend funerals with their arms full of flowers, which are reproductive organs — because life is fleeting and death eternal, and they long to vanquish eternity with fugacity, to drown the colourless odourless neutrality of permanent non-existence with the brilliant hues and smells of the here and now — sex, flowers, body, excess, wetness, redness! sense, sweat, crotch, juices flowing, bodies jerking, panting, moaning, ah! we're alive now and knowing it and crying out

— oh look my love just look, we're not yet dead!

I once came upon on an article about My Lai — an entire village of Vietnamese civilians massacred by American troops who'd gone berserk and shot into the crowd. The article was written by a woman. She told how, a few weeks after the massacre, she and several other journalists had travelled to My Lai to see what there was to see — and, having reopened the mass grave into which the corpses of more than a hundred men, women and children had been flung, they'd indulged in an orgy at the edge of the pit. And I believe this woman when she writes that *their bodies did it all themselves* — that, confronted with this flagrant proof of mortality, they'd been galvanized by an unprecedented sexual urge and begun to fuck at random, responding to the basic impulse to hurl *life! life! life!* in the face of death.

Without comparing my own emotion to anything so extreme, Your Honour, I was overcome with desire for Cosmo that night. But the children were present — even more so than usual, given Fiona's illness and Frank's vile mood. I love my children, Your Honour, God knows I love them, but that night I wouldn't have minded dispatching them off to the Alps with their father. They were a burden on me. There. I've said it. A burden.

By ten o'clock, everything I could do for and with them had been done. Stuffed with medication, Fiona was nodding off in her bedroom. Frank had had his supper. The hostility emanating from him was so powerful that I scarcely dared to go wish him goodnight. Ah... if only I could have read him a bedtime story! But he didn't want to be read to anymore... If only I could have cuddled him or wrestled with him (we used to roll around on the living-room rug, in pseudo-wrestling matches that drove Michael up the wall), but he wasn't four years old anymore, or five, or six; he was eleven. And eleven-year-old boys are too big for physical games with their mothers.

How should a mother behave, Your Honour, with a father-less son on the brink of adolescence? How break through his barrier of taciturnity — gently, gently — and get a grip on any inner part of him? How reassure him, when you no longer have the right to take him in your arms and press him to you, when even a goodnight kiss makes him blush and turn his face away?

Latifa

If I for once can give my opinion without being interrupted, my opinion is that bringing a lover into the house is not the best thing a mother can do to help her son. I'm shocked, Your Honour, by what I'm learning here about how French mothers live — Madam Elke and Madam Vera — to me and my friends it's hard to understand, we do all we can to hold the family together, and they blast it apart on purpose, we try to give our poor husbands support, watching sick at heart as they subside into silence, unable to be men in this country... and *they* chase their husbands out of the house! If Kacim had had a father, he'd never have gone to prison; I'm saying nothing but the truth — and no matter what Kacim did I love him — just as your mother loves you, Your Honour, exactly the same. We love our sons... But a boy without a father is like a firecracker, there's nothing for it, the fuse has been lit and all you can do is wait for it to go off.

Elke

Yes, Latifa. Our sons, unfortunately, had a lot in common, and they were destined to pool the worst of their resources. But at the time we're discussing right now, they haven't yet met.

Latifa

What? They haven't yet met? Why do you say that, Madam, when you swore to tell the truth? My Kacim doesn't know your Frank?

Elke

We're telling the story for the judge, you understand? First one thing happened, then another.

Latifa

Ah. All right, I understand. First one thing happened, then another. All right. Kacim and Frank haven't met. They're not even born. So listen to me: when my husband Hassan came to live in the medium-sized city, it was the mid-sixties, long before what you're talking about now, so it must be my turn, I don't know why someone didn't tell me.

Hassan was twenty-four at the time. He had a thick black mustache and his dark eyes glinted like a bonfire in the desert night; I'd known him forever because he was my cousin and to me he was a god, even if I was just fourteen I was in love with him, he didn't know how to read or write but he could recite poetry by heart and I loved poetry: *She captured my heart today, / The gazelle who came from Arafât. / At an indolent pace, her friends / Walked with her towards the Stone. / She wore clothes of the purest silk, / Richly coloured and brocaded. / How could I ever forget / This gazelle? She is my life.* So when my father called me to him one day and said: Latifa, my brother and I have decided you shall marry your cousin Hassan, it's a good match, my heart started leaping in my chest like a little goat, but right afterwards my father said: You know times are hard, very hard, things have gotten even worse since the end of the war, so as soon as you are married Hassan will go overseas to France to make tires, because all the people in this city are making military planes and there aren't enough of them left to make tires, he won't be gone long, just until he earns enough to support a family here, and meanwhile you'll live with his parents... Don't worry, Your Honour, I'm not going to tell you every little detail but on the eve of his departure, I was already settled into his mother's house, Hassan came to wish me goodbye. Look, Latifa, he said — withdrawing from his jellaba a magnificent knife with a long tapered blade and a handle sculpted in goat's horn — this knife has been in my family for more than a century, I received it from my father who received it from *his* father, I leave it in your keeping, as a token of our love, and one day it will belong to our son.

That is what he said, and then he went to France.

The Knife

It was a firm, steady hand indeed that guided me that day into Cosmo's entrails — you would have thought my handle had been modelled especially to espouse its inner curve. It was quite marvellous, Your Honour, to feel myself thus clasped between palm and fingers, neither too loosely nor too tightly. I do appreciate being held in a steady grip. Nothing is more unpleasant than a clammy hand, a twitchy, trembling hand that's not yet sure what it wants to do with you, or even if it should do anything. That day, moreover, there was no risk of sweating and slippage because the hand was gloved — yes, there was a thin layer of pink silk between it and me — so thin that I could feel the quivering of every muscle... Ah, Your Honour — you wouldn't believe how many muscles there are in a human hand!

Latifa

Would you please tell the knife to be quiet, Your Honour? Its turn is still a long way off.

So that was in 1965. Kacim, my oldest son, was born in 1966. Every two years my husband would come home to visit, then go away again, leaving me with a new baby in my womb, God is the greatest, so when he told me to come and join him in France in 1974 there were four children already, two boys two girls, we took the boat, then a train, then another train and arrived in La Chancelle. When I was still in Algeria my husband told me the word *Chancelle* meant luck, *la chance*, but when I began to live there and learned French a little better I found out the real meaning of the word, it comes from *chanceler*, to totter, because everyone totters around here, Your Honour, it's impossible to stand up straight. Look, with my hands I'll draw you a map of the middle-sized city and you'll understand what I mean: here's the city centre, you see, with the cathedral, the Renaissance palaces and the ancient half-timber houses, La Chancelle is up here to the north. To get there, you have to cross the railroad tracks — and then, just beyond the tracks, you have the cemetery, the prison and the goods station. That's the southern limit of our neighbourhood. Here to the east is the highway to Paris, and then in the back, this line running across at an angle is a river! So La Chancelle is this flattened triangle cut off from the rest of the city, with some thirty thousand people squeezed into it. *Woe is me! How is it I've become a lonely wanderer / Amidst so many strangers / Each person must live out his own destiny / And your fate is in the hands of the merciful Maker...* In the early years it wasn't so bad, the neighbourhood was full of life, Wednesday morning in the marketplace you'd see people of all different colours speaking many different languages, my friends and I were not unhappy, even if we couldn't help pining for our village... But if you don't mind my saying so, Your Honour, it was a strange idea to bring over the families of the immigrant workers just when the economy started falling apart. I hope I don't need to give you a lesson in history — oil crisis, lay-offs, unemployment — La Chancelle got poorer by the day, everyone who could afford to moved out, and eventually only the Arabs were left. *The contingencies of Time are many and sundry / Time is the source of both wealth and misery...* Hassan lost his job at the tire factory, and the only new job he could find was garbage collector, it's nothing to be ashamed of but the salary was low for a big family, we'd had four more children in the meantime and ten people is a lot in a four-room apartment but we couldn't afford a bigger one; as it was it cost us six hundred francs a month — no, Your Honour, please don't tap your foot with impatience, I know you're wondering what this has to do with Cosmo's death but there is a connection, everything is connected and I want you to understand *why*, over the years, Hassan grew more and more silent and withdrawn.

In 1979 destiny struck, my husband slipped off the garbage truck and fell on his back, right on one of those concrete markers on the sidewalk, three vertebrae broken, now he was really tottering, they had to operate but even after the operation his body was all twisted, he couldn't jump up on the garbage truck anymore so they gave him a job sweeping the streets in the old part of the city and that was hard on him, he had to take two buses each way, what with his back pain and the commute in addition to the job itself he was exhausted by the time he got home and he didn't feel like talking, either to me or the children, he just changed into his jellaba and sat down — outside on a bench if it wasn't raining, inside at the kitchen window if it was — he sat and stared but there was nothing to see, Your Honour, nothing but high-rise apartments and the sky which was almost always grey or white, still today he sits there for hours with one leg crossed over the other, smoking cigarettes and staring into the void, he's forty now, his mustache has turned grey and he doesn't say a word but I know he's thinking about Boussâada and the old poems and the nighttime in the desert, *My eyes weep for the land of my Ancestors / The love of my Homeland lives deep within my heart* — no, I'm not trying to move you to pity, it's not that, I just want you to know why it was that Kacim almost never heard the sound of his father's voice...

He took off early, my eldest son — by the age of ten he was already hanging out with the older boys in the streets, by eleven he was smoking cigarettes and hashish, and by twelve he was robbing stores and getting picked up by the police, I was ashamed but what could I do? Go ahead and tell me, Your Honour, I'm waiting, what could I do?

All right, I'll stop there, I talked for a long time but it's because I kept getting interrupted before, so a lot of things built up.

Elke

With all the respect a mother owes another mother, Latifa, despite the fact that the connection between us is a most painful one, I'd should like to pick up my story where I left off. Given the length and intensity of Latifa's tale, Your Honour, you've probably forgotten where that was, so let me refresh your memory — I was leaving my son's bedroom on tiptoes, about to join my lover.

Ah... Silence. Silence at long last.

To prevent mother worries from entering my lover space, I now had to change gears, undergo a metamorphosis, surround my bedroom with a thick marble wall.

Having turned the key in the lock, I remained facing the door for a moment with my eyes closed, so as to empty out my head. When I turned round, I saw to my enchantment that Cosmo had lit candles here and there around the room. It reminded me of the Christmases and Easters of my childhood — and without wishing to offend the pious, Your Honour, I must say that what I felt now was much like what I used to feel in church — namely, the approach of something sacred and the knowledge that for the next hour or so every second, word and gesture would be filled with significance.

Cosmo slowly removed my clothes, while himself remaining fully dressed. Lingeringly, he kissed the skin of my shoulders, stomach and thighs — and I began to melt, the melted snow went rushing through my veins — but I won't prolong this description, Your Honour, because I can tell you want me to get on with it; after a while he rose and I listened, eyes closed, to the sounds of his own undressing — clink of belt buckle, brief buzz of zipper, faint rustle of shirt dropping to floor — all accompanied by his heavy breathing and my own spaced whimpers of impatience. At last — warm, naked, not heavy — his body came to lie full length on mine, he kissed me on the lips... and once again, everything ceased.

I'm sorry, he murmured.

And I: But what is it?

And he: It's a thing that happens.

Lying side by side on our backs, we stared up at the ceiling, where shadows flickered in the candlelight. Are those shadows real? I wondered. It wasn't a rhetorical question, Your Honour.

I wasn't asking it just to change the subject in my mind, as it were. Are shadows real? Is candlelight real? And the candles themselves... before, during and after their consumption by the flame? And my love? The overwhelming love I feel for this young actor?

Always? I ventured after a lengthy silence, not knowing which answer would upset me more, a *yes* or a *no*.

No, said Cosmo in a normal voice — his usual, soft, cracked, ever-so-beloved voice.

A different silence blossomed between us, teeming with different words, ideas, images. (I wouldn't have minded being somewhere else. Mightn't Fiona need me for something? Shouldn't I check to make sure that Frank was asleep?)

It's like stage fright, he said at last. The more you dread it, the more likely you are to get it.

My body is not a stage, Cosmo, I told him. There's no need to dazzle anyone here. Love is not a performance.

He made no answer, and my own sentence echoed hollowly in my head: *Love is not a performance.*

And... when *can* you?

Frank

May I ask what effect all this is having on you, Your Honour? Seriously. How do you feel about the fact that the fornicating clown couldn't get it up for my mother?

Come to think of it, there's a great deal to be said for the peasant philosophy of minding one's own business.

All the stuff we're unloading here... what's it to you? Who

are you anyway, that we should tell you our most intimate secrets, whereas *we* know nothing about you! Neither your name, nor your nationality, nor even your sex! Mum's the word! Oh, yes, it's convenient for you to hold your tongue, isn't it? Well, you can go fuck off!

The Novelist
Now, now, do calm down, Frank. Those are the rules of the game. No judge, no hearing. That's the way it is.

Still, Your Honour, I admit that I can understand Frank's outburst. The asymmetry between you and us is flagrant: whereas we lay ourselves bare before you, both literally and figuratively, you just sit there, impassive and unruffled, concealing your face, your marital status, and every detail of your past... Yet by definition you, too, are a specific individual! You, too, have a particular life history, made up of parents, potties, kisses, disappointments, blows, humiliations, encounters, caresses, books, meals, sunsets...

If I know nothing about you, how can I convince you of the things I care about most? How entrust you with the lives of my characters? Will you be able to comprehend them, take them into your heart, render them immortal through your love? Are you even worthy of making the attempt?

Your silence terrifies me, sometimes.

Elke
And... when *can* you? I asked him.

Is this an interrogation?

No.

Almost always.

Recently?

Yes, Elke. Recently, of course.

Another echo in my mind — his phrase, this time — *Yes, Elke. Recently, of course.*

Was it a cruel thing to say? Was Cosmo treating me cruelly? I didn't think so. I could scarcely breathe but my heart was thumping wildly.

Who... with? I whispered.

Propping himself up on one elbow, Cosmo stroked my face with his gaze — just as he'd stroked my body that first evening at *La Fontaine*. One hand supporting his chin, he gently pushed my hair away from my forehead with the other. I tried to read what was in his eyes, but his face was in shadow.

Are shadows real? I wondered. Is his face in shadow still his face? Is the man in bed with me still Cosmo?

Françoise

Forgive me for interrupting, Your Honour, but... as it happens... only three days earlier, Cosmo and I had made fantastic love together.

Elke

Françoise, he told me, worked as an usherette in the Montparnasse theatre where he'd been performing this past month. She was a small, apparently insignificant woman in her mid-twenties — but to Cosmo, no one was insignificant.

She does her best to conceal her beauty behind a fringe and glasses, he told me, but you can't fool me; I know beauty when I see it...

Françoise
He asked me out for a drink at *Le Sélect*, and we got talking...

Elke
Françoise's father was a painter — one of the innumerable failed painters who gravitate around Montparnasse — and her mother supported the family on her modest salary as a postal clerk. When Françoise turned fifteen her father asked her to pose for him, on pretext that he could no longer afford to pay for models. Her mother firmly opposed the idea, but since a fifteen-year-old girl rarely cares to please her mother, Françoise agreed.

Françoise
Yes.

Naked, then, and alone with my father for long hours in his studio, with variety programs playing on the radio and rain pattering on the windowpanes, I felt... so many things. It was beautiful, clear and calm. My father was aroused. His desire for me passed through his arm, hand and brush, then flowed directly into the painting. As the hours went by, his strokes grew brisker and his choice of colours surer, he worked more and more feverishly, plastering the paint onto the canvas with an ever-firmer hand... These moments were unforgettable, Your Honour.

Elke

Since then, a decade had passed. Françoise's father had died and her mother had remarried; Françoise herself was completing a thesis in linguistics and working as an usherette to pay for her studies; the moments we've just evoked were already ancient history. But desire is a mysterious thing, Your Honour. Mysterious... and contagious. I shall leave it to you to imagine (not necessarily right now — whenever you like!) how I responded that night to my lover's description of the pleasure he'd taken with a Parisian usherette — a pleasure which was in turn enhanced by the ten-year-old, sublimated desire of a failed painter for his daughter...

Sandrine

This is disgusting!

As it was, I thought Cosmo treated Elke pretty offhandedly, but *this* — no, Your Honour, frankly, I am shocked! In the first place he betrays her, in the second place he boasts to her about his betrayals — and in the third place, if I understand correctly, she gets off on it! No, you can call me a prude if you like, but... For god's sake, Elke...

By this time I was well into the eighth month of my second pregnancy; I often stopped off at *La Fontaine* to chew the rag with Elke between two calls. When I hoisted myself up onto one of the high wooden stools, my huge, swaying stomach would bump up against the counter but I didn't know where else to put it, which way to turn. One day I said to Elke, Listen, dear, it's your life, but you've got to think of your future, your children's future, you can't just go on living like a bird on a branch! You're still young — how old are you? — yes, well, you're still fairly young and attractive, you should remarry, you don't want to tend bar at *La Fontaine* for the rest of your life, do you? All right, so you love Cosmo, I know that, I doubt there are three people in the county who aren't aware of it, but I mean... what kind of love are we talking about? Forgive me for saying so, but you can't go around behaving like a starry-eyed teenager. Sure, Cosmo's sweet, I'm not arguing with that, but you've got to take reality into account. I mean, have the two of you made plans? What are your plans?

She answered me in a low voice, leaning over the counter with a conspiratorial air: If you must know, we plan to be in love *forever.*

And I: But in that case... why not get married?

And she: Whatever for? We've got exactly the number of children we want: two for me and none for him.

And I: But at least you'll live together?

And she: No more than we already are.

And I: Elke, forgive me for being prosaic and down-to-earth, you probably think I'm reasoning with my hormones, but from everything you've told me, I gather this man will be spending something like, er... two weeks a year with you? Is that correct? Come on, wipe that enigmatic smile off your face — am I right or wrong? You mean to tell me that two weeks a year of loving is all you deserve? All you need?

The conversation took an unfortunate turn at this point, because Elke said, When Cosmo's here, Sandrine, I don't think of his presence as an hourglass with the sand running through it, running through it, running out, soon to be over, soon to be gone again, leaving me alone, poor little me, yearning, mooning and nostalgic, condemned to count the days until he returns.

And I said: So how *do* you think of it?

And she, with a shrug: He makes me happy.

So then I said: You live in a dream world, Elke.

And she: I like the world I live in.

And I: Dreams can be dangerous, my dear.

And this is where she went too far; she said: So, I gather, can reality.

At once she was contrite and tried to take it back, saying, I'm sorry, I apologize, please forgive me — but the harm was done.

Her *I gather* referred to the fact that I was wearing dark glasses that day, to hide the black eye my husband had given me the night before. Elke knew that for the past few months Jean-Baptiste had started drinking and hitting me when he got home from work — sometimes even in front of little Eugene. I'd confessed it to her as an absolute secret and she had no business throwing it in my face, it wasn't a friendly thing to do and I found it hard to forgive her. I mean, it's easy to feel superior with an imaginary lover, right? *He* doesn't give you lumps and bruises, that's for sure! Anyway, I stormed out of the café and didn't speak to Elke again until my baby was born; she came to see me in the hospital and we pretended nothing had happened.

A daughter this time! she exclaimed.

And I: Yup. A daughter.

And she: What will you call her?

And I: Leontine.

And we looked at each other, wondering what the future held in store for this new little person whose father battered her mother.

The Cosmophile

If you don't mind, Your Honour, I feel we're devoting a bit too much time to the detailed description of Cosmo's private life — which, after all, is merely incidental...

The Chorus of Women

Incidental!!!

The Cosmophile

...and not enough time, objectively speaking, to what made him great in the eyes of the world, namely his genius as an actor.

If I understand correctly, we have now reached the mid-seventies, when war broke out in Lebanon, and I'd like to at least mention the remarkable sketch he did on that theme — the one about the old fisherman who runs into one of his cronies in the port of Biblos and is informed, to his astonishment, that he is at war.

He scratches his head.

Me? At war? At war? Me?

He proceeds to scrutinize his hands from every angle,

study the soles of his feet and rummage about between his toes. With an expression of mounting terror on his face, he examines his teeth in the mirror, then begins to contort his body in an effort to see his own back... His eyes strive to look at one another and he goes cross-eyed. In the end, his eyeballs roll all the way inward, as if his pupils were desperately trying to check out what was going on inside his brain...

I am at war.

The Psychiatric Expert

But in fact, Your Honour, *nothing* can be described as incidental because it all holds together: as the cosmophile himself pointed out earlier in reference to the actor's *lifework* and *work-life*, the private and the public were inextricably intermingled in this individual — or rather, in perfect continuity, like the two faces of a Möbius ribbon. Torn between his mother and his father, it is as if Cosmo had decided (unconsciously, of course) to *be* no one, but to carry all sorts of other people around inside of him — male and female, French and foreign, old and young... At age sixteen, renouncing the names his parents had chosen for him, he achieved a sort of rebirth by deciding to call himself *Cosmo* — a name which at least has the advantage of being frank! Not content with being merely an artist, one creator among others, he aspired to become *the* Creator par excellence, capable of embodying any element of His creation, whether animate or inanimate. According to all witnesses, Cosmo's capacity to embody others verged on the uncanny: in the course of a single evening he might adopt a hundred different identities, each recognizable to the audience within a fraction of a second. By his voice, posture, facial expressions and hand movements, he would literally *become* the perplexed Lebanese fisherman, the horrified little girl, the Chinese border guard, the dromedary, the pyramid... He projected himself into people he'd never met, his substance became their substance, his marrow their marrow. If I may have recourse to a metaphor (as Freud himself was wont to do), Cosmo borrowed thousands of coloured threads and wove them into an enormous tapestry which he called his personality. In classical terms, it might be said that he aspired to illustrate Terence's motto *Nothing human is foreign to me.* In clinical terms, this behaviour is known as megalomania.

Latifa

I speak French, but what is this man talking about? Do *you* understand anything?

The Psychiatric Expert

This being said, it is worth pointing out that the woman named Elke played a highly singular rôle in Cosmo's life. She held exclusive sway over two, interconnected realms: his sexual impotence and his hometown. As far as we can ascertain, she was the only woman with whom he experienced difficulties of erection as an adult, and the only one directly linked to his rural origins. Moreover, she alone had the right to know everything about him, from his amorous conquests to his professional plans. In their relationship, in keeping with an equivalence familiar to all psychoanalysts, words took the place of sperm. Cosmo himself, you will recall, compared his impotence to stage fright, and indeed the sexual nature of his acting was quite obvious. For two, three, sometimes four hours running, he would flood his spectators with an uninterrupted stream of language (I'm sure I need not remind you that *semantics* and *semen* have the same rootword). The audience — plunged into darkness, passive and silent yet filled with desire, electrified with expectancy, as compliantly eager to respond, laugh, weep or swoon as a woman in the hands of her lover — was in effect an enormous fertile vagina in which Cosmo planted his pearls of wisdom.

Over the many years their relationship lasted, Elke became, if I may have recourse to a pun (as Freud himself was wont to do), a sort of primal scene. Cosmo was unable to make love to her because she lived in the same village as his parents, because she knew everything about him — and especially, as she herself has repeatedly implied (I've been taking notes), because *he was like a son to her.* She told him fairy tales, as she did with her own children; when he fell asleep he looked scarcely older than Frank; his body weighed almost nothing, and so on and so forth. Thus, it is quite clear that from Cosmo's point of view, making love to Elke would have been symbolically equivalent to committing incest and...

Elke

Forgive me, Your Honour — I know we're supposed to allow each witness to express himself fully, but what the psychiatric expert is saying is, quite simply, hogwash.Cosmo and I made love *many* times. *Many many many many* times.

So far, I've merely attempted to describe our somewhat hesitant beginnings. I'm sure lots of love affairs start out this way, but people are loath to talk about their fumblings and bumblings. As a rule, things improve with time. Between Cosmo and me, at least, to say that they improved is an understatement.

The Wisteria

I can neither confirm nor contradict this version of the facts, Your Honour. Following the night I described to you, the shutters on Elke's bedroom windows remained obstinately closed.

Elke

He loved me greedily, tenderly, totally. No detail of my life left him indifferent. Once — I remember it was the evening of Frank's twelfth birthday — he even asked me what it had been like to give birth. Do you see what I mean, Your Honour? Can you imagine such a thing? A man asking his mistress to tell him *how another man's children burst from the sex he so adores?*

The Chorus of Women

Oh, yes, that's exactly how Cosmo was!

We'll all have our chance to testify, won't we? We've been waiting a long time, the days keep going by and we're getting a bit nervous because we've got so much to say! It wouldn't be fair if Françoise alone had the right to tell of her passion for

Cosmo. All of us loved him, all of us were loved by him, and we're dying to tell you about it!

We weren't jealous of one another — you couldn't ask a man like that to curtail his freedom, quell his curiosity, deny his needs, thwart his appetites, and limit himself to loving a single woman. We wouldn't have dreamed of it! We felt no frustration because Cosmo gave each of us more than she'd ever had before. Sure, he juggled with us, but he never pitted us against each other, and it was a privilege to be a ball in the hands of such a juggler. Other men treated us like punching-bags, pencil sharpeners (no? you don't know what we mean?), mothers, whores... whereas *he*...

Oh dear, Your Honour, how can we describe it? He knew the most important thing of all: that physical love is the miraculous revelation of the soul by the body. Each person so sexually different from each other person. To give a woman *that*...to offer her *that*... is beauty itself. What about your own body, Your Honour (for you do have one, there's no getting around it)? Did anyone, male or female, ever celebrate it fully? We hope so; we doubt it; we pity you. In a word, what was unique about Cosmo in bed was his presence. Most men are absent in bed, and he was present. He looked at us, do you understand? More surprisingly still, he looked at himself — his own body — *with* us and laughed at its imperfections. He loved our intimate odours, each woman her own. He loved our stomachs, whether they'd borne children or not, whether they were flabby and wrinkled or silky and smooth.

Don Juan

Good Lord, it stinks to high heaven in here, my stomach is beginning to heave. This is revolting, Your Honour, I must ask your permission to leave.

Farewell!

The Chorus of Women

Ah... you see? Don Juan withdraws, as usual. Don Juan never loved women, Your Honour; love is not his department, and he knows it. His goal is a metaphysical one, and women are merely a means by which to achieve it. Cosmo, on the other hand... Ah! Cosmo! He loved each woman's body because it contained and reflected her unique story. Her skin colour bespoke the peregrinations of her ancestors; her scars were the echoes of illnesses, childbirths, brushes with death... In Cosmo's hands, beneath Cosmo's gaze, no woman could feel ugly. Each life is beautiful because each is a quivering fragment of infinity, set on a finite arc of time. With Cosmo, everything about our bodies that usually shamed us became a source of pride, because we could *talk* about it. When someone's there to listen, the stories unfold, and the telling of them makes you beautiful. The more intently Cosmo listened to us, the more arousing and aroused we grew! We came to him and kissed his penis, Your Honour, it swelled and hardened beneath our lips, between our hands, and he let us see his pleasure, and when desire took over and language disappeared we trusted him, for we knew that in taking his pleasure he would not be moving away from us as most men do, but only coming closer, entering us — yes! — penetrating to the very heart of our beings, each of us pierced, transported, joined in that deepest inner place wherein she loves herself and is, herself, nothing but love.

Not used. No. Not one of us.

The Novelist

Believe me, friends, I can hear the passion behind your plea. I know that when a woman has been loved by Cosmo, she longs to bear witness in front of Heaven itself. Your stories are beautiful, I'm familiar with a number of them, but it's *impossible* for us to listen to them all! Some other time, perhaps, in the course of some other hearing! But not now — no, it would be sheer madness. As it is, the main story line has led us into an alarming number of digressions; the river whose course we're trying to follow keeps branching out into streams and rivulets... I'm sorry, believe me, but that's the way it is — the only statements we can take are those which have a direct bearing on the tragedy.

The Baguette

Ah, but what is a direct bearing? *That* is the question, Your Honour! I myself had the honour, so to speak, of playing a minor role in this story, so allow me to introduce myself, just as an example, of course, or a matter of course... er... I'm not as gifted at verbal expression as some of the other witnesses — the Lebanese cedar quite took my breath away — *what eloquence!* But then, he's ancient, he's been rooted in a scientific neighbourhood for centuries, whereas my own existence is fleeting to say the least; my life expectancy rarely exceeds twenty-four hours: fresh and crusty in the morning, I'm digested by sundown; in a word, I tend to be superficial, but this by no means means (sorry, I shouldn't say by no means means, I should say either by no means signifies or in no way means) that I have nothing to say — so here, if you don't mind, is a small instance of the way Cosmo's mind worked, and it will also allow us to hear the tale of at least *one* more woman from the Chorus of women.

One day, it was in the heart of winter (but the winter of what year? not easy to say, for a baguette), Cosmo was over at Elke's place and they were roasting chestnuts sitting in front of the hearth. I mean *they* were sitting, naturally, not the chestnuts. What a rustic scene, you're probably thinking. Well, never judge too quickly — that's one thing I learned in the course of my short existence. Frank had bought me that day at the baker's — at Elke's behest, albeit unwillingly — and when he got home, instead of setting me gently on the kitchen table, he threw me across the living room in the direction of his mother. Heavens, what a sensation! It's not often a baguette gets treated like a weapon! Fortunately, Elke caught me in mid-air; she registered her son's hostility, but made no comment on it. Well, this tiny event plunged Cosmo into a spiral of memories which would eventually lead to a new show.

Here's how it happened.

There was a brief silence. I was lying calmly on the couch, waiting to be eaten, when suddenly, even as they peeled and ate the hot chestnuts, Cosmo started telling Elke the story of one of his mistresses.

She was one of his oldest and dearest friends in Paris, a Jewish actress by the name of Avital. Her mother was a failed dancer from Austria, and her father, a failed writer from Poland. In 1939, the two of them had managed to escape to London, where Avital was born. When the war finally ended and they returned to Paris, so many of their friends and neighbours had been deported that they never again quite managed to believe in the reality of their lives. They lived in a hotel near the Luxembourg Gardens, ate out in restaurants, and paid only the scantest attention to the so-called necessities of life; both were more or less anorexic and insomniac; neither did housework.

Time passed, Cosmo went on. Once Avital had grown up and begun to live on her own, her parents moved to Israel and settled down in Tel Aviv.

That's practically the anagram of their daughter's name! Elke pointed out.

Since that time, they'd sunk into a sort of harmless lunacy. As the mother had health problems (phlebitis and a zona, if I remember correctly), the father did all the shopping and cooking. Whereas he himself ate almost nothing for supper (two yogurts were plenty), he went to the supermarket every day and bought a half chicken for his wife. Being unable to eat a half chicken, she gave most of it to the dog. Ah yes, I forgot to tell you they had a dog. Storytelling is not my forte, I apologize. Anyway, it was a very cute dog when they first got it, but by this time it had grown neurotic and obese; Avital's mother kept it on a leash even inside the house; she would lead it into the kitchen and force-feed it with a spoon, and when it couldn't swallow another mouthful she'd empty the contents of its tins directly onto the kitchen floor; the apartment reeked of dogfood, and when the father got up barefoot in the middle of the night for a glass of water, he would step in squishy stuff. Moreover, the mother was worried the dog might catch cold so, even in the summer, even in ninety-degree weather, she would cover it with blankets, mountains of blankets, until all you could see was its poor little nose sticking out. She fretted and fussed about the dog so much that her husband finally exploded — I'll KILL that dog! he roared. I swear, I'm going to KILL it! And he would pretend to step on the dog and crush it beneath his feet...

The Cosmophile

Cosmo played the Mother. He played the Father. He played the Dog.

The Baguette

Apart from the father's daily jaunt to the supermarket, they virtually never left the house. They had no friends at all in Tel Aviv. Or anywhere else, for that matter. Each had the other and that was it. Or that was that, I'm not sure which is correct. The mother worked on her dance steps all day long, alone in her bedroom, and the father worked on his novel. He'd been writing the same novel for the past thirty years — a life of Jesus which was also his autobiography in disguise. When they came to visit Avital in Paris in the summertime, he would bring all his

Bibles, dictionaries, and various drafts of the book with him...
and swear he'd put the finishing touches on the manuscript
the minute he got back to Israel. Then he'd return to Tel Aviv,
work all year long and announce his firm intention to com-
plete the book in Paris. Over the years, Avital had read bits and
pieces of her father's book. The tragic thing, she told Cosmo,
was that it was good.

Their hysteria worsened with time — and now, from what I
could glean, they screamed at each other from morning to night.
They quarrelled over anything and everything, including how to
cook eggs. Her father had read somewhere that colza oil was
good for the health, so he would fry his eggs in an inch and a
half of colza oil. Her mother refused to eat eggs cooked in this
manner. Indeed she liked only the yolks, not the whites, and
would not so much as touch the eggs if the yolks had been
broken. Unfortunately, her husband liked to shake the eggs vig-
orously before cracking them open; then he would knock them
repeatedly against the edge of the bowl, then drop them into the
bowl to study them carefully before slipping them into the
frying pan, so that more often than not, by the time they started
frying, the yolks were no longer intact. This caused his wife to
yell at him and, in exasperation, he would throw the eggs out
the window. (I forgot to tell you they lived on a fifth-floor walk-
up; fortunately the kitchen window gave onto an empty lot and
not onto the street.)

One day, she lit into him for buying a new loaf of bread
every day without checking to make sure the previous loaf was
finished, so he threw the bread out the window, too. Not

window number two, you understand, I mean he threw it out the window *as well.*

The Cosmophile
Cosmo played the Eggs. He played the Bread.

The Baguette
Well, that's all I wanted to tell you. Frank threw me across the room, and that reminded Cosmo of the Avital tale (I mean story, it wasn't a tall tale) — which, in turn, because Elke was there to hear it, became the departure point for a whole new show.

The Cosmophile
I'd like to thank the baguette for having revealed to us the origin of the famous *Fried Eggs* number.

When Cosmo used a situation like this onstage, Your Honour, the point was obviously not to make fun of the poor couple. The more comic it was, in effect, the more tragic it was. The spectators laughed, but their laughter was laced with pain, bad memories, and anxiety for their own futures.

The same went for Ribeaudeau — you could laugh at a raving drunk who pulled up his shirt to show off his scars, but only if you knew nothing of his past. The minute you learned his story, your laughter died on your lips.

I think we're finally beginning to get at the specific nature of Cosmo's genius: he was *a story addict.*

Elke

Exactly. And that's why I disagree with what the psychiatric expert said earlier about Cosmo's wish to be God. Nothing could be further from the truth — precisely because, from God's point of view there's no such thing as a story. Indeed, God *has* no point of view, He has no view at all, He's blind and deaf and mute and all-powerful; we humans, on the other hand, being not only mortal (even slugs can boast as much!) but *aware* of it, *do* have a point of view, and this is what's so moving about us — because we realize, stunned, at least those of us who stop to think about it, that we have no choice but to be in a particular time and place, and then, more moments having elapsed, in *another* particular time and place. Hence the fact that we all tend, even those of us who *don't* stop to think about it, to construct our lives inwardly as if they were stories — this, indeed, is the most beautiful thing we do. Stories don't exist in and of themselves; we make them up, and cherish them, and depend on them — because, no longer believing our paths to have been mapped out in advance, or our fate to be in the hands of our Maker, stories are what turn our lives into destinies! All of us are walking novels, teeming with main and secondary characters, punctuated by moments of drama and long, boring descriptions, ellipses and suspense, climaxes and dénouements... You tell me your story and I'll tell you mine, your story becomes a part of mine...

Nancy Huston

Frank and Fiona

Stop it, Mama, for the love of God! You're driving us up the wall!

Elke

My dear children... Can I help it if the novelist singled me out to be her spokeswoman? It's not an easy job, let me tell you! I realize this speech is didactic and overblown, but what can I do about it?

Frank and Fiona

But it's dangerous! This isn't the nineteenth century anymore, you know! We're not allowed to annoy the judge with abstractions and repetitions; he's got better things to do! If you keep this up, he's liable to hurl the book across the room and go watch television — and *then* what will become of us?

186

Sixth Day

The Footbridge

Personally, I have a hard time following the lady's flights of oratory but if there's one thing I do know, it's that time produces weird effects on human beings. I've been around since the end of the nineteenth century, so I've seen quite a few people pass by... I don't want to boast or anything, I wasn't constructed on a strategically important site from a geopolitical point of view so I don't have as many stories to tell as the hero of *The Bridge on the Drina*, I don't know whether you've read that novel by Ivo Andric, Your Honour? No? It recounts several centuries in the life of a stone bridge located at a cultural crossroads — in Bosnia–Herzegovina, if I'm not mistaken. For my part, all I do is span the little Arnon River between two pastures dotted with grazing cows, and today's peasants have probably forgotten why the peasants of yore felt the need for a bridge at this particular spot — so have I, for that matter, but I can testify that time, passing over me, has worn me down little by little. The elements — rain, frost, wind, heat — have nibbled away at me, my cement steps have begun to crumble and my iron bars to rust, several varieties of weeds sprout freely in my cracks, but this is all a part of normal evolution and therefore scientifically predictable — whereas the effect time has upon human beings is, I can only repeat myself, weird.

For instance. At the point we've now reached in the hearing, you're probably convinced that Frank's resentment towards Cosmo is one of the invariables of the story — that it began the day they met and did nothing but worsen as the years wore on — expressing itself, at this hearing, in epithets such as *fornicating clown*. You may even have surmised, deep down, that Frank was in some way implicated in Cosmo's murder, even if he didn't actually wield the knife (otherwise he would never have brazenly proclaimed, as he did at the outset, *I curse Cosmo...*).

Well, I can formally testify that this is not the case. Given the fact that time acts unpredictably on human beings, with zigs and zags, surprises and reversals, sudden crises and prolonged stretches of calm, there was also a period during which Cosmo and Frank got along quite well; indeed, I think one might go so far as to assert that they were friends.

Take the day in the summer of 1976 when they came and picnicked at my side — a summer characterized, Your Honour, in case you're too young to remember it, by drought and a scorching heat wave...

I'd known Cosmo since he was knee high to a grasshopper. I was fortunate enough to be loved by him, and I can only repeat what the chorus of women said earlier, namely that when Cosmo loved someone, he knew how to make them feel it. So it was only natural he should have wanted Elke and her children to meet me. That year, if I remember correctly, Elke would have been pushing forty, Frank was thirteen and Fiona, eight.

Elke parked the car in the grass, right next to me.

I love this little bridge, said Cosmo. When I was a kid, I

used to come here alone and talk to myself.

(It was true! A poignant memory indeed, Your Honour! I was privileged witness of Cosmo's first theatrical monologues — in an embryonic state, to be sure, but already an impressive one. He would stand on me as if I were a rostrum and shout himself hoarse for hours, haranguing the Charolais cows, the fish and the wildflowers... Sometimes, oblivious to the passage of time, he'd go on declaiming long after the sun had set, dazzling the very stars with his eloquence.)

Cosmo and the children removed their sandals and mounted my steps; as trees met overhead, my cement was cool to their feet. Cosmo suggested they play at dropping stones into the water — from my height, some three feet or so — without making a splash, not at all, not the least little upward spurt of water.

How do you do it? marvelled Frank.

It *was* surprising. The stone was simply swallowed up by the water, as if the Arnon had opened its mouth to receive it, then shut it again. Cosmo taught Frank the trick, but try as she might, Fiona couldn't seem to get the hang of it. Then Cosmo showed Frank how to hook his legs into my lower bar, swing his head downwards and watch the water rushing past just beneath his nose. At thirteen, Frank was already taller than Cosmo; his nose all but grazed the water. As Fiona was too small to even *attempt* this feat, she felt left out and began to pout. Paying no attention, the men now started skipping stones over the surface of the water. Five times, six times, their stones skipped. Even seven, once, one of Cosmo's. In the many years since I was built, I've watched humans play this game on numerous occasions and, with all due respect to feminists, whose cause I staunchly support, I must say that the flick of the wrist required for skipping stones is a virile trait; women just can't get it right. I'm sure there are exceptions to this rule, but I don't know of any. Fiona, in any case, was no exception. She tried and her stone went *plop!* The men laughed at her. Cringing, she turned her back on them and stomped away, hitting me as hard as she could with her bare feet. She headed straight for the spot beneath the trees where Elke was seated, grabbed a few stuffed animals out of the picnic basket and went to sulk a little further on.

Elke

As the footbridge has said, it was a very hot day. Thin streams of sunlight filtered through the overhanging trees and struck the water, sending brief floating flashes into my eyes... It was Vincennes, it was the lights on Daumesnil Lake in the forest of Vincennes; Monsieur Denain had taken us all there on a Sunday outing one autumn long ago, he'd held me by the hand and we'd stood side by side on the little footbridge looking down at the fallen leaves floating on the lake, sharply serrated flecks of red, yellow, orange, rust, I remember the photo Yvette took of us that day, me so tiny and my father so tall at my side, so very handsome in his dark suit and bowler hat... Oh, I adored my father, Your Honour — almost as much as my mother! I loved it when he would pick me up and carry me on his left hip, I can still feel my little thighs squeezed tightly around his waist

— I weighed nothing, nothing at all, and he could carry me forever, it was wonderful... That day in Vincennes, he pointed out the different flowers to me and told me their names, the bright bushes of azalea and colchicum, and a vast sea of nasturtiums bobbing gently in the faint wind, saffron on green, dancing with their shadows in the lovely, low-angled light of autumn, the air was as tepid as tears, and how did it happen that the sensations of *then* had come to mingle with those of *now*? You see, Your Honour, this is what the footbridge meant in referring to the weird effect time has on human beings: the steadily advancing river of chronology is forever perturbed by powerful ripples and undertows from the past and future. To be in the *hic et nunc* is the heaven of Buddhists and the hell of Alzheimer patients, but the rest of us are continually, invisibly, being tugged to and fro by other times and places... Do the flowers at Vincennes still exist? I wondered. And these brief flashes of light on the Arnon River — do they, truly, *exist?* They may be an optical illusion — but when you come right down to it, what is an optical illusion? *What you see is what you see,* and in a sense everything is illusory, isn't it? The sky isn't really blue and the sun neither rises nor sets...

Frank

Cosmo is dead, Mama.

You can introduce as many red herrings as you like into the discussion; nothing will ever change that fact.

Elke

Please don't interrupt me, darling. Let me go on. You may think they're red herrings but in fact the words I'm uttering now are the heart and crux and core of the discussion, the most intimate essence of the story, the very sap of Cosmo's life, so please let me finish, it will only take a minute, Your Honour — here's the question I asked myself that day: *Are those flashes real?* Would they be there if I weren't on the spot to see them, or if the sky happened to be cloudy? Ah — so fortunate, and so fortuitous, to be witness to the glittering of the water: this is the way things appear, here, now, in this tremor of time thanks to which a thirty-nine-year-old woman on the banks of the Arnon can also be a four-year-old girl in the Bois de Vincennes — there you are, I've finished, and the footbridge can resume its tale.

The Footbridge

Where was I?

Ah yes.

Right. Frank went on skipping stones on the river beneath me, but Cosmo went over to join Fiona where she was sulking a little ways off. She was lying on her stomach and he stretched out next to her on his back. Above them, the leaves of a silver poplar tree flipped this way and that in the almost-no-wind.

Which way is right side up for those leaves, do you think? asked Cosmo after a while. Do they prefer to show off their silver sides like a queen, or would they rather hide and hoard them like a miser?

Fiona remained silent.

I mean, insisted Cosmo, do you think they prefer to show the world their ordinary green sides and keep the silver sides a special secret for themselves, or...

I think they don't give a damn, said Fiona firmly.

Another silence. Then she changed her mind.

No, I bet they show the green to humans and the silver to the birds, tantalizing the humans who prefer silver and the birds who prefer green.

Tantalizing, that's a nice word.

But the *real* secret is deep inside... and it's *black!*

Oh yeah?

Yeah. Everything's black inside.

How do you know that?

None of your business.

That's true. Except that my business is sticking my nose into other people's business. Sniff, sniff, sniff — I love it. Everybody's so *interesting.*

I don't think so. I'd rather be alone.

Oh, come on. I bet you're curious, too.

No I'm not.

Yes you are. What about all your furry friends?

They don't count. They're me, too.

Then where do their different voices come from?

Oh, Mama made them up when I was little, and now I can do them, too.

Will you do some for me?

Relenting, she introduced him to Fuchsia the little lady

dinosaur and Bill the buffalo, imitating their respective voices.

Hey, you're *good*, you know? said Cosmo. Maybe you'll be an actress, too, when you grow up.

No, I won't.

How come?

Because I have to be a... spel... speleologist.

A *speleologist*? Who decided that?

Silence.

Who said you had to be a speleologist?

Silence.

Do you know what a speleologist is?

...I found the word in a newspaper once, in the bathroom. And — Fiona went on in a very low voice — the Head People said it was an order.

Oh, so you've got Head People ordering you around, too?

She nodded almost imperceptibly.

We can whisper if you want, said Cosmo. No, because I used to know those guys, too, when I lived around here. I grew up in this town, did you know that?

Of course I knew that. Mama told me. It's none of my business.

What's this business business? Can't I tell you about little-boy Cosmo? Who knows, maybe he left his Head People behind when he went off to Paris, and when you moved here they took one look at you and said, Hey *there's* a great head, let's set up housekeeping inside it.

Fiona was listening closely now.

Let's see if it's the same ones... My Head People told me I

always had to set my fork down on the table like this.

He turned his left hand into a fork, tines curved downward.

Nope, said Fiona.

They told me never to step on the threshold between rooms. If I forgot and stepped on a threshold I had to say *sorry sorry sorry* under my breath, five times in a row.

Fiona chortled. No, it's not the same ones, she said. They give *me* different rules.

Maybe girl heads get different rules from boy heads? Let's see... Mine used to forbid me to sleep on my right side.

For me it's the left! Fiona blurted out.

Ah, but maybe that's because I'm left-handed. Are you right-handed, by any chance?

Yup!

You see? So we're not allowed to sleep on the side *opposite* the hand we write with — it's the same rule! What else?

I have to clean house every night.

You get up after your mama goes to bed?

No, I mean, I lie in bed and my nose is the house and I have to clean it out completely.

Ah, *I* get it. For me it was the navel, not the nose. And what do we do with all the dirt?

We eat it, they said simultaneously.

Peals of laughter.

We eat it, we eat it, chanted Fiona.

That's right! Down the drain with it!

Down the drain with it! squealed Fiona — tense now, fairly bursting with excitement.

And what else?

Uh... she cast about, eager to go on.

Tell the truth, now, Cosmo warned. No making things up.

Well, she whispered, if I burp, I have to spell *antidisestab-lishmentarianism* out loud to myself, and if I fart, I have to spell it backwards.

Can you spell it *backwards?*

Yup: m-s-i-n-a-i-r-a-t-n-e-m-h-s-i-l-b-a-t-s-e-s-i-d-i-t-n-a.

That's pretty amazing. I was always a terrible speller, so my Head People must have given up on *that* idea.

What did *you* have to do?

If I burped?

Fiona nodded.

Well, if I burped accidentally, then I had to burp on pur-pose, and the intentional burp would cancel out the unintentional one.

Same for farting?

Same for farting.

Can you still do it?

Sure.

He did so and she giggled.

It's not that hard. But I'm not sure your mother would appreciate my teaching you.

I hear *her* fart sometimes.

Cosmo laughed.

Anything else? he asks. What about the speleologist? Maybe they told you to be a speleologist because you could spell so well?

Fiona nodded slowly. What about you? she asked. Did they tell *you* to be an actor?

They didn't exactly tell me, no. But I put so much effort into getting around their rules and regulations, behaving like this, behaving like that, changing my voice, disguising myself so they wouldn't recognize me, pretending I was someone else... that before I knew it, I was onstage.

How can you pretend you're someone else?

You already *know* how! It's easy! Like... when we played *Jack and the Beanstalk* together, who were you?

THE GIANT!

Right! And you sure scared the dickens out of me!

Eyes wide, fists clenched, Fiona sizzled with pleasure.

I could do it again...

No, no, please don't do it again!

Fee...

Oh, stop at *fee*, please stop at *fee*, I'm already having a heart attack! If you say *fi*, I'm done for!

Fiona

Enough! That's enough, Your Honour. What's the point of all this? What's the footbridge trying to prove? That I got along well with Cosmo? All right, so I got along well with Cosmo, I admit it, I've said as much myself... So what? We're not going to let any old baguette, wisteria, or footbridge run off at the mouth for hours while the rest of us sit here twiddling our thumbs.

I think I know why we're dilly-dallying around like this — it's because we're scared to let events move forward. We prefer to go on basking in those days of happiness because we know that in the next part of the story, as of 1980 or so, things are going to turn sour, and everybody's afraid of hearing about that — everybody but Frank and me, who are afraid of nothing. But we'll have to get around to it sometime — that's what we're here for, after all; there's no point in pretending the story is nothing but honey and chocolate, skipping stones and rippling laughter to the end of time!

The Footbridge

It's true, Your Honour, I did get a bit carried away by the memory of that conversation... The purpose of my intervention, as I'm sure you've gathered, was to show that for a time, even Frank was quite taken with my old friend Cosmo.

Frank

Oh, a game of skipping-stones hardly implies any great intimacy. I'm still the only one in the room who *never* compromised himself with the fornicating clown.

Sandrine

Fiona is right, Your Honour. Time must go on.

Elke

I'm not afraid to let the story move forward.

Here's what happened.

Cosmo was to leave the following day. I'd offered to pick him up and take him to the train station in the middle-sized city. But when I arrived at his barn early that afternoon, I found the shutters closed and the door locked.

How can I describe the effect it had on me? It was like plummeting into the void — like the day I first arrived at the orphanage — like a nightmare in which everything suddenly vanishes; you madly flail your arms and legs but they touch nothing, you scream but not a sound comes out of your mouth... You know, Your Honour, my most painful memory of the orphanage involves not me but another child — a toddler eighteen months old, the same age as my little brother Yves. He arrived at the orphanage one day, I've never seen anyone look so lost and forlorn. His nose was running, his eyes darted nervously to and fro, he whimpered and whined all day long and no one came to comfort him, no one bent down to pick him up, ruffle his hair and tell him, as I so longed to tell little Yves: Now now, don't worry, it's not as bad as all that, everything will turn out fine. The ladies of the Depart-ment of Health and Social Service weren't exactly soft-hearted — besides, they, too, were cold and hungry; there was no heat at all in the orphanage that winter. So the little boy was gradually submerged by fear. In small children, everything is infinite and within a few days he was nothing but fear...

Forgive me. I promise to get hold of myself — I'm fine, really. I know exactly where I was in the story — standing in front of Cosmo's locked barn.

I turned around — Josette was framed in the doorway of the house, with her face in shadow. As I moved towards her she said, Excuse me, Miss, I should have telephoned but I didn't know your last name. Philippe won't be able to leave today. He's ill.

I was taken aback — as much by the word *Miss* as by *Philippe*.

Ill? I stammered stupidly.

He's got his migraine headache, Josette went on with obvious satisfaction, almost with pride — as if to say: Mistresses have no role to play here; this is the mother's exclusive realm.

I'm sorry, she repeated, but I can't let you see him. Light or noise of any kind are intolerable to him.

I'll be quiet, I said. I'll be dark.

Josette was preparing a smile for her final refusal when André's voice reached us from the front room.

Let her in, Josette! Charles told you to let the barmaid in when she came to pick him up!

The barmaid! It took my breath away. So that's what I was to these people? *The barmaid?*

The bedroom was plunged in darkness. I entered on tiptoe and stayed for less than five minutes. Cosmo was stretched out full length on a narrow bed, his hands completely covering his face. The minute I came in, he begged me to remove my watch because its ticking was a torture to him. I slipped the watch into my handbag but he could hear it still; I stuffed the bag under a pile of cushions and at last it was all right. I came over and sat on the chair near his bed. Afraid to touch him, I stretched out a tentative hand and he grabbed it, squeezing it tightly and repeating Elke... Elke...

What's it like? I asked.

To tell you the truth, Your Honour, I can no longer distinguish clearly between what he confided to me that day and what I learned later. But the gist of it was this: having come home in the middle of the night, he'd begun working on a new number... *Tolerance*, it must have been. You know that one, don't you? No?

The Cosmophile

Oh, surely you know that one, Your Honour! *I am tolerance incarnate, I value cultural differences, I can tolerate anything at all, I tolerate Israel building more and more colonies in the Gaza Strip, I tolerate the ablation of the labia and clitorises of little African girls, I tolerate the permanent poisoning of Lombardy by dioxine from Seveso, I tolerate white policemen shooting down black schoolchildren in Soweto, human diversity is a great and beautiful thing — you wouldn't want everyone to be alike, now, would you? What a boring world it would be! I tolerate my upstairs neighbour beating his wife and my downstairs neighbour beating her husband — they're expressing themselves! I tolerate the young man down the hall shooting heroin into his veins — it's a free country! I tolerate gangs of young blacks in the United States tearing each other to pieces — let them die in their filthy ghettos! I can tolerate anything, anything, I'm the most tolerant person in the world...*

That sort of thing.

Elke

Elated and inspired, he'd gone on improvising until dawn. And then, hideous and familiar, the pain had set in. The chirping of the early birds seemed to attack him personally, sneaking into his ears and reverberating in his spinal cord; the morning sunlight was a brilliant knifeblade that slid beneath his eyelids and drove itself into his brain; even the hues of the flowers seemed garish and belligerent, and the contour of their petals was intolerably precise. Upon entering the house, Cosmo smelled the toast Josette was making for breakfast and was overcome by a wave of nausea; the spasms of his vomiting exacerbated the pain in his cranium... Then the inner images began: monotonous, repetitive, threatening.

What is it? I asked him. What do you see?

It's indescribable, he said... If I close my eyes, purple bars flash across my field of vision... And when I open them, everything is bathed in a strange, seething aura...

Like your father at Fontainebleau, I murmured.

I've gone over the scene countless times in my memory, Your Honour, and I still don't know what happened. Perhaps involuntarily, Cosmo's hand flew up and struck me on the mouth; I leaped back, incredulous at the pain, and at that very moment Josette burst into the room. I feel certain she'd been eavesdropping on us.

I'm sorry, Miss, she said, but you really must leave now; the doctor will be arriving at any minute.

And without a word, Cosmo turned his face to the wall.

I don't know if you have children, Your Honour, but I can tell you it's a good thing, after a scene like that, to have small people at home who depend upon you, who are waiting for you and counting on you to do ordinary things for them such as brush their hair, smooth over their quarrels, lend them a hand with their math. It's a good thing, too, to be able to throw yourself into the preparation of a meal, shelling peas and beating eggs and stirring pudding over a low flame until it thickens — and then, after the meal, to go out of doors and work in your vegetable garden, which requires precise and coordinated movements: bent over from the waist, you go along the row of carrots, thinning, each carrot must have enough room to grow downwards and outwards, extending itself firmly in the earth to become good food for you and your family the following winter. And it's an excellent thing to have a job, to be expected in a given place at a given time, and to perform specific tasks there with grace and gusto. I smiled at the customers, giving them my full attention — and indeed, I said to myself, I'll be forever grateful to *La Fontaine* for it was here that I first set eyes on Cosmo and I refuse to let the word *Cosmo* send my mind skidding and crashing into panic, I'll just wait for him to call and tell me the crisis is over; that he's in Paris; that all is well.

He didn't call me, as it turned out. He wrote to me, from Paris, in the middle of the week. It's the only letter I ever received from him; let me read it to you.

My Elke, wrote Cosmo. *Now you know.*

Now you've met your one and only rival. Migraine is my wife. She alone is more deeply imprinted on my being than you are. We've been unhappily married for long years, and divorce is out of the question. When she takes over, it's as if my head were being split with an axe and I were literally two different people.

Elke, another man lives inside of me — a dark, ferocious, hate-

filled stranger. His hatred is that which has always divided and united my parents. His axe is the hatchet of war — the stealthy, surreptitious war André and Josette have been waging on each other ever since I was born. Being the offspring of these two extremes, I can only bear the contradiction by acting upon it, acting it, using it, being perpetually on the move so that I'm never where people think I am. Still, every now and then the dark man catches up with me. And when that happens, everything I've learned about the world suddenly overwhelms me and I find myself at the mercy of the most baneful images... God, Elke! if only you could be inside my head at times like that, and film what's going on!

Thanks to that short paragraph, Your Honour, I finally understood Cosmo's all-devouring passion for the stage. To him, theatre was neither a pastime nor a profession — it was a vital necessity. He worked like a madman. When he had a new idea for a show, he was capable of rehearsing sixteen to twenty hours a day, going without food and sleep, spending his last drop of energy, then drawing strength from his very fatigue — fresh, incredible, terrifying strength. Always he feared he would fail, always he doubted, always he felt crushed and awed by the immensity of the task he'd taken on, but he persisted, using his rage, using his fear, setting himself against himself, spending his physical and mental energies, offering himself up in holocaust to redeem what he found intolerable about reality — the lack of love, the lack of love, the lack of love.

There's a second page to Cosmo's letter, but it's a series of almost random notes, floating obsessional images; the handwriting is chaotic, so written over as to be illegible in places...

*words seethe and buzz at my lips electric bumblebees   cluster
and swarm over my teeth   fill the moist pink cavern of my mouth
hover and alight upon my tongue   then sting their venom causes
my tongue to swell I choke on it   a battlefield young dead soldiers
lying on their backs   as far as the eye can see   naked gaping
wounds in chests heads limbs   morning mist in the distance
the pale corpses mingle with the crop of new spring wheat   very
young woman   bleach-blond hair   miniskirt   high-heeled shoes
dancing   frolicking in the streets   carelessly kicking around   not a
ball   the head of a man   the head rolls and bleeds   she hums and
frolics well aware of what she's doing   getting off on it   human
and animal heads   long necks of stone ribbed and rigid   thrusting
from a cathedral arch   dragon-dogs   heads tilted to one side
mouths agape   howling   but not in pain   in abandonment? urns
and amphoras   spewing out naked women   their long hair dangling
earthward   Greek goddesses   chopped off at the thighs planted
in goblets   headless torsos stuck onto plates where they twist and
turn   living creatures wending their way   amongst decorative
whorls   babies and leaves lions and vines birds and waves   desperately climbing youths   geometrical designs   surround and
intermingle with   the moving flesh sculpted in cold stone*

The Psychiatric Expert

Your Honour, I think we need to question the authenticity, not
of this document itself, but of the images it contains. Knowing
Elke to be relatively uneducated, Cosmo could count on her
being unfamiliar with these images — to us, on the other
hand, their lack of originality is obvious. We cannot help but

recognize the *inhabited cames* on the capitals of Romanic churches, any number of which Cosmo must have seen in the course of his travels... Or the doors of the Gothic cathedral which is the middle-sized city's greatest claim to fame... Or again, Rodin's famous *assemblages*, which anyone can visit in the sculptor's studio at Meudon...

So, what is most striking about this letter is that not only Cosmo's public persona but even his imagination was vicarious — the chaotic juxtaposition of other people's fantasies! The man, in other words, was a stranger to authenticity. He was like the mirror inside a kaleidoscope: himself deprived of colour, he was past master at reflecting the motley glints and glimmers of other people's stories.

Elke

Your Honour, it's up to you: either the psychiatric expert quits the hearing once and for all, or I'm the one who's leaving.

Thank you.

Jonas

Cosmo's suffering was authentic, Your Honour, I can testify to that. The pain of his headaches, his migraine auras and his anguish — all these things belonged to him, and to him alone.

Though at the time I knew him only from a distance, he'd already had a decisive impact on my life, and perhaps this is the right time to tell you about it. It was Cosmo who gave me the love of language.

I grew up, as you know, in a gypsy camp. In the 1960s,

Romany children attended school sporadically if at all, and the great majority of the adults were illiterate. My father was no exception — we earned our living selling baskets, and I noticed that when he drove his minibus from town market to town market, he could barely decipher the road signs. Fortunately, Vera had taught me the rudiments of reading and writing when I was a child; she used to let me read the comic books in her newspaper shop, provided I washed my hands thoroughly before and afterwards; sometimes I even helped her out with her crossword puzzles! But it was just a way of staving off boredom.

I didn't really grasp the importance of language until the day I happened to see one of Cosmo's shows on television. I'll never forget it — the spectators were literally weeping with laughter, and I couldn't follow, because I only recognized about one word out of two. It blew my mind. Suddenly my own uncouthness was unbearable to me. I started going to the library every day in secret. I'd sneak out of the camp early in the morning and walk the six kilometres into town; then I'd ask the librarian's advice and read whatever she recommended, looking up the words I didn't know in the dictionary...

Fiona
I have no idea where all this is taking us...

Jonas
It's taking us to Rodolphe.

Rodolphe, Your Honour, is the last major character in this

hearing. A man of considerable refinement — professor of medieval history, music lover, and my official boyfriend at the time Cosmo entered my life. For a while, he was even the prime suspect in Cosmo's murder. Motivation: jealousy. Ironically enough, if it hadn't been for Cosmo (who, however indirectly, had bestowed the gift of language on me), Rodolphe probably wouldn't have fallen in love with me in the first place. When you're a history professor, a night of wild sex with a young gypsy is all well and good, but if you want to set up housekeeping with him, he's got to be able to hold up his end of a conversation...

Having received a grant to study the violin full-time at the Conservatory, I'd come to live in the middle-sized city at age sixteen. The gulf between me and my family kept widening; every time I went home I felt more uncomfortable. Things about the camp I hadn't even noticed as a child now bothered me enormously — the poverty, the terrible manners, and especially the cramped living quarters, the total lack of privacy. As I found it hard to hide my discomfort, my gypsy cousins started calling me a snob — they accused me of putting on airs, talking like a city-dweller, and I felt increasingly lost and bewildered. A bit like Cosmo, I was divided against myself. I longed for oblivion — the bliss of forgetting who and where I was. Sometimes I achieved this in my music — my bow would seem to move over the strings all by itself, I'd close my eyes and let myself be carried away by the torrent of notes... Less frequently, I'd achieve it in my encounters with men out at the Val d'Auron.

I loved the promises of that place. The curve of male thighs in tight white pants, fleetingly glimpsed amongst the shadows. The deft, swift choreography of young male bodies as they moved around the lake — it reminded me of the scene at the beginning of *Mutiny on the Bounty*, when, preparing the ship for departure, the sailors go running along the railings, leaping onto the deck, shinnying up the masts... (*God,* is Franchot Tone gorgeous in that movie — especially by contrast with that phoney macho, Clark Gable!) At sea there are no women as far as the eye can see and men can breathe freely at last, they don't have to watch their tongues and be forever on their guard; freedom — salty, muscular and pure — invigorates them, swelling up their chests just as the sea wind swells the sails; when you touch a man you can feel his tendons tauten under the skin of his stomach, arm, or shoulder, and your sex goes hard, your whole body stiffens with desire... Once contact has been made, you breathe together and move inside each other and the pleasure is *there*, nothing lacy or hypocritical or vaporous about it, you can give and take of it wholeheartedly...

That, at least, was how I fantasized the nocturnal encounters with men at the lake's edge. When it came to reality, nearly all the men I met there were either middle-aged gays eager to get it on with an ephebe, or straight men curious about passivity — either way, the exchanges tended to be furtive, guilt-ridden and disappointing; this way of loving left me starved for love.

Rodolphe was the first man to really love me and the way we met was like a fairy tale. It was Christmas 1984. I'd gone home for the holidays as I always did, and found the camp even more appalling than usual — a mixture of religious drivel, bad wine and family quarrels, with snivelling brats everywhere underfoot, their faces streaked with dirt and snot. During the Christmas service, even as he sang hymns to the glory of the Virgin and Child, my father kept pawing the young women in the row in front of him; by midnight I was on the verge of imploding. I knew I wouldn't be able to stay overnight as planned. I also knew that if I left, my father would be hurt and angry — he'd light into me, telling me not to bother ever setting foot in the camp again if that was how I felt, if I'd gotten too clean and pure and holier-than-thou for the rest of the family, if I preferred to reject my ancestors and traditions and go over to my bitch of a whore of a red-headed devil of a mother, all right then, that was fine with him (he still didn't know what his brother Armand had done to me; even today he doesn't know about it)... Well, my fears were confirmed. The minute I announced my intention of biking home, my father lit into me. He yelled at me for a good ten minutes; it was like having the chamber pot dumped on your head on a winter's morning, after a dozen people have slept in the trailer...

A disaster. I went home utterly depressed. Knowing I wouldn't be able to find sleep, I decided to fool around on the Minitel for a while — and *that*, Your Honour, was when the miracle occurred. A true Christmas miracle. I hadn't been at the keyboard for more than five minutes when I stumbled upon a man who, by the most incredible coincidence, lived only half a mile from my place. Come on over, he told me electronically; I want you. He gave me his address and door code, told me what floor he lived on, said he'd leave the door to his apartment open and be waiting for me in the bedroom. And so it was, Your Honour. Every fantasy we'd first seen printed on the screen turned into reality. I found the right building, punched in the right door code, took the elevator to the right floor, found his apartment, and in the apartment a bedroom, and in the bedroom a bed, and in the bed the body of a man with a beautiful hard-on. Within seconds my clothes were off and we were going at each other, we fucked for hours in the dark, exchanging not a word, nothing but groans and shouts of pleasure until, exhausted, we fell asleep in each other's arms. Upon opening my eyes the next morning I saw a handsome, fortyish man bending over me with a smile:

Merry Christmas! What's your name?

Jonas. And you?

Rodolphe.

Yves

Well, that's quite a story. I must say that in my own life, Your Honour, the Minitel played just the opposite sort of role. Negative. Catastrophic.

Come on, Your Honour. Don't tell me you've forgotten who I am. For shame! You pretend to be paying attention but in fact your mind keeps wandering — you can't help thinking about other hearings, or even about the events of your own life, your plans and memories; perhaps Jonas reminded you of someone you know and you drifted into a daydream about that person, and now you're completely disorientated; you have no idea where you are... Yves? Yves? The name rings a bell... Oh, for heaven's sake — take *notes*, if you've got such a lousy memory! You're in a position of responsibility, don't forget; all of us are counting on you to pronounce your judgment at the end; if you listen with only half an ear, whatever will become of us?

No? You still don't know who I am? Well then, I'll have to introduce myself but frankly, you disappoint me — I'm the long-lost younger brother of the woman you know as Elke.

Yes, of course, *now* you remember!

Right. So. Listen carefully. Given that I played no role whatsoever in Cosmo's destiny, I'll testify only this once, but I want you to pay close attention to my words because I march to a different drummer than all the other witnesses.

Right. So. All these years, Elke had been wondering what had become of me. She'd kept in touch with her older brother — who, like her, had been raised by a foster family (and whose name was...? whose name was...? Oh, you're hopeless, Your Honour, his name was Maxime). As for me, I'd been adopted as a baby — and, in their great wisdom, my parents had not only given me their name, they'd refrained from telling me I was not their biological child. There was no reason for anything to change — but Elke, who has an unfortunate penchant for meddling in other people's affairs, was unable to forget my existence. It ate away at her, to think she had a little brother somewhere in the world and to not know where. So she asked Cosmo to check out the archives of Paris's Third District, and he did so — God know who gave him the *right* to do so, I suppose celebrities have all the rights in the world, most likely he chatted up the secretary in the archives office; in any case, he managed to walk away with the name of my adoptive parents — Robert and Anne-Marie Brunet. He even looked them up in the Paris phone book but they weren't there, for the simple reason that we lived in Nice.

Meanwhile, like everyone else, I'd grown up. I'd spent a couple of years wog-bashing in Algeria...

Latifa

What did he say, Your Honour? He said *wog-bashing*, and you let it pass? You don't even react? You're not going to pound your hammer and tell this racist to hold his tongue?

Yves

Wait a bit! I said I'd only testify this once, but I insist on having my say without being interrupted by filthy foreigners. *Oh, my husband isn't happy in France, oh my husband doesn't talk to me when he comes home from work, oh my husband has stopped reciting poetry...* All I can say is, if your husband had stayed where he was, we wouldn't have had all these problems and there'd be nothing to be racist about. First you say *Algeria for the Algerians,* then you come and clog up our cities in France! I mean, make up your minds, for Christ's sake! I don't need to be polite to you, lady. Who knows, maybe it was your father who left five of my buddies with the Oranese grin — are you familiar with that grin, Your Honour? The one that goes from ear to ear — but *below* the chin, *below* the jaw, with lots of

blood gurgling out of it? In Philippeville I saw five of my buddies die with that grin on their faces, and I will not put up with
being interrupted by a fucking wog.

Where was I? Ah, yes. Right. So. As I was saying, I'd grown
up. When I returned to Nice after Algeria, I was hired by the
city as a cop, directing traffic. I went through three marriages
and two divorces, I hit fifty, my parents died, I already had
four children and two grandchildren... when one day, all of a
sudden — a bolt out of the blue — the phone rings.

Hallo? I say. And I hear a woman's voice. A perfect stranger.

Excuse me, Sir, she says, but is your name Yves Brunet?

And I go: Yeah, why?

And she says, Excuse me, Sir, but were you by any chance
born in 1939?

That should have put me on my guard but I wasn't
thinking fast enough, so I say, Yeah, why?

And she says, Siddown.

So then I get mad and I say, Who the hell is calling?

And she says, I'm your sister.

At fifty, Your Honour, I didn't need a sister. Maybe Elke
needed a little brother — someone had just bumped off her
actor boyfriend, that's probably why she decided to bang away
at her Minitel until she'd dug up every Yves Brunet in the
country. Apparently there were three of us and I was the third
and last, her final hope. She'd asked the other two the same
questions and they were lucky enough not to have been born
in 1939. All right, so she could prove I was her brother; she
had an official photocopy of my adoption papers; I don't see

why that gave her the right to come and mess up my life.

I mean, it really disturbed me, you know? It's disturbing to be told, at age fifty, just because somebody found you on the Minitel, that your life is an enormous lie, that you were born not in Nice but in Paris; that your parents, who aren't even around anymore to defend themselves, were not your real parents, that your mother was a hatmaker — a *hatmaker*, for chrissake! — and your father a banker, and that you, you... are a bastard.

I mean, I didn't want to know, you know what I mean? I didn't give a shit! As far as I was concerned, my parents were the Brunets, the people who had brought me up — good people, faithfully married, practising Catholics — not this hodgepodge of adultery and variety programs. When I finally did meet Elke, everything she told me about our parents, the photos she showed me — *Look, that's you right there! We called you Yvou, if you'd been a girl they would have named you Yvette, like our mother. Boy, did she ever spoil you! She used to stand you on the kitchen table and dance with you — don't you remember?* — Monsieur Denain's love letters... the whole thing made me sick.

I didn't even want to meet these people. I didn't see the point. But when Elke sets her mind on something, there's no talking her out of it. She's like a dog that gets your pants cuff between its teeth and refuses to let go — she went on and on until finally, like an idiot, I gave in. So I came up here with my third wife and children and grandchildren, we'd never set foot in this godforsaken part of the country before and I hope we never do again, Elke was there with her shifty little brats, big brother Maxime drove up with *his* rowdy tribe, and then

Trabant the fat reporter for the local newspaper came to do a sob story — here we go, interviews, photographs, flash, pop, flash, and he splashed it all over on the front page — *Siblings separated for over half a century... boo, hoo... incredible family reunion... thanks to the Minitel...*

I wish the fucking Minitel had never been invented. Seriously. I wish I'd never learned about my connection to this crowd of freaks.

Well, that's it, Your Honour. I've had my say and I'll be off.

Seventh Day

Sandrine

Your Honour, we simply must stop leaping about from one time period to another; the family reunion Yves just described took place in 1989, whereas when we left Cosmo with his migraine a while ago, we were still back in 1976. I suggest we return to the chronological order of events and do our best to stick to it from now on.

Elke

We can try, my dear Sandrine.

...Time passed. What else is it supposed to do? What else *can* time do, poor thing?

The effects of its passage are now comic, now tragic; they are what they are.

Monsieur Picot, the owner of *La Fontaine*, catching up with an already outdated fashion, renamed his café *Le Zodiac*. When I told Cosmo about this over the phone he burst into laughter — and then, after thinking it over for a few seconds, said musingly, That's really beautiful, you know. That's magnificent. Wandering around Montparnasse, I often look at the people sitting on restaurant and café terraces, drinking, laughing, chatting, and, I think how each of them is constructing the story of his life in his head — the specific concatenation of events, days, places, people, thanks to which he recognizes himself as *himself* when he wakes up in the morning... All these thousands of individuals will integrate the evening spent in this café or that restaurant into their life stories... And now you tell me that the bistrot in my hometown, which has been called *La Fontaine* since the beginning of the century, will henceforth be known as *Le Zodiac* — what a clever, subtle choice, do tell Monsieur Picot what a brilliant man I think he is — and it's under this name that it will leave a trace in the minds of today's youth. They'll say to themselves, Yes, I remember, I tied one on at *Le Zodiac*, I chatted up the sexy barmaid at *Le Zodiac*, I heard Jonas play the violin at *Le Zodiac*... and it won't be the same memory as if the café were still called *La Fontaine*...

I remember this speech of his, Your Honour; it struck me.

Anyway, as I said, time continued to pass. I did nothing to hold it back. I watched as my children grew and changed — not only their looks, but their voices, their opinions, their personalities... Frank entered high school in the middle-sized city — it was a boarding school, so I saw him only on weekends. After Christmas, he would sometimes stay in town weekends as well. He'd begun to hang out with Kacim and some other boys in the neighbourhood to the north of the city, but he never introduced me to his friends, nor did he breathe a word to me about how they got their kicks — burglary, car theft, cocaine parties when the pickings were good. I didn't meet Kacim until a while later, when he and Frank spent their first night in jail, and Latifa and I arrived simultaneously at the police station to pick up our sons.

As for Fiona, she ripened early — by age ten her breasts

were sprouting; by eleven she was menstruating and boys had begun to paw at her during school recess; one day after school a whole delegation of teachers descended on *Le Zodiac* to complain to me of her behaviour in class — she alternated, they told me, between insolence and somnolence... I felt helpless and alone; Cosmo was on a triumphant international tour at the time, winging his way from western Africa to Quebec and from the West Indies to Guyana: I was glad for him but almost a year went by without our seeing each other at all...

Time giveth, Your Honour, and time taketh away.

I knew this. I'd always known it. Nonetheless, it was a shock to me every time I looked in the mirror and saw a woman who was no longer young. I turned forty-one, then forty-two, then forty-three. I remember a conversation I had with Cosmo the day I turned forty-three, in January 1980 — he'd rung me up early in the morning to be the first to wish me happy birthday, and I said, You know, I've got crow's feet around my eyes now, even when I'm not smiling... Do you still love me?

And he said, I've got nothing against crows.

And I said, What about later, when I need to wear reading glasses... will you still love me then?

Fiona

Your Honour, you really must ask my mother to cut it short. These details are of no interest to anyone.

Latifa

To me they are interesting, because I remember — also when I got to be forty-two or forty-three — I said to myself, Oh, look at you, Latifa, you're getting old! But I couldn't bother my husband Hassan with these questions, the way Madam Elke talks to her friend Cosmo over the phone... On market days at La Chancelle, my friends and I started buying beauty products to lighten our skins and take the liver spots away, Hassan would have said it was a waste of money but it made us feel prettier and we liked to compare the different brands...

The Cosmophile

Less than a week after this phone call with Elke, Cosmo gave a public performance of the dialogue which would eventually be called *An Adoration*. I happen to have a cassette recording of this sketch, Your Honour, and I suggest we take the time to listen to it.

It took off from Elke's question about reading glasses.

Cosmo plays a married couple. At the beginning they're in their forties, but with every exchange they age by a few years and at the end of the number their voices are quavering and feeble. In turn, they enumerate the blows time has inflicted on their minds and bodies.

Listen — it begins with the woman.

Do you love me any less, now that I need to wear reading glasses?

Ha ha ha, my darling, you must be joking! What a silly idea! Those glasses suit you perfectly — they make you look like a sexy young schoolteacher — to me, they're a turn-on!... What about you... I hope you're not bothered by the fact that a few grey hairs have sprouted at my temples?

What are you talking about, darling? They make you look so distinguished and mature... Now, tell me... I've been laughing at your jokes for so many years that I've got crow's feet at the corners of my eyes — do you still love me in spite of them?

Oh, you turn me on, baby, you really turn me on. I love those little lines at the corners of your eyes, they look like sunshine, they illuminate my life... And.... er... you have no objection to the flab which has started to appear around my midriff?

Oh, don't be daft... Don't you know that the more of you there is to kiss, the happier it makes me?... But tell me, sweetheart, you know I've got this little problem with arthritis, they tell me my cartilage is shot and I shouldn't go dancing anymore... Won't you miss our waltzing together?

Miss it? Are you kidding?! I never was much of a dancer; I'd just as soon stay home and chat with you by the fireside... Speaking of chatting... are you quite certain my worsening deafness doesn't get on your nerves?

Oh, don't worry about that, darling... You know, most of what I say is frivolous nonsense anyway; the main thing is for us to be together... And... er... you must be at least a little bit upset about the ablation of my right breast?

Oh, no, not at all — I've always preferred the left!... What about you... when you see how hump-backed I've gotten... Doesn't it make you a bit nostalgic for the good old days?

Not in the least, my love. I simply have the impression you're

leaning down to listen to me. And... tell me... tell me the truth now...
My memory lapses must bother you, don't they?... Some days I'm
not even sure who you are.

Come, come, dear! Just think what an honour it is to be a dif-
ferent companion for you every day! What more could I ask for? On
the other hand... I know that ever since my prostate operation I've
grown irascible, incontinent and impotent — it can't be much fun
for you...

Now, honey, don't even think about that. You bring out the best
in me — munificence, tenderness and maternal solicitude... But...
tell me, sweetheart.... and no cheating, huh? Promise? Doesn't it
upset you... at least a tiny bit, you know... from time to time... that
I'm dead? Do you love me still?

...I love you still.

Fiona

Ah, my mother's blubbering again. That exchange — *I'm dead,*
do you love me still? Yes — makes her blubber every time. She
keeps clutching onto the past, but what she refuses to
acknowledge is that the seeds of the future were already
planted there.

That's the truth, Your Honour, and no one can make it
untrue.

My mother's problem, you see, is that she's so busy marvelling at the way things glint and glimmer, shift and
shimmer, refract and reflect that she's grown incapable of
looking plain reality in the face. At the time we're talking
about now, for instance, she was completely out of touch with

her own children and she didn't even realize it.

Frank and I had always had our own world — but now, entering adolescence, we might as well have been living on a different planet. Literally, Elke no longer knew whose mother she was.

Frank was my hero. I didn't want to listen to Mama's bedtime stories anymore; I didn't want to read books or even comic books — the only stories I cared about were the adventures of Frank and Kacim in La Chancelle. I could hardly wait for the weekends when Frank would come home and tell me how they'd smoked dope together, then gone around the neighbourhood painting graffiti on the walls and puncturing tires. One Saturday when Mama had some shopping to do in the middle-sized city, I convinced her to let me visit Frank in his boarding school and it was just fantastic, you should have seen the ruckus the students made in the cafeteria, they used their spoons as catapults to send pats of butter flying, some of them stuck to the ceiling, others hit the neon light tubes — they must have smashed half the lights in the cafeteria that day, I laughed until my stomach ached! After lunch, Frank invited a group of his pals to come up to his room and get acquainted with his little sister, so we all went upstairs together, he locked the door and put on a Lou Reed record and turned it up full blast, I could feel my heart flip-flopping in my chest because this time it was for real, not like when we were little kids at the edge of the Arnon, these were young men, they had nascent mustaches and deep voices and they weren't ashamed of what was between their legs, I could feel a lump forming in my throat and I glanced up at Frank because I didn't know what he had in mind but his face was made of stone, he said, My kid sister does whatever I tell her, don't you, Fiona? Yes I said, at least I tried to say yes but nothing came out, just a little gasp, and then he said, Take off your clothes, Fiona, and lie down on the bed with your legs apart, and I obeyed, I felt like I was in a dream or a movie, I was divided into two, part of me was myself and the other part was like a camera set up above the bedroom door. I could see the eleven-and-a-half-year-old girl remove her top and shorts and underpants with trembling hands, then lie down on the bed and spread her plump white thighs, I could see her budding breasts and her scant pubic hair, I could even zoom in close-up and see the goose bumps on her skin, then the big sixteen-year-old boys formed a circle around her, I could no longer hear what Frank was saying, because my heart was beating as loud and fast as Lou Reed's drums, but he must have told his pals to go ahead without touching me so they went ahead, in time with the music, and meanwhile Mama was out shopping on the highway to La Charité where all the discount stores are and look what a pitiful sight she makes, my poor Mama, she just can't stop blubbering.

Latifa

I understand you, Madam. You weep, yes. You can only weep when you see what has happened to young people today. I also wept, all those years when I had to go to the prison to see Kacim, it made me so ashamed... And then destiny struck again, *Against God's judgment what can man do? / Oh, my eye, bemoan thy fate with abundant tears / Dig furrows that will fill up with water...* our youngest son died of a drug overdose, and this time, for Hassan, it was the end. We went back to Boussâada to bury our boy, and ever since then my husband has taken his meals in his room, he's stopped saying his prayers, he just lies on his bed all day long staring up at the ceiling, saying nothing, nothing, as if he could build a tomb with his silence, a mausoleum for his beloved son.

Sandrine

The century had now entered its next-to-last decade. Soviet troops were advancing across Afghanistan; America was arming the Islamic resistance. Elke's ex-husband Michael finally got in touch — not only was his career as a photographer flourishing, but he'd remarried, and his new wife, a young heiress from Switzerland, had just given birth to a charming Laetitia.

In my own family life, things were considerably less brilliant. Eugene and Leontine were in school now and less of a drain on my energy, but in the meantime I'd had twins — Karine and Kevin — and after that delivery, Your Honour, I must admit, I had trouble getting my figure back.

Latifa

Oh, you shouldn't worry about that, Madam! I put on weight, too... After five or six children it's only natural, Your Honour.

Nancy Huston

Sandrine

Jean-Baptiste almost never had dinner with us anymore. He usually got home at ten or eleven o'clock, dead drunk, and he no longer came to me at night, my body repelled him, he'd probably found someone else but I didn't question him about it, I was too frightened — what if he stopped coming home entirely? How would I manage without his pay? How could I support four children on my wage as a visiting nurse? You're probably wondering why I'm telling you all this, Your Honour, but in fact it's relevant — it's to explain why I hesitated when, on the evening of February 14, 1980, Josette called me about André.

I remember the exact date because it was Valentine's Day. Back in the days when we were courting, Jean-Baptiste had sent me a white rose to ask me to be his Valentine and it had melted my heart, but now he didn't care anymore, Valentine's Day it was just a day like any other — that is, morose. My life had become morose. I spent most of my evenings weeping and eating potato chips and watching TV — anyway, that particular evening, it must have been about nine o'clock when the telephone rang. I answered it, and it was Josette.

Something's wrong with André, she said. Do you think you could stop by?

I can't remember if she pronounced the word *emergency* but her voice sounded different — much less hysterical than usual — almost like a normal voice, in fact.

Wouldn't you prefer to call the doctor? I asked.

No, no, she said. I'm sure you can handle it, Sandrine.

I'm alone at home with the kids, I said. I'm sorry...

I beg of you, she said.

I could tell something was wrong, Your Honour, because Josette never said things like *I beg of you*; it wasn't her style... As I was wondering what to do, Jean-Baptiste staggered home.

An emergency call, I told him — and with no further explanation, I rushed out. Given the state he was in, it was tantamount to leaving the children alone, but I wasn't really worried — the twins usually woke up at around midnight and I was sure to be home by then.

I knocked on Josette's door and she let me in. She was very pale. How shall I put it? She was like a normal woman who is afraid, and whose life is about to fall apart. When she spoke, her voice was very soft and again I was struck by her change of tone; it was the voice of an extremely frightened, normal woman. She clutched at me — literally, I could feel her fingernails sinking into the flesh of my left arm.

André went down to the basement after supper, she told me. He said he wanted to do some tidying up... though what could possibly have needed tidying up at that hour, heaven only knows... I started doing the dishes, I heard a noise and... well, he still hasn't come back upstairs yet. He's been down there for nearly two hours now, I'm beginning to get worried.

You haven't gone down to check? I asked, to be polite. Two people now, instead of one, knew with certainty that a tragedy had occurred.

No, she answered. It's silly of me, but there are mice in the basement and I'm terrified of mice. So I thought of you,

Sandrine. I said to myself, Surely Sandrine isn't afraid of mice, she's the sort of woman who fears nothing...

Yes — a woman. That, I believe, was why she'd called *me* rather than a doctor — because I was a woman. An irrational idea flashed through my brain — it's like a delivery, I said to myself. She's going to bring a corpse into the world and she needs me to be the midwife. Only women are allowed in maternity hospitals. It was a completely irrational idea, Your Honour, I admit it.

Okay, let's go see, I said, very softly. And then I led the way down the steps.

When she saw her husband in a heap on the basement floor, Josette cried out in surprise.

Oh, my God! she said. That's my grandfather's hunting rifle! André must have been cleaning it, and then it went off accidentally. But for heaven's sake, André, why would you take it into your head to clean grandpa's gun? You always hated hunting!

Again she grasped my arm; again I felt her nails dig into my flesh. As I bent over the body — just as a matter of course, for I knew there was no hope — she began hissing into my ear: Save him, Sandrine! You can do it, I know you can. Don't worry, André, you'll be as good as new in no time. Come on, Sandrine, let's wake him up! All he needs is a little injection...

At last the gendarmes arrived, and Josette, still refusing to acknowledge her husband's death, tried to convince them to take him to the hospital...

Frank

I happened to be at home that night — it was February vacation and I was too broke to go anywhere else. I was awakened, I remember, by the phone ringing. I would have gone straight back to sleep — the fornicating clown often called in the middle of the night — but my mother let out a cry that woke me up for good. Sneaking out of bed, I came and leaned up against her door to listen. She was in tears. She was asking Sandrine questions, and it didn't take me long to figure out what had happened — Cosmo's father had blown his brains out. I don't recall my mother's exact words, but *rifle* and *mouth* must have been among them: in my mind's eye I saw the little old man, all bent and shrivelled, sliding the barrel between his lips...

The Lebanese Cedar

...those same lips which he'd pressed so ardently against my bark, that night long ago...

Elke

It was up to me to tell Cosmo.

I was acutely aware of being the meeting point between two violent events — the bullet that had just exploded in André's head and the news of it, which would soon explode in Cosmo's. For the moment, here in the interval, all was calm. I got out of bed and, despite the cold, threw open the shutters at my window; outside, the moon was high in the sky, its light glowing eerily through tatters of fog... I thought of André, his communion with the moonlight and the murmuring trees.

Some seven years earlier, Cosmo had given me his number in Paris; I'd never used it. Now, very slowly, I dialed it for the first time and listened to the strident ringing in his apartment — five times, ten times, like a reiterated question to which the silence answered no, five times no, ten times no, Cosmo isn't here. Where was he? He could have been anywhere, but (as on the day when Frank was hiding in the basement) I knew instinctively where to look. Avital... I called the operator and obtained, with mind-boggling ease, the number of his actress friend Avital Blum. And so it was that I, a little country barmaid hunched shivering in her bed in the middle of the night, twirled my telephone dial in such a way as to set off, in a city of three million inhabitants more than two hundred miles away, the ringing of another telephone, belonging to a woman whom I'd never met but whose story I knew well — London, Tel Aviv, dogfood, flying eggs and bread.

I told Avital it was urgent, and she believed me. She gave me the number of a café in Place Blanche, not far from the theatre where Cosmo had performed that night. Within five minutes the beloved voice was on the line, and I'd delivered my terrible message.

Silence.

A long silence — so long that I began to worry — had he fainted?

Cosmo?

I'll take the six o'clock train, he said.

His voice was altered, almost unrecognizable — it had

blanched, so to speak — like when some dreadful shock or sorrow makes a person's hair turn white overnight. I myself have never seen this happen, Your Honour, but that's what his voice sounded like.

He hung up before I could tell him that I'd meet his train. But I *would* meet his train. And I *did* meet his train — forgive me for expressing myself so clumsily, Your Honour, forgive me for getting emotional again, it's because I'll never forget the way Cosmo looked getting off the train that day — gaunt, absent, aged, much older than his thirty-seven years. Throughout the whole trip to the village, he scarcely opened his mouth... with one exception. I'd been railing against Tabrant because André's death was already in the papers — it was only a three-line notice, with no details, but just to say something I lit into the journalist, calling him a fat pig, accusing him of gorging on other people's misery — it's his favourite food, I said, he can't get enough of it, the bastard probably sleeps over at the police station to make sure he'll get the scoop on all the town scandals — I let my tongue run away with me, saying whatever came into my head because the sound of my own voice made me feel better... But suddenly Cosmo broke in.

He went to Australia once, he said.

And that was it. Not another word.

It shut me up, which must have been his intention.

And when I dropped him off at his place, he scarcely cast a glance in my direction.

A three-day silence ensued.

Meanwhile the journalists, heeding the advice of the mayor

and notary public, had reached a consensus — a cerebral accident, it was to be called.

I guess you could put it that way.

Vera

My turn has come at last.

On the day of André's funeral, the weather was abominable — cold, wet and windy all at once — and the procession, pitifully small. Standing at the edge of the grave, the red-nosed priest muttered a few hollow phrases about the sins of the deceased, and I felt a monstrous anger rising in my chest. *Nothing was going to happen, nothing at all!* We'd lost André, and no one was going to pronounce the words that should have been pronounced. I glanced around at the other mourners — all of us looked elderly, ugly, sad — and above all, defeated... At the thought that André's dreams had come to this, my whole body turned into a block of hatred against Josette.

As the men began slipping the ropes under André's coffin to lower it into the hole, I whispered a few words to Cosmo about his father and myself. My tongue freed at last by the poor man's disappearance, I added: The date André chose for his death is no accident. It was on February 14th, 1951, that your mother had him locked up at Chezal-Benoît because he was in love with me.

Cosmo stared at me, and I saw he had suddenly understood a number of things — in particular the reason for which, when he was eight years old, his father had disappeared for nearly a year.

Josette had lied to him, of course — *this whole story is rid-
dled with lies, Your Honour!* — she and her family had told the
little boy that his father was suffering from tuberculosis and
had been sent to a sanatorium in the Alps... whereas the poor
man was *right here* — *a mere six miles away*, moping, fretting,
stagnating in an insane asylum... Even today, the idea is intolerable to me.

That's when little Charles began paying regular visits to the
tomb of Marie-Louise Cottereau, having grasped the fact that
no one in the world could listen to him better than his mother's
dead sister. I'd see him walking through the village square
sometimes, with a bereft look on his face... What had happened to his father? Why didn't he come home? And I was in
no position to answer — because for me, too, Your Honour,
André's absence contained a painful mystery...

The mystery was not to be dispelled until some thirty years
later, after his death.

Josette

Objection, Your Honour! All of this is totally irrelevant! You
must order this woman to sit down!

Vera

I'll sit down, Josette, when I've had my say.

True, the episode I'm about to relate dates back to long
before the events we've described so far — before the Algerian
war, before Hassan's arrival in France, before the birth of Frank
and Fiona, Jonas and Kacim — perhaps even before your own

birth, Your Honour... Yet the seism it provoked in Cosmo's destiny was a violent one, and it has had repercussions on all the protagonists, whether they know it or not.

Because of what I'd whispered in his ear, Cosmo went to Chezal-Benoît the day after the funeral, and asked for his father's file. A very thick file it was — *Uncommonly* thick! the dynamic new director of the hospital exclaimed, as he handed it to him with a smile. Had he known what was in that file, he would probably never have given it to Cosmo, and Josette's treachery would never have been revealed.

What did it contain? Naturally, there were the nurses' daily records, the patient's weight chart, and the weekly report of the head psychiatrist, describing the man I loved as neurasthenic and listing symptoms such as *dizziness* and *fainting spells, thickness of speech, fits of rage* and *dysmnesia* — do you know what that means, Your Honour? I looked it up in the dictionary; it means defective memory. André's file also contained a list of the drugs he was being given, morning, noon and night, and their (essentially sedative) effects on his behaviour.

It was not, the medical records, however, which made his file so voluminous. It was the correspondence. Some fifty letters from me to André, and more than a hundred from André to me — written over the course of six months, between February and August 1951.

The first few weeks, he wrote to me daily, sometimes several times a day. I'd like to read you a few excerpts from these letters, because it's important you know what sort of man he was back then. He was not always the man described by

An Adoration

Clementine — spluttering and stuttering, choking with rage, incapable of expressing himself... Nor, at the time, did he resemble the twitching, muttering, melancholy individual whom Elke met later on... No, the André I fell in love with in 1947 was a man of exceptional intelligence and grace; an avid reader; a brilliant if fragile mind; 1950 was I think the happiest year of his life — not only because of our love, but because of the hope he'd begun to place in his young son...

At the beginning of his forced confinement at Chezal-Benoît, for instance, André wrote: *Just think how ironic it is for me, a peasant who rebelled against the back-breaking labours of rural life, to find myself in an agricultural colony amidst six hundred madmen sent down from Paris on the assumption that fresh air and strenuous farm work will do wonders for their mental health...*

Other of his early letters were passionate and erotic, filled with the joy of our recent encounters — these I shall keep to myself.

Yet another letter evokes the origins of the place-name. *Many centuries ago*, wrote André, *the only building on this wild, ill-favoured spot was a miserable little shack called* Casale malanum, *the devil's house. When an Italian monk came along and founded an abbey here in the eleventh century, he named it, by opposition,* Casale benedictum *or the blessed house — whence* Chezal-Benoît.

I'm willing to bet that no one in the room was aware of this etymology — am I right? Fiona?

Fiona
Right.

Vera
But it has reverted to being the devil's house, the letter goes on. *The monks' cells are now used for solitary confinement — the most violent patients are locked up there and left with a heap of straw, like wild animals.*

Sandrine
It's true that the general atmosphere in mental hospitals was far more chaotic in the early fifties than it is today... Neuroleptics have changed all that.

Vera
From my window, André wrote, *I can hear one of them screaming. Every day he screams, sometimes for hours on end — his screams are monotonous, interminable and heart-breaking. No one ever tries to console him — and indeed, any attempt to console that scream would be a lie... It seems to express a form of misery hidden deep within us all — even the nurses recognize it... Oh, Vera! to think that if I hadn't met you I might have ended up like this, screaming my days away in an insane asylum...*

Kacim
Uh — that scream? That scream you just described, Madam Vera? I know it. I know it well. You hear it day and night in prison. Sometimes it's you, sometimes it's another guy — you

can't even tell the difference, it doesn't matter. You're locked up behind bars — like your friend, there, André — you can't go anywhere. Men, deprived of their freedom. Young male bodies fairly bursting with strength and sexuality — arrested, locked up, told where to go, what to do and when. Also told, over and over, that they're worth shit. I'm sorry — there's no other word for it.

You've got no choice but to scream. My father Hassan could scream that way, too. His silence *contains* that scream, you know what I mean? Even if he's not behind bars, it amounts to the same thing — he's a prisoner in France. He goes back and forth between La Chancelle and the Cathedral, but he might as well be pacing a cell — he's stuck, stopped, immobilized, silenced. Belittled as a man, ignored as a human being. In France, his own wife and children have learned not to respect him — he's lost everything, including his dignity. If my father's not in prison, I don't know who is.

Vera

But as the weeks went by, the tone of André's letters began to change. They became less passionate and more poignant... then anxious... then aggressive... And finally they stopped altogether. There are no letters dating from the last three months of his confinement.

Now, Your Honour. Since you're an excellent judge, a consummately clever and experienced judge, you must be wondering what André's letters were doing in his hospital file, rather than in a secret drawer in my bedroom. The answer is quite simple. On orders from Josette, *they were never mailed* — and my own letters were never delivered to him. When Cosmo opened the file in 1980, *all of the envelopes were still sealed.*

Shall we recapitulate? You take a perfectly harmless man, you lock him up against his will in a psychiatric hospital, amidst several hundred patients suffering from epilepsy and senile dementia (the two specialties of Chezal-Benoît), you give him massive doses of sedative drugs — and then, over a period of several months, you allow him to believe that his letters have been posted and that no response has been forthcoming, not even a postcard or a request for a visit; you plunge him into a solitude he can only find baffling and frightening, and then you calmly describe this man as displaying symptoms of *anger, dizziness* or *neurasthenia* — perhaps even a bit of *dysmnesia* from time to time? Subjected to such treatment, Your Honour, who, I ask you, would *not* go mad?

Josette achieved her goal: she destroyed our love. Stewing in the poison of silence, both André and I began to doubt. After six months I was in despair, and rather than kill myself, I killed the part of me I valued most — namely, my tenderness for André. He must have done the same. By the time he was released in late November, we'd ceased even to mourn our lost intimacy. For the next three decades, we lived less than a mile apart without exchanging a word. We passed each other in the street like strangers. We'd suffered so much that we no longer knew each other.

Yes, Elke. This, too, is part of the truth. Love can thrive over great distances, but it can also wither and die close at hand.

As you can imagine, Cosmo was deeply shaken by his reading of the letters. He brought them to me the next day. They're yours, he told me. Forgive me, Vera — I opened them and read them all, I couldn't stop, I was up all night reading them, do forgive me, I've brought them to you straight away, they're yours.

And believe it or not, Your Honour, right there in the middle of my *pigsty*, as Josette so tactfully called it, Cosmo began to sob. He grasped both my hands, lifted them to his face and wet them with his tears.

Well, I told him, at least now you know where you got your ability to love.

We stared at one another... Your Honour, it was the worst moment of my life.

Everything was too late.

Eighth Day

Josette

How moving. How extraordinarily moving. Everything was too late. And who's fault was that? Why, Josette's, of course.

A convenient explanation — and such an *original* one! The true guilty party is not the hero's murderer, it's his mother. Oh, God... I'm so alone... For forty-four years I did everything in my power to help my husband, and look what happened, and people hold *me* responsible! They're willing to identify with anyone but me. They're prepared to see the world through the eyes of a baguette, a wisteria, a dying doe... *anything*, just so long as it's not Josette.

Well, Your Honour, I'm fed up to the teeth with this treatment. I've been the laughingstock of the hearing ever since it began. The novelist has given all her other characters complex, nuanced personalities; I alone am a stereotype, a caricature. *What has she got against her mother,* that's what I'd like to know!? But the answer is obvious — grievances, like everyone else. Huge, irreparable grievances. Ah, yes. We mothers are a lamentable lot, aren't we? Ridiculous. Grotesque. Our every word and gesture denotes stupidity. We strive to protect our children, save their lives — what could be stupider than that? They grow up and move away from us, take risks, take flight... and we sit there trembling stupidly for their safety, fearing stupidly for their lives, and when they get themselves killed, we weep for them — stupidly, once again!

Forgive me... Not only do I mourn the loss of my loved ones, I have to take the blame for it. It makes me furious.

No matter what you say, André was *ill*. If mental illness exists, my husband was ill. All of the specialists agreed, whether at the Salpêtrière in Paris or at Chezal-Benoît down here — he suffered from acute anxiety attacks. He was anxious all the time; he didn't know what to do with himself. Of course it's infinitely more romantic to claim, as Elke and Vera have done, that so-called madmen are in fact exceptional human beings, and that the real madmen are those we generally consider to be normal. Yes, it may be romantic — but, unfortunately, it's not true.

None of you had to live with André, day in, day out — neither you, his mistress, nor you, the novelist, nor *you*, Your Honour. None of you had to deal with his fits of melancholy, his explosions of rage, his endless silences. Rather than talking to me, he'd talk to himself. *He couldn't function.* He never found his place in society.

God knows I put my faith in him, at first; otherwise I would never have married him! My family was firmly opposed to the match (they said I was marrying down) but I was convinced André would make something of himself. After all, he'd travelled all the way to the capital on his own! He'd found employment in the hotel and restaurant business! That set me to dreaming, Your Honour... I thought the two of us might return to Paris someday... or else open up a restaurant here on the village square... I was prepared for anything, and his compliments went to my head.

So we were married.

My father's own parents had just died. He gave us their property as a wedding present, though he was under no obligation to do so — an old farmhouse and barn at the edge of town. People looked at us askance — a healthy young man is not supposed to live off his in-laws — but I defended my husband, telling them he hadn't yet found his path in life. To André himself, I said nothing; I wouldn't have dared. I simply waited to see what he would do, and in the meantime I tried to make our home a pleasant place to live — for which, I've been rewarded by Clementine's mockery...

Frankly, Your Honour, don't you find it shocking that the novelist should be so incapable of seeing things from my point of view?

Can't she understand that when a rural family finally rises to just *barely* above the subsistence level — when the eldest son, my father, after considerable striving and sacrifice, manages to pass his law exams and set himself up as a notary public, it makes every member of the family proud? Can't she comprehend the love these people then feel for the first, timid signs of affluence — because after centuries of hard, filthy, exhausting, monotonous peasant existence, *at last* they can cease to live like animals, *at last* they can lay down tiles on the earthen floor, *at last* they have a bit of leisure time and money to spend, *at last* they can hitch themselves up to the lowest rung on the ladder of civilization and display a few modest symbols of success, silverware, porcelain, factory-made furniture... Yes, Clementine, you're right! They lavish huge amounts of attention on these symbols, polishing the silverware, scrubbing the floor tiles, admiring their reflections in the furniture...

Latifa

I understand the lady. I would have given anything to have some silverware to polish. I know what she means.

Josette

It was *my life*, Your Honour — can you hear what I'm saying? I, too, come from a specific background — I didn't materialize out of nowhere. The Josettes of this world are *also* the results of their experience, and that was my experience: a father who was a peasant's son, proud as pie to have the right to hang the prestigious notary public's sign over his door; a mother who was a peasant's daughter, relieved at no longer needing to wring chickens' necks, drain them of their blood, pluck out their feathers by the handful, and pass a blue flame over their cold white pimply skins to burn away the last quills — to be able, instead, to purchase chicken pieces under cellophane in the supermarket — yes, these things were a source of pride to us: cellophane, Formica, everything the novelist sniffs at, calling them *kitsch* or *tacky*. It may not be the Sixtine Chapel, but it's a start! When you come right down to it, the novelist is a snob — wealth meets with her approval only when it is extreme, sumptuous, maximal, grandiloquent! But the first, hesitant signs of it elicit nothing but her sarcasm... Sorry not to be Tolstoy yet, sorry not to be Beethoven or Michelangelo — but we did our best, we were a notary public and his wife and daughter, and I shall not put up with the novelist's disparagement for one second longer!

The Novelist

I apologize, Josette. You're quite right to be angry. In fact, without this added nuance to your character, the rest of the story would be incomprehensible.

A while ago, Elke said she was not afraid to advance in the narrative... But ironically enough, Your Honour (given that the hearing itself is unfolding at my initiative), *I'm* the one who's now afraid to advance. I'm loath to embark on the story's final spiral — the one which will lead to Cosmo's death.

Frank

Don't be ridiculous! Everyone already knows the ending, so what's there to be afraid of?

Come now, let us all form a circle, join hands, and merrily dance the death of the fornicating clown.

Elke

I've been silent for quite some time, Your Honour, but I'd like to take the stand again at this point.

What I'm about to reveal will come as a surprise to many of you.

Though it's true that Cosmo was deeply affected, in 1980, by his father's suicide and the discovery of his correspondence with Vera, it would be a mistake to see these events as the sole cause of his collapse. This is why, a little while ago, I told you about a migraine headache which occurred several years *prior* to André's death.

From then on, however, the attacks did grow more acute. And more frequent.

Sandrine

Yes — I've checked my files, and I can confirm that the first time Cosmo saw a local doctor for his headaches was in 1970, shortly after the scene at the foot of Clementine's grave. He was only twenty-seven at the time.

Elke

In his letter to me, Cosmo had described his sense of being split — as by an axe — between his two parents. Now, with André dead and Josette all alone, bereft, overcome with grief and tenderness (yes, tenderness, for there's no denying she loved her son in her own way), this sense of splitting grew intolerable; Cosmo feared it would drive him mad.

If only he could have firmly proclaimed his mother guilty and his father innocent — or the other way around — he would not have lost his balance as he did. But the truth was that he had serious doubts about his father's sanity, and it wasn't hard for him to see André through Josette's eyes. As far back as he could remember, he'd been a helpless witness to his father's fits of rage and periods of prostration. Indeed, he and Josette had often spent long evenings alone together when André was too depressed to come to the table. Now, as an adult, watching me struggle to raise two young children by myself, Cosmo could only admire his mother's courage in retrospect. André's weakness appalled him. And it appalled him still more to think that Josette might have had him committed partly for *his*, Cosmo's, sake.

Whenever he found himself on the verge of despair, he'd bring to mind his father's letters to Vera and this would make him furious with his mother. He'd ring her up and berate her at length, reducing her to tears and threatening never to come and visit her again.

Then he'd change his mind. Filled with contrition, he'd hop on a train, throw himself at his mother's feet and beg her forgiveness.

One day he was André, the next he was Josette; then the oscillation accelerated. His position would change from hour to hour, from minute to minute... It was enough to make him bang his head against the wall — and on occasion, Your Honour, that's exactly what he did.

My brain is splitting in two, he'd tell me over the phone, in a voice broken by pain. My parietal sutures are ripping open!

Naturally, I took this to be a figure of speech. Not for an instant did I suspect that it corresponded to a physiological reality...

A man with Cosmo's professional commitments could not allow himself this sort of lapse. To keep up with his hectic schedule of performances, he took quantities of painkillers and consulted costly medical specialists.

Ironically enough, throughout this period, his popularity did nothing but increase — indeed, it began to get out of hand. He had the disagreeable impression that his career was going on without him — that he would get rave reviews and standing ovations no matter what he said or did onstage. He was persecuted, as it were, by his own success. Wherever he went, people would stop him in the street and thank him profusely, drowning him in a flood of compliments...

It's a catastrophe, he told me over the telephone. I'm a brand name, like *Mister Clean*. People know my face as well as his. Cosmophile clubs are proliferating everywhere — not only in France but abroad... People are writing theses about me, teaching courses in Cosmology... The other day I met a perfectly pleasant young man from Toronto who recited to me, word for word — get this — one of my sketches dating back to *1962!* It scared the living daylights out of me. He played me better than I did!

The Cosmophile
That was yours truly, of course.

Elke
They analyse me! he said. They put me in a box and stick a label on it. Worst of all, they seem to *understand* me, whereas I myself no longer have the faintest clue who I am or where I'm going — or, especially, *why*. Elke, whatever will become of me? I don't know how to be Cosmo anymore. When journalists come to interview me, I'm convinced they've got the wrong man. I feel like an impostor — someone who's trying to *pass himself off as Cosmo* — it's dreadful! So far, I can still play my role convincingly, but what will happen when I start forgetting

my lines? People will talk to me about one of my old shows and I'll sit there with a vacant smile on my face — Ah, so you liked *I Am at War*, did you? How kind of you, delighted to hear it, thank you so much. And, thinking back to *I Am at War*, I'll say to myself Hm, yes, that wasn't half bad, but that was *then*... The words don't come to me anymore, I've forgotten how to improvise, I'm *through!* Oh, Elke, where can I hide? I can't go on like this, I wish everything would simply *stop*...

The dark man was gaining ground inside of him. The other name for the dark man was doubt. Once he himself had been devoured, Cosmo turned on *me*. You think you're in love with me, he said, but it's all in your mind. What you're really in love with is my *image* — some guy you saw on TV. You get off on my celebrity — being able to boast that you sleep with a household name — whereas you don't even *know* me — you don't even *want* to know me, you *prefer* for me to be far away, that way you can fantasize about me to your heart's content. Even when I'm with you, more often than not I can't get it up, and that allows you to feel superior and magnanimous by con-soling me... The rest of the time I betray you left and right, I sleep with other women and you know it, they're younger, more beautiful and more cultivated than you and they turn me on more than you do — almost anyone turns me on more than you do — and yet you go on pretending, how could you seriously believe I would take an interest in a middle-aged barmaid from the sticks and her perverse, violent children?

I didn't find this amusing, Your Honour. I didn't find it pleasant.

However, as my despicable younger brother Yves pointed out a while ago, I am nothing if not stubborn. My love for this man was an absolute in my existence; nothing could incite me to give it up. I was determined to find some way of bringing Cosmo back to life, back to himself... It was unthinkable that all our moments of happiness and shimmering light should go down the drain like this!

The Cosmophile

Onstage as well, starting at about this time, his behaviour grew erratic and disconcerting. Had he lost his talent or was he purposely undermining it? He'd launch into one of his old numbers, desperately improvising in the hopes that inspiration (what he used to call *the divine breath*) would take over — and sometimes it did, yes, sometimes the silvery genius bubbled from his lips as it had in the past, but he couldn't count on it anymore; within a few minutes his eloquence would abandon him; like a mountain-climber suddenly seeing he is unroped, he would lose his balance and plummet to the ground. It was a scary thing to watch. He'd stare distractedly at the audience, playing on his anxiety and on theirs... Would he be able to remember where he was, get the show back on its feet, convince them that the whole thing was part of the act — his new idea of *entertainment?*

In August 1985, I attended a performance he gave at the community arts centre of the middle-sized city. He stood motionless beneath the spotlight at centre stage, in white clown-face, with his arms at his sides, the very image of desolation and

despair. And then — very slowly — he began to talk. Excruci-
atingly long silences separated each sentence from the next.

I've lost something, he said.

My genius.

I was rather attached to it.

Where on Earth might I have put it?

He turned his pockets inside out and mopped his brow.

I know I had it, I'm nearly a hundred percent sure!

No later than yesterday.

Now, now, mustn't get all het up about it, let's think this through.

When did I have it last?

Ah... well, maybe it wasn't yesterday...

He scratched his head.

Maybe it was... ah... the day before yesterday?

I know for certain I had it two years ago.

I did a sketch — oh a great little sketch it was...

I swear it's true!

*And then, well, I woke up this morning, I flipped the light switch
in my brain and...*

Nothing.

I couldn't believe it.

I flipped the switch again...

Total darkness.

Not even the faintest glimmer of an idea...

A prolonged silence. Consternation in the audience. Did
Cosmo still know he was onstage? And then:

*Does Cosmo still know he is onstage? you're wondering. Has his
mind gone blank? Good for you, hurrah, bravo, you've come up*

with the right answer. My mind has gone blank... There's not a word left on it, or in it... Well, you've got only yourselves to blame! You ate my words, now they're all gone... Do forgive me, ladies and gentlemen, but... try to understand... I mean... deep down... one does this sort of thing in order to be loved... and the horrible thing is that it works... it works... people love you, they adore you... you make them laugh... ha! ha! ha! ha!... but it doesn't help... by the end of a show you're even hungrier for love than you were at the beginning... but you keep at it... you put your heart into it... you outdo yourself... and it works, that's the horrible thing... people cheer, they applaud, they praise you to the skies... but it still isn't enough... it doesn't help... it makes no difference at all... deep inside of you there's still the same godawful lack... and the more they love you, the worse the lack, and after a while all that remains of you is one, enormous LACK... Do forgive me, Ladies and Gentlemen, for telling you the truth, for once... a pity it hasn't made you laugh... but that's just the way it is, that's what you're going to hear tonight because I'm the one who's onstage and you poor jackasses have paid good money to listen to me... Besides, if you knew how to love, you wouldn't need to come to the theatre to watch a stupid asshole clowning around onstage...

And so on and so forth. For ninety minutes.

Was it funny? Did he intend for people to laugh, or was he asking them to take him seriously? The spectators were at a loss. More than half of them walked out before the end of the performance. When the curtain came down, even those who remained scarcely dared to applaud.

Following this fiasco, Cosmo was so depressed that he

decided to have a drink in one of the downtown bars — something he never did.

By pure chance, the bar he walked into was the one which had hired Jonas to perform on Saturday nights. The two men had always known each other by sight, but it was on this occasion that the true meeting between them took place. As of the very first notes that rose from Jonas's violin, Cosmo was... how shall I put it?... thunderstruck... transfixed... mesmerized... no, Your Honour, I'm afraid there's no word strong enough to describe the effect produced by the young musician on the aging actor.

Jonas was... *it*. What? *It*, at long last — the chance to heal the godawful split.

Jonas was his brother, the son of the woman his father had loved.

Jonas was the solution, the key; he was reconciliation, fulfillment and salvation; he was love, beauty, youth retrieved...

He was music.

As for Rodolphe, the elegant history professor who'd been living with Jonas for the past three years, and who was seated that evening at a table near his own, Cosmo didn't see him. Even afterwards, when he saw him, he didn't see him. Nothing existed but Jonas.

He had to have him.

He had to have him at all costs.

Frank

In the meantime, Your Honour — to distract you briefly from the tragic turn events seem to be taking here — I'd dropped

out of school and rented a room not far from Kacim's place —
on the Avenue Charles-de-Gaulle, which is also the eastern limit
of La Chancelle and the road to Paris. It wasn't the most restful
place in the world what with the continual stench and roar of
traffic beneath my window — but I'd had my fill of rest in the
village; now it was something else I was after — namely, thrills.

Kacim and I had become bosom buddies: he had taken on
a job in the Total gas station just down the road. He was nineteen years old, three years younger than me, tall dark and
handsome with good biceps on him, whereas my own
strengths were more in the verbal field, the two of us made a
good team if I do say so myself and we were pretty inventive
when it came to making ends meet. Kacim had a chip on his
shoulder against society. He taught me a line of poetry in
Arabic that said, *We grind our wheat but get no taste of it* — his
father spent all day making the downtown streets spic and
span for tourists but when Kacim would walk down those
same streets, people would look at him askance and mutter
things like Why don't you go back where you came from? —
whereas he came from less than a mile away. And Latifa's right,
Your Honour, when she says la Chancelle isn't exactly con-
ducive to dreaming — the place would win first prize in a
contest for bad urban planning. My mother is right too, for
once, when she says that people need dreams as badly as they
need bread and water.

Okay, so let's dream! is what Kacim and I figured. The
society we live in is rotten to the core, the *last* thing we want to
do is fit into it! We'd see these corrupt politicians on TV — they

kept stuffing millions into their pockets and nobody stopped them, whereas the cops were constantly harassing Kacim, pushing him around, taking him in, checking his papers, frisking him, making him strip to the skin — come on now, bend over, let's see what you've got up your asshole — cops are all a bunch of faggots, I hope you're aware of that, Your Honour... So we figured, okay, if they're going to treat us like criminals we might as well go commit some crimes!

That's when I finally realized how wrong the peasant outlook is. *Every penny counts* but be careful not to earn too many of them, just hang on in there, pull in your belt a notch, show everyone how long-suffering you are, go on, keep on working, keep on suffering — without even believing in God or pie in the sky after this vale of tears — without believing in *anything*. Nine human beings out of ten on this planet are up to their necks in shit, I told Kacim, and there's no point in deluding ourselves, we'll never be able to do anything about *that*, so we might as well have a good time. And to do that, we'll have to... help ourselves! I trotted out all these ideas in front of Kacim and he listened to me, wide-eyed with admiration — he was more than just a sidekick to me now, Your Honour, he was a disciple. As long as we're young and good-looking, I said, let's enjoy ourselves to the hilt! And so we did.

We weren't crazy, though. Back in those days, 1984–1985, more and more kids at La Chancelle were getting high on crack — that's how Kacim's little brother died, and his death made a big impression on us, so we were careful: mary-jane, cocaine, nothing but the best. However, the best costs money

— and, not having been born yesterday, Your Honour, I'm sure you know how kids like us get their hands on money.

We called it living on charity — I don't know if you get the joke — it's because there's a town called La Charité some thirty miles east of the middle-sized city, and there's a whole slough of discount stores on the highway going there, where everybody flocks to do their shopping on the weekend. Furniture stores, shoe stores, tool stores, you name it. We'd show up at the cash registers shortly before closing time, never the same store twice, and I'll leave the rest to your imagination. No, no; we didn't need guns; we did just fine with Sharpie — the knife Hassan had entrusted to Latifa when he left for France, telling her it would one day belong to their son. True, Kacim had jumped the gun a bit by appropriating the knife before his father's death — but we took really good care of it, polishing it and sharpening it just about every day — in fact it was sort of our mascot.

Man, did we have some good times together! I'd probably make a better impression if I said we felt wretched and pathetic but I'd be lying — every time I think about those days, I get a pang of nostalgia. When the takings were good, we'd splurge on a weekend up in Paris — fancy hotel on the Champs Élysées, hookers, champagne, nightclubs — you name it, we did it. I wouldn't have minded settling down in the capital for a while — but not alone, not without Kacim; and he didn't want to hang around, he was the eldest son and his father didn't earn enough to feed ten mouths. At least you could drop your lousy job at the gas station, I told him, but he just shook his head. The pay may be lousy, he said, but at least it's clean money; I can give it to my mother.

I'd been out of touch with my own mother for ages, to say nothing of her friends and everyone else in the village — the only person I cared about seeing was Fiona. At sixteen, my little sister could have passed for twenty — her tits and ass were pretty amazing. For a while I even considered taking her cherry myself but then I decided against it, I already possessed her in every other way and I wasn't sure I felt like fucking her because when you fuck somebody you lose control, and I wanted her to see me as a hundred percent Rambo, *eyes of stone, body of stone, heart of stone,* as we used to say when we were kids, so I let Kacim take her cherry and then the three of us celebrated afterwards with a line of C, following which I put a want ad in the local bi-weekly, a word to the wise is sufficient and it certainly was, my phone started ringing off the wall. For two years, Fiona put out for us — not full-time of course, only on the weekends; during the week she was still living at home with Mama and attending high school. She'd receive her johns in my room and Kacim and I would hang out in the hallway with Sharpie in case anything went wrong. Sure, it bothered us to picture those guys panting and slobbering all over our sweet Fiona — it bothered Kacim even more than me — I think he must have had a crush on my little sister for real, but Fiona herself didn't seem to mind, she handed the cash over to us with an elegant little laugh — like the girl in Cosmo's letter, the one who hums and capers as she kicks a man's head around with her high-heeled shoes. Really elegant. And it worked — man, we were raking it in! Between Fiona's income and our own, we could buy anything that took our fancy, it was the dolce vita, let me tell you...

Latifa

I'm sorry, Madam Elke. I'm so sorry I don't know what to say.

Fiona

No, don't be sorry, Latifa. It didn't kill me! Look, I'm still here, I'm doing fine! I can tell you now — I was really in love with Kacim, and his love protected me far better than Sharpie ever did! There again, Elke's wisdom came in handy, though it did so in a way she'd probably never have foreseen. It didn't bother me to lie there on Frank's bed and let men use my body, because *I wasn't there*... I'd learned to go elsewhere in my head. I was with Kacim, pressing my lips to his lips or swooning with pleasure in his arms or listening rapturously as he spoke to me in Arabic. I loved the music of his mother tongue, Your Honour (for some reason I feel like being polite to you again); it was like my childhood dream come true — a language which, to me, was only music. Kacim wasn't fluent in Arabic but Latifa had taught him suras from the Koran when he was little and that's what he'd recite to me in a soft voice, over and over again, as we lay together in bed. I doubt if any religious text has ever been such a turn-on...

Frank didn't know it, but Kacim was my lover throughout those two years. You can be proud of your son, Madam Latifa, he's really wonderful... It made me laugh to see how he scared people just by walking down the street, whereas he was the kindest, sweetest guy I ever met... At one point I was even pregnant by him (yes, I'm sure the child was his — I never took risks with my johns) — but we agreed it wasn't a good idea, we weren't exactly in a position to become parents. Since I was underage and didn't want to get my mother involved, I had to find a backstreet abortionist. Kacim came with me and when I lay down on the table, I could tell he was on the verge of fainting — it was funny, Your Honour, you should have seen him, he was more upset than I was...

As it turned out, I was lucky; the abortion went smoothly enough... but it changed me, somehow. *I'd had a human being inside of me,* you know what I mean? *There'd been another person in my stomach.* These things were more important than I'd thought. Making love... And life in general... I don't want to sound pompous or anything, but it's true. You don't look at the world quite the same way, afterwards. Not that I stopped putting out the next day or anything, but *in my head* I'd stopped. In my head I was already making plans for the future. I decided to pay attention in class. I passed my baccalaureate exams — which is more than either Frank or Kacim could boast. My youthful hijinks are over! I told them, as we downed a bottle of Veuve Clicquot to celebrate my high school diploma — I'm going up to Paris to study theatre.

I'd been thinking a lot about Cosmo. He embodied everything I now aspired to — wealth, talent and fame... And I remembered what he'd told me, that day next to the footbridge, *You could be an actress, too, when you grow up...* He'd give me some good contacts, I was sure of it. He'd help me get my foot in the door.

I blush, now, Your Honour, to think I was so naïve. But all eighteen year olds are self-centred. In a way, to them, adults don't really exist. I mean, they exist, of course — but in the same way as the walls of your house exist; they're old and solid, you count on their being there; you don't go check them out every morning to make sure they haven't crumbled during the night.

Cosmo was crumbling, and I hadn't noticed a thing. At most, I may have been *vaguely* aware that he was less talkative than he used to be. Or that his blond hair had started turning grey when he entered his forties. If I really turn my memory upside down and shake it, I *might* be able to recall overhearing some quarrels between Cosmo and my mother, in the middle of the night. But I was far from suspecting, day by day and month by month, the dramatic developments in their relation-ship, and in Cosmo's brain.

If you look at it from a distance, it's almost comical. In the summer of 1986, when I finished high school and turned eighteen, I packed all my belongings — including a few large banknotes I'd somehow neglected to hand over to Frank — and went to the capital to be close to Cosmo.

At exactly the same time, Cosmo moved out of the capital and purchased an apartment in the middle-sized city, to be close to Jonas.

Ninth Day

Elke

That, Your Honour... That...

I'd put up with everything from Cosmo. From day one. Never had I voiced a complaint. I'd accepted his megalomania, his incompetence in daily life, his absences, his infidelities, his egoism, his impotence... Over the past few years, I'd learned to accept and even embrace his nastiness, because it was a part of him, and I loved the whole man — *all Cosmo*. I took pride in being the only person in the world who knew and cherished every facet of him — his childhood, his mother, his father, his dear departed, his memories, his other women, his talent, his stage fright, his nightmares, his migraines... *everything*. But that he should fall in love with a man... No. That I could not accept. It was... oh, what can I say?

At *Le Zodiac*, rumours were flying. A ladies' man is only moderately interesting as a subject of gossip; people soon tire of discussing his conquests. A man's man, on the other hand, is much spicier — moreover, *both* Cosmo and Jonas had grown up right here in town, and each was famous in his own right... There was no way I could avoid hearing the speculation and commentary; and my nerves rapidly began to fray.

I never did find out what Vera thought about it. Had she even fully grasped the fact that André's son and her own were spinning an idyll together? I wouldn't swear to it. Though not yet seventy, she'd aged spectacularly since the asylum letters had been brought back to her: she'd stopped using henna on her hair and dressing vivaciously; she'd even shut down her newspaper shop. When I ran into her in the town square, she'd stride past me with long, ungainly steps, her hair floating in the wind, her blue gaze lost to the world. The village children (and not only the children) thought of her as a witch.

I was alone, Your Honour. Never had I been so alone. I had no parents, no children, no husband, no lover... Worse yet — for the first time in my life, I had no dreams.

This I had not expected.

I tried to tell myself he'd get over it, but I didn't believe it. Cosmo was nothing if not loyal. That was the biggest difference between him and Don Juan — he did not toss people out after use. When he loved, he loved.

He still called me on the telephone, and dropped by to see me once in a while, but we found it hard to talk. Jonas had changed things between us as no member of the chorus of women had ever done — for the simple reason that Cosmo told me nothing about him. Their love could not be turned into a story; he was *inside* of it.

Over one part of Cosmo's life, however, I still held full sway — his health. Early in 1986, one of the specialists he'd consulted for his migraines prescribed a spinal tap. As you know, this examination entails withdrawing a small quantity of cerebrospinal fluid. In Cosmo's case, it brought about an instant lessening of the pain.

Sandrine

That's news to me!

If it's true, Your Honour, what it implies is that there actually *was* intracranial brain pressure — that the cerebrospinal fluid couldn't circulate freely in the brain because of an increase in the mass contained within the skull. In a word, it would strongly indicate the existence of a tumour.

Elke

Just so. They went on to do a biopsy and Cosmo brought me the results. There was, indeed, a tumour.

Sandrine

But...

Elke

Following this, he underwent an IRM — ironically at the Salpêtrière Hospital, where his father had been interned for full-moon ecstasy more than half a century earlier... Once again, he brought me the results and we went over them together. The tumour was perfectly apparent, lodged at the heart of the hypothalamus. It was not removable.

Once Cosmo had left, I went on poring over his file, smothering the images of his brain with my kisses. My darling. My darling. Was his love for me still hidden somewhere in those dark whorls? Was this all that remained to me? Where was Cosmo?

Jonas

Cosmo was where he'd always longed to be — namely, in music. Frankly, Your Honour, I find the whole tumour story pretty hard to believe. I was seeing Cosmo on a daily basis throughout this period; if he'd been ill, surely I would have noticed it! I mean, some illnesses you can hide, but brain cancer?

Certainly Cosmo had changed. There's no denying that it was a time of crisis for him. He'd stopped running around like a chicken with its head cut off, stopped hating himself so much that he had to be twenty different people every night... But in my opinion, that was a good thing. He was learning to be himself. At last. With me.

Though I continued to eat, sleep, and keep my things at Rodolphe's place, I spent the better part of my days with Cosmo. Confronted with this new presence in my life, Rodolphe did his best to grin and bear it. I'm deeply grateful to him for not threatening to bash the actor's face in or throw me out into the street. True, monogamy had never been part of the understanding between us — we'd both had flings; that had never been a problem. But Rodolphe could tell that, this time, something very different was involved — something that could jeopardize the delicate balance of our couple. Yet he chose to wait. He managed, somehow, to control his jealousy... Maybe it was thanks to all the books he'd read; or maybe men are less hot-blooded after forty; I don't know. Later on, he confessed to having literally *prayed* that this new passion of mine wouldn't last too long.

Cosmo had bought a large, opulent apartment in the heart

of the old city. I went over to see him and play the violin for him almost every afternoon. My studies at the Conservatory had greatly broadened and diversified my repertory; I could play pretty much anything, from baroque suites to gypsy *czardas* — and no matter what I chose to play, Cosmo would listen to me with burning intensity. It was as if he'd been dying of thirst for years, and my music was the river of milk and honey they talk about in the Bible... He *received* it, Your Honour. Sitting calm and motionless in an armchair, he'd close his eyes and listen to me with all his might. One day, after playing the "Largo" from Bach's *Sonata N°3 in F*, I turned around and saw that his cheeks were bathed in tears.

When I had finished playing, I'd set aside my instrument and taken him by the hand. Though I was much younger than he was, he allowed me to guide him in the coming together of our bodies. He was like a child taking its first steps in thrilled disbelief — is it possible... no... yes... really... oh my God, I'm actually able... to... walk?!

He was so grateful, Your Honour... Just talking about it brings tears to my eyes... I'll stop there.

Fiona

Cosmo's illness is news to me, too. I can't believe how blind we all were.

For my part, having arrived in Paris fairly brimming over with hopes and dreams, I learned in the course of a single day, firstly, that Cosmo's phone had been disconnected, and secondly, that he no longer lived in the capital. It shook me up a bit, Your Honour, I won't deny it. But I'm not the sort of person who throws in the towel...

For a whole year I struggled to keep my head above water — making phone calls, visiting theatres, doing interviews and auditions... As I didn't want to compromise my chances of getting a rôle I had to learn how to fend off wandering hands while keeping a smile on my face. I had the same problem as Marilyn Monroe — my breasts drew so much attention that I had a hard time being taken seriously. It was a drag, but I refused to give up — Cosmo's words kept coming back to me — *maybe you'll be an actress, too...* I intended to prove it — to myself, to him, and to the world.

Towards the end of that first year, I finally started getting minor roles — mostly in radio plays, which is pretty ironic for a woman of my endowments... Anyway, all this is just to explain how it is that I was so completely unaware what was going on back home. In the wilful way of eighteen-year-olds, I'd broken off all contact with my mother. Between you and me, Your Honour, I think I resented her having divorced my father. (It's funny: now that I'm divorced myself, I don't resent it anymore!) One day I happened to be in the Third District, not far from the Rue Au Maire where Elke once lived with her hatmaker mother, and I ran into one of my johns from the middle-sized city. Jack, his name was. A very respectable, well-dressed gentleman. He's the one who recognized me as we passed each other in the Rue Quincampoix, and he leaned over and whispered in my ear: Well, well, Gina — so business is better in Paris, is it?

Gina was my *nom de guerre* from back then. At first I almost jumped out of my skin; but then I got angry. For the past year I'd been working to *become somebody*, and this guy couldn't even tell the difference; he talked to me as if I were still in the gutter. But he apologized, and asked if he could earn my forgiveness by taking me out to dinner in Les Halles. He didn't need to ask twice — it had been a while since I'd had a good meal, and the prospect of some sauerkraut and white wine was a cheery one indeed. We downed two bottles of Gewürztraminer between the two of us, and when Jack's hand slipped between my thighs at the end of the meal I didn't bother to push it away. I was too content to be sitting in a fancy restaurant with hot food in my stomach. Even when he invited me up to his hotel room for a nightcap, it didn't get my suspicions up; I can't believe how gullible I was. Things degenerated rapidly, of course.

Come on, Fiona, he told me. I'm sure you're a terrific actress, but if there's one role you can't play it's the offended virgin. It's just not in your repertory, I'm sorry! Now come on, dear, take off your clothes, I'll pay you. So saying, he slapped me playfully on the rump — and, seeing that I continued to resist, he turned mean. He picked me up and threw me onto the bed. And believe it or not, Your Honour, it was Cosmo who came to my rescue.

It must have been because of the name Jack. All of a sudden I remembered how angry I'd been able to get, the day Cosmo and I played *Jack and the Beanstalk* together. I'd been the most awesome giant in the world! And now, fifteen years later, finding myself alone in a luxury hotel room with a bastard who was planning to rape me, I became the giant again. *Fee, fi, fo, fum*... My body swelled up, my muscles flooded with adrenaline, I was like Popeye when he eats his spinach or Asterix when he guzzles down the magic potion... Believe me, Your Honour, that Jack didn't know what hit him. Three seconds later, he was on the far side of the room with the breath knocked out of him, and I'd closed the door behind me.

Thanks, Cosmo.

Anyhow.

After that, it was back to the old rat race. More interviews, more auditions, more minor roles for *another* whole year — following which, with a sigh of relief, I agreed to marry Jean-Claude. He was a radio-play director, he'd been running after me for months and finally I said to myself: Come on, he's a nice guy, he's got a good salary and at least this way you'll have some time to breathe. The breathing part didn't happen, though: I got pregnant a few weeks after our wedding, and this time there was no way I was going to get rid of the kid.

I called my mother to tell her the news. She burst into tears of joy, and suddenly everything was all right again between us.

My son Xavier was born in June 1988; I'd just turned twenty.

Frank

It bugged me to have fallen out of touch with my little sister. I'd always thought she depended on me — but now, ever since she'd moved up to Paris, I realized I depended on her, too. Without her, my little schemes weren't half as amusing — or half as lucrative.

Fortunately, Kacim was still in the picture. The two of us had become thick as thieves — well, the three of us, counting Sharpie. We always stashed the knife in the same place, near an abandoned garage halfway between our two homes. The cops kept a close eye on us; we'd already spent quite a few nights in jail and every so often they'd come bursting into our homes with search warrants, but they could never come up with any hard evidence; our apartments were pure as the driven snow.

Fiona

I brought Jean-Claude and Xavier home with me for Christmas that year. Mama hit it off with them right away, but with Frank it was a different matter. Something felt wrong between us. I got pissed off because he kept casting these disparaging looks at my husband, as if he were some sort of square, and as for my son, for all the attention Frank paid him, he might as well have been invisible. I didn't know how to revive our old sense of closeness. And when he suggested the two of us go take a spin in the middle-sized city, I was unenthusiastic to say the least. I knew he was leading the same dumb-ass life as before — what we used to call the Four C's: Chancelle, Charité, Cash, Cocaine. The only new thing he had to show me was the hiding place he'd found for Sharpie... Terrific, I sighed, shrugging my shoulders. Frank's face sort of clouded over and I realized I'd hurt his feelings. But I wasn't going to congratulate him on *that!* Maybe knives are less exciting, once you've had a baby.

It moved me to see Kacim again, though. The guy was such a looker — handsome as a god, and a real man now, too. But we both felt pretty shy, I could hardly look him in the eye, and even to kiss me hello he didn't dare take me in his arms — I think he was afraid of brushing up against my breasts, because I'd become a mother since I last saw him and my breasts meant something different now...

Kacim wouldn't have hurt a fly, Your Honour. He was polite and soft-spoken, he never raised his voice... Anyone who's met him will tell you the same thing. The only problem is that some people never met him. His lawyers, for instance. For obvious reasons, he only got court-appointed lawyers... I know those guys. I haven't forgotten how they behave. They're a bunch of arrogant, incompetent pricks. They're not too busy to screw hookers and eat out in four-star restaurants, but they're way too busy to meet their clients. They don't get around to opening their files until the trial has already begun — it's true, I'm not kidding! Then they take one look at the case and say, Er, let's see, the knife belonged to the boy's father. What more proof do we need? They glance at the accused — Ah, you see how shifty his eyes are? Can't look you straight in the face... Very suspicious... Where there's smoke there's fire... Okay now, we've wasted enough time, let's put this kid behind some nice French bars; fifteen years — who's next?

Fifteen years in prison! My Kacim! I don't believe it! My first lover? The dark-haired boy who made me swoon by murmuring suras in my ear? And meanwhile those bastard lawyers and that asshole judge can gad about as they please? *They can* burp and fart in their beds at night, whereas they never learned a line of poetry in their whole lives?

Deep down, Your Honour, I think Frank killed Cosmo. I don't see who else could have done it.

Jonas? Impossible. He'd had lunch that day in a bistrot near Cosmo's place; he'd left the restaurant at two o'clock sharp and returned three minutes later in a state of shock, his body convulsed with the horror of what he'd just seen. He was the one who called the police. According to the autopsy, Cosmo had been dead for at least two hours; rigor mortis had already set in.

Rodolphe, then? Of course he was the ideal suspect, and the police questioned him for hours... But it turned out he'd spent the morning with his mother; the retirement home employees had seen him leave at about one.

Besides, neither Jonas nor Rodolphe had any way of knowing where Sharpie was hidden.

Kacim

Thanks for believing me, Fiona. I didn't kill Cosmo, I promise you, I'd never have done a thing like that.

I swear it's true, Your Honour — just because Frank was my best friend doesn't mean I killed his worst enemy. I can't stand the sight of blood. I'm more like Cosmo as a little boy, when he picked up the dead magpie so Clementine could fix it...

The knife was just for show. People's eyes would widen when they saw it, and they'd empty out the cash registers at top speed — *that* was a good feeling. So was the money itself, I won't deny it — but killing someone, no. I never even wounded anybody with the knife — not once — it was just to make an impression. I don't know if you're aware of this, Your Honour, but in our tradition you're not supposed to unsheathe a weapon like that without drawing blood, my father told me this long ago, back in Algeria, when I turned seven and he showed me the knife for the first time — it's cowardly, he said, just to threaten and not to act; it's an insult to the knife. But Frank and I were proud of Sharpie, we took good care of him and always stashed him in the same place — I could even show you exactly where, on General-Charles-de-Gaulle between Apollinaire and Stendhal... I can tell you all this without batting an eyelash because I was not the one who went to get the knife on the day of the murder. *I didn't do it, I didn't do it, I didn't do it!*

Tenth Day

Latifa

You see, Your Honour? My Kacim is innocent! He's not the one who killed the actor, everyone agrees, they all say the same thing, he didn't do it! I'm not saying he's an angel, he made some mistakes, I know, big ones, small ones — but that, no. *That* he didn't do. He paid for someone else's crime, I swear before God it's true.

Elke

It's hard for a mother to admit she's lost her son — that all her efforts at educating him have failed. Despite the differences between Latifa and myself, I felt the same dreadful impotence every time I thought of Frank. When I considered his trajectory of destruction, from the savaging of the hi-fi to his current chronic delinquency, I had no idea how to get close to him again. I loved him, that goes without saying — you can't not love the fruit of your own womb — but he now belonged to a universe I found both foreign and hostile. With Fiona, things had gotten better, I was happy to see her reconciled with life... but to tell you the truth, Your Honour, my mind was not primarily on my children at this time; I was anguishing over Cosmo day and night.

His health was deteriorating rapidly. Only to me did he show the results of his monthly tests, and changes which were imperceptible to other people seemed dramatic to me. His gait had grown clumsy and uncoordinated. He could no longer fold his newspaper properly. He'd lost his sense of smell. The first biopsy had caused him to lose all sensation on the right side of his mouth and part of his right hand; his smile was asymmetrical. Fortunately, being left-handed, he could still fake good table manners — but often a dribble of saliva or a fragment of food would remain on the right-hand corner of his mouth because he couldn't feel it there. Worse, his personality was changing. He who had always been so sweet and funny and attentive was now irascible. He heard criticism in the most innocuous remark and responded to it with violence.

Jonas
This is making me dizzy, Your Honour. Elke warned us that her testimony would surprise us, and I must say she was right... I don't know whether Cosmo folded his newspaper properly or not, but if that's a criterion for brain tumours this is the first I've heard of it... As for the other symptoms, I'm certain I would have noticed them, living at such close quarters with his body...

Sandrine
You could knock me over with a feather, Your Honour. True, Cosmo had stopped consulting local physicians, but if there'd been anything as serious as this, I'm convinced we would have heard about it...

Elke

At best, his speech was confused; at worst it was downright delirious. Other people could chalk up his verbal shakiness to his loss of confidence in himself as an artist, but to me there was no room for doubt: he was losing language. Cosmo was losing language. *That's* when the real collapse began — when he realized he'd never be able to go back onstage.

Until then, I'm convinced, Cosmo had thought of his idyll with Jonas as a parenthesis — or, more accurately, as a vacation. He never took vacations, you see. In the fifteen years I'd known him, scarcely a week had passed without his performing in public at least once. Now, unable to channel his fear through acting, he was bearing the full brunt of it.

The Footbridge

Cosmo made one last attempt to put together a new show, Your Honour. I was the sole witness to it, and I must say it was one of the saddest things I ever saw — it will be centuries before I can forget it.

He came to see me in May of 1989. Physically, as far as I could tell, he hadn't changed. He greeted me in a soft voice, climbed up on me and began to improvise. Ah! just like in the good old days! I thought. But it was *not* like in the good old days. It was terrifying.

The show was called *Questionnaire on Last Judgment Day*. It was about what happens after people die. They find themselves all crowded together in a huge, intimidating amphitheatre, *infernal academia*, he called it. A jury of angels stands waiting for them onstage, arms crossed, features set in an expression of implacable severity. Then an insane god starts drilling them about what they've learned during their stay on Earth. It's the quintessential examination, you understand — a sort of paroxystic *Trivial Pursuits. What is the meaning of life?* thunders the god, for instance; or *Whence cometh Evil?* — and the poor human beings, scared out of their wits, forgot everything they know, shit in their pants, mumble answers at random, and endure abominable punishments...

Oh, Your Honour! I found it so painful to hear Cosmo talk that way...

That was the last I ever saw of him.

Frank

Well, well, aren't we learning a lot today!

I don't know who killed Cosmo, Your Honour, but it sounds as if nothing could have made him happier!

It might very well have been Kacim; I just don't know. He could have done it out of friendship for me. In my opinion, it's even more than possible, it's plausible.

Let me tell you why.

Kacim and I were tired of living off of Charité. Even delinquency gets tedious after a while. I felt frustrated and out of sorts, forever on edge and impatient, though I couldn't have said what I was waiting for. I wasn't getting any younger — I was twenty-five, I had no idea where my life was headed. *Variety is the spice of life*, my father always used to say. Well, the problem was, our life was beginning to lack spice. Then we hit on a new idea and everything got interesting again.

One day in July of '89, a day of stifling heat and smog, Kacim suggested we take a dip out at the Val d'Auron when he got off work at the gas station. But then there was some mix-up; apparently his boss accused him of taking money from the cash register and Kacim sort of lost it — like he said, it was important to him that this job stay clean, it was for his mother, he wouldn't have touched the cash register — anyway so he blew his top, the cops arrived, usual routine, handcuffs, ID check, body search, the whole bit, and by the time they let him go it was already past midnight. But the day's heat remained in the air, and since Kacim was all steamed up about what he'd just been through, I suggested we go to the lake anyway for a midnight swim.

What we didn't know was that real men weren't welcome at that hour — the place belonged to the local fairies. You'll remember Jonas's description of how they mince and prance around the lake at night. At first it made me want to puke, but then I had a brainwave. I told Kacim my idea and he agreed: objectively, it was brilliant. We'd brought Sharpie along with us just in case... To make a long story short, we started mugging faggots.

Ah, you should have seen us, Your Honour! The poor guys didn't know which way to turn! Lots of them were married men on an escapade (I even recognized a member of the municipal government); their situation was delicate, not to say compromising, and the last thing they wanted was to bring the police into it. Fuming and cursing, they handed over all their valuables — credit cards, watches, gold chains — it was fantastic.

When I got home, I was so excited that I rang up Fiona to tell her about it, but her reaction was a letdown, just like the day we showed her Sharpie's hiding place. I mean, I know she was pregnant again, she probably didn't appreciate being woken up at three in the morning, but the least she could have done was *laugh!* She's gotten so conventional since her marriage, I can't believe it. She used to like to live dangerously; she's not my little Fiona anymore. Now, over the phone, she started telling me about Xavier's first steps. What did I care about a little brat taking its first steps? I was so pissed off that I hung up on her. She really disappointed me. At least Kacim and I had remained faithful to the ideals of our youth, and now we were having more fun than ever before.

We had fun, precisely, until August the 3rd.

That night we went down to the lake as usual, and the very first couple of faggots we stumbled upon — sitting there on the beach, in full view — were Cosmo and Jonas.

I can't tell you what a shock it was to me, Your Honour. I hadn't seen the fornicating clown in years — and to come upon him like that, at the edge of the lake, a fag among fags... I mean, there was no doubt about it — he was lying with his head in Jonas's lap, and Jonas was stroking his hair, they weren't there to study ducks... I saw red. Literally, a sort of red curtain came down in front of my eyes. I was so angry I felt as if my head was on fire, and my breath came in ragged gasps. That day, I understood why dragons are always portrayed with flames leaping from their throats and smoke pouring from their nostrils... I grabbed Kacim's arm and dragged him to the nearest bus stop.

What's the matter? he asked. You know those pansies?

Yeah, I know them...

And in a few words I told him the story.

Kacim

Frank was mad that night, all right; I'd never seen him in such a state. Of course it made an impression on me — it's only natural, he was my best friend... He kept ranting and railing against the guy down at the lake and how he'd humiliated his mother — first by making love to her and then, if I understood correctly, by not making love to her anymore. I'm not sure I caught every little detail but all men are sensitive on the subject of their mother's morality — it's only natural; I think Fiona would be well-advised not to tell her son too much about what she was doing at age seventeen... I mean, why else would Christianity have invented a saviour with a virgin mother? Whoever thought that one up was a genius!

Latifa

What are you saying, my son? Now you start to believe in the Virgin Mary? Oh God, oh God, what did they do to you in prison? *The old woman wept and her liver was on burning coals / For her poor son, lost to her...*

Kacim

So as I said, Your Honour, I could see Frank's point of view, but in my personal opinion when two people are in love it's their own business, and who cares if they're men or women.

Even if Frank was my friend, I felt I had to tell him that.

Frank

The more I went on about Cosmo, the more at a loss Kacim looked, and that made me even angrier. By now I was foaming at the mouth; I had to find some way to express my hatred and there was only one person in the world who could hear it, so the minute I got home I rushed to the phone and rang up Fiona in Paris...

I'll kill him! I'll kill him! I'll kill him! I must have screamed it into the receiver a hundred times. Kacim was at least as impressed by my rage as by the event that had sparked it off.

Calm down, Frank, he told me, when I hung up the phone at last. Come on, calm down, we'll take care of him.

He really worshipped me, you know what I mean? He couldn't stand to see me beside myself like that. That's why I think he's the one who killed Cosmo on August 4th. I don't have any proof, I'm not a hundred percent sure. But apart from the two of us, no one knew about Sharpie's hiding place... Except for Fiona, of course. But Fiona had a solid alibi — at the time of Cosmo's death, she was in a maternity hospital in Paris's Fifteenth District, giving birth to a little girl.

Fiona

Frank's phone call scared me out of my wits. He was hysterical. I was sure he was going to kill Cosmo. I couldn't get the idea out of my head; all night it kept me from sleeping. The tension got so bad I started getting contractions, so early the next morning I called Mama and told her the whole story. She didn't seem surprised when I mentioned Jonas, so I gathered she already knew about him. I told her that Frank was raging mad and Kacim couldn't make him listen to reason. I told her exactly where they hid the knife during the day and begged her to go get it at once. There's this abandoned garage, I told her — on Charles-de-Gaulle, between Apollinaire and Stendhal — you can't miss it. They slide the knife between two slats in the back wall, on the right-hand side — *please* go get it, Mama! Right away, *please, do it,* it's an emergency! Frank is out of his mind, I'm scared to death he'll do something stupid, you've got to stop him!

But she wasn't able to stop anything...

Elke

Don't cry, sweetheart, don't cry, my little girl, my darling Fiona... Please don't blame yourself... It's not your fault — you did exactly the right thing... In fact, darling I'm grateful to you — I thank you from the bottom of my heart...

Poor Cosmo was so ill, Your Honour. So very ill. His tumour wasn't removable, he needed emergency surgery and at that stage of the illness only love could save him... I prepared for the operation meticulously... Thanks to Fiona, I found the scalpel of love; then I slipped my hands into the surgical gloves — those selfsame, pink silk gloves which had been a gift of love from my father to my mother and which I'd always treasured...

Josette
Aaaaaaaaaaaaarrrrrrgh!

Sandrine
Oh my God, Your Honour! Call for an ambulance at once!
Josette is having an apoplectic fit and Latifa has fainted!

The Novelist
I am surprised. I am *very* surprised.

The Doe
And... tell me, Elke... How did he look at you? What did you
see in Cosmo's eyes as life ebbed away from him?

Eleventh Day

Elke

Cosmo is alive, Your Honour, he is resurrected!

He's the one who had Frank released.

The minute the police recognized the knife, they arrested the two youths — any number of people in town could testify to having seen the weapon in the hands of one or the other.

Over the ensuing weeks, I managed to get in touch with virtually every member of the chorus of women. Two were married to lawyers, a third to a minister, a fourth to a journalist who was privy to the secrets of the Elysée palace, and a fifth to a man whose sister, by the most delightful coincidence, was the mistress of the very judge who would be sitting at the trial. Ah, it was something to see, let me tell you! Pulling strings, greasing palms, wielding subtle political and financial threats, it took Cosmo's cuckolds only six short weeks to get the man whom they firmly believed to be his murderer released from jail. Kacim, on the other hand, was maintained in custody. Though there was no real evidence against him, the legal system needed a murderer, especially for so famous a victim, and he was the only plausible one left. The sentence was heavy — fifteen years.

Should I have turned myself in, Your Honour? Of course not. I was invested with the sacred mission of spreading Cosmo's love; getting myself locked up would have meant failing that mission. Naturally, it was painful to me to know that someone was paying for a crime he hadn't committed, even if the so-called crime was an act of consummate mercy — but to be perfectly honest, and without wanting to cause poor Latifa to faint again, I felt that doing a bit of time might actually be good for Kacim. In the first place, I told myself, it'll keep him away from Frank. And in the second place, it will give him the chance to discover something that has been lacking in his life since birth, namely solitude. In his jail cell, he'll be able to think, read and dream to his heart's content. And who knows? Maybe he'll decide to take his life in hand.

As it turned out, Kacim took even better advantage of his prison term than I'd expected. His behaviour was above reproach — *exemplary,* in fact — and he was released on parole after only eight years. He survived thanks to his mother's love, of course — but also thanks to the visits of one of his former professors from La Chancelle. Month after month, the latter brought him books and discussed them with him; by the time Kacim was released he could quote whole pages of Verlaine, Herman Hesse and Kateb Yacine, verbatim... He began to give creative writing workshops — first in La Chancelle, then in other immigrant neighbourhoods here and there throughout the country... He became a public figure, sought out for his erudition and admired for his charisma... A far more edifying destiny, I must admit, than that of my own son Frank — about whose shady affairs, the less said the better. Unfortunately, Hassan was not able to rejoice in this turn of fate — he died of a heart attack at age fifty-five, a mere few days before his son's release from prison.

But what I wanted to say, Your Honour, is that I'm happy.

Cosmo is alive! And in so many different ways... it's quite incredible!

Look at this portrait of him as an adolescent, which I inherited upon the death of Josette. It's a charcoal drawing by Aleo — yes, you remember, Marinette's deformed son — dated 1960. Isn't it simply beautiful?

And here's a cassette tape with the first message Cosmo left on my answering machine (the machine itself was a gift from him, for my fiftieth birthday, in 1987). A miracle, yet another miracle: I come home from *Le Zodiac* in the middle of the night, press a button, and lo and behold — my lover is there with me in my bedroom! Listen: *Elke, where are you... I'm in Aix. What am I doing in Aix. What am I doing anywhere. Walking down the Cours Mirabeau this afternoon, I rubbed the inside corner of my eye and suddenly noticed that my face didn't feel familiar... Exploring with my fingertip, I discovered there was a dent there, between the corner of my eye and the top of my nose -no, it was more than a dent, it was a hole... My finger slid into it... and before I knew it, I was hooking out great gobs of my own brain... Now my brain is empty. I have nothing left to say.*

Would you like to hear it again? *Elke, where are you... I'm in Aix. What am I doing in Aix. What am I doing anywhere. Walking down the Cours Mirabeau this afternoon, I rubbed the inside corner of my eye and suddenly noticed that my face didn't feel familiar... Exploring with my fingertip, I discovered there was a dent there, between the corner of my eye and the top of my nose — no, it was more than a dent, it was a hole... My finger slid into it... and before I knew it, I was hooking out great gobs of my own brain... Now my brain is empty. I have nothing left to say.*

It's just his voice, you say. Yes, of course. But when he was alive and I'd be speaking to him over the phone — or even lying next to him in the dark — then, too, his voice. I loved... *I love* his voice, Your Honour.

And when I curl up on the living-room couch and watch a tape of one of his shows, there's more than just his voice! There's his face as well, and his body, and the way he moves! Warm flesh is missing, you say. Yes, you're right. But even with a warm, throbbing, perspiring body, it's impossible to really *unite*. The other person remains irremediably opaque. Only love can efface the borders between two people — and the love between Cosmo and myself is indestructible.

I can rent a film he mentioned to me long ago — *The Misfits* by John Huston, for example — and watch it with him, and feel, as the images glide past, not only my own emotion but *his* at the sight of sweet, broken Marilyn Monroe...

Often he comes to visit me at night.

In a recent dream, I entered the room where his body had been laid out, I knew he was dead but I thought he might nevertheless consent to appear to me and speak to me. And so he did — even as he lay motionless on his death bed, he rose and walked towards me, smiling. You know, Elke, he said, death is not at all what it's made out to be, it's not frightening in the least, indeed it's rather pleasant... And with a shout of laughter he added — incorrigible seducer that he is — Ever since I got here, the angels have been fighting over my soul!

Cosmo is alive, Your Honour, he has risen! Sometimes, in the street or at work, I catch a brief glimpse of him in other people. This man has his wild blond hair, that one his stick-out ears, the other his knobby nose or chin... From a distance, I see someone holding his head at the same angle, or walking in the same way... Once I even heard his laugh! Far from resenting all these people for not being Cosmo, I'm grateful to them for carrying small fragments of him around with them, thus prolonging the vibration of his being in the universe...

The other day at *Le Zodiac*, he actually brought me to climax while I was on duty! A customer glanced up at me as I served him and I noticed he had Cosmo's eyes, hazel flecked with gold. Blushing, I turned away. But a few seconds later, realizing the unique opportunity life was offering me, I turned back and plunged my gaze into his, and for ten seconds the two of us made full, magnificent, *creamy* love; it was a perfect moment, with no frustration on either side. Thanks to Cosmo, this stranger and I had been given a dollop of heaven.

He's everywhere!

I received fresh proof of his presence the other day. Old Tabrant came in to *Le Zodiac* for a beer. Since the place was empty, and since his fat stomach now prevents him from sitting on a stool at the bar, I took pity on him and decided to keep him company for a while. But no sooner had I pulled up a chair than he began slandering the mayor, fishing nasty bits of gossip out of his memory, making fun of people whom he knew to be my friends... I grew tense and annoyed, inwardly cursing this ruddy-cheeked, flabby-jowled boor and searching for some pretext to get up and walk away... when all at once I remembered what Cosmo had said about him years before, on the way home from the train station — *He went to Australia once.*

Excuse me, I murmured, interrupting him, but... I hear you once visited Australia?

Instantly, the journalist's expression changed.

Ah, yes! he sighed. I won a three-week trip to Australia when I was twenty-two, and while there I discovered my true passion in life — cetaceans.

Fiona

Who needs citations? We're already in a law court!

Sorry about that.

Elke

Dolphins and whales.

In the course of my wanderings along the east coast, Tabrant went on, I happened to go past a Dolphin Centre in Wollongong. It was late afternoon, almost closing time, and... anyway, to make a long story short, I struck up acquaintance with the dolphin trainer, a girl by the name of Sally, and it was love at first sight. Total, absolute, mutual *love* — just like in a novel! She locked up the centre, but the two of us spent the night there and I can tell you I learned a great deal that night. Not just about cetaceans, either!

I didn't even feel like laughing, Your Honour; it moved me to think that at least one woman in the world had found this man attractive. Come to think of it, he rather resembled a whale himself — how could I not have noticed it before? If you looked at him that way, he wasn't so monstrous after all. By now I was hanging on his every word, because I knew that one day long ago *he had told the same story to Cosmo...* With him as with everyone else, Cosmo had known the right questions to ask.

For the duration of my stay in Australia, Tabrant went on, Sally and I were deliriously happy together. She took me out to sea with her once... It was a gorgeous day, the water was emerald green, and the two of us went swimming amongst the dolphins. It's the most unbelievable experience, Elke. There were hundreds of them, and they were thrilled to have us there, I'm not kidding! They played with us, diving between our legs, rubbing up against us, bumping us this way and that... As for the sensation of their soundwaves passing through your body, it's simply indescribable... By the end of the afternoon, I felt as if I'd had a six-hour orgasm!

The journalist had undergone a metamorphosis before my very eyes; he seemed to be lit up from within by the beauty of what he'd experienced forty years earlier on the opposite side of the Earth, and when he finally stopped talking my eyes were filled with tears.

Thank you, Cosmo, I breathed.

Do you understand, Your Honour?

What has changed, since Cosmo's death, is not that I can receive nothing from him but that he can receive nothing from me — my *thank yous* will never take their place among his moments of being.

There's another way in which Cosmo has ceased to exist — current events. Having died in the summer of 1989, he won't have registered the crumbling of the Berlin Wall, the end of the Cold War, the dismantling of the Soviet Union. He won't need to include in his *Explanation of the World to a Little Girl* the genocide in Rwanda, or the second intifada, or the pulverization of Manhattan's twin towers... He won't even have lived to see the Internet... whereas his name now flashes on thousands of sites!

The years slide by, huge but imprecise, like the ship in Fellini's *Amarcord*, and fade into the fog one after the other. I've stopped counting them... Monsieur Picot eventually gave up the ghost and I took over *Le Zodiac*, I bought the place with my savings, though admittedly there weren't many bidders... The countryside is emptying out, Your Honour. Red-nosed peasants with dirty caps have become a virtually extinct species; my clientele is far more diverse than it used to be. There are Parisians who come down on school vacations to play at being country folk... Belgian, Dutch and German tourists, making a detour through George Sand country on their way to the Côte d'Azur... Even women! Yes, women feel quite at home in cafés nowadays; you even see very young ones — skinny teenagers like Fiona's daughter Milena — sipping apricot juice and smoking Menthol cigarettes...

Life goes on, Your Honour!

Twelfth Day

Frank

When Fiona rang me up in September of 2020 to tell me Mama was dying, I rushed to her bedside and remained there to the end. For two long nights and a day, almost without interruption, I watched the flickering flame — the one Papa used to do his best to catch on film. At last, early on the morning of the second day, I saw what I'd been longing to see for so many years — the extinction of the last spark of life in my mother's eyes.

No, Your Honour, it was not my mother's death I wanted to see — it was *his*.

Cosmo was gone, at long last. I heaved a sigh of relief.

Exit the fornicating clown.

I decided to celebrate with a glass of whisky at *Le Zodiac*. But no sooner had I walked out of Mama's house than I realized my mistake.

For one thing, the café had been renamed again — it was now called *Le Cosmo*.

I hitched myself up onto a stool at the counter, next to Asimon, the old blacksmith. He was a miserable little troll, twisted with age and ravaged by alcohol, but when he raised his glass to my mother, I could tell he still remembered that goddamn birthday party almost half a century before, when Cosmo had asked him to slip a note to the pretty barmaid.

A week later, I was in Paris for business and I happened to overhear a conversation between two women in the metro. One of them kept crossing her eyes and repeating, *At war? Me? I am at war?* and the other one giggled hysterically.

Later that day, I dropped by Fiona's place — she lives in the same cushy suburb as our banker grandfather used to, way back when — and I found her sitting on the front steps with her granddaughter Giulia; coming down the sidewalk I waved at the two of them but they didn't even notice me. Approaching, I saw they were playing cat's cradle, the stupid string game Cosmo taught Fiona, that long-ago day when she was sick in bed...

He was everywhere! It was like a prairie fire... you stamp out the flames here, they reappear there — and there — and over there... No matter how fast you run to stamp them out, the minute you turn your head you see they've spread, new fires have broken out in ten different places... *Fu——u-u-u-u-u-uck!*

Elke

Of course I'm dead, Your Honour. Does that surprise you?... Ah... But you see... these events took place a very long time ago...

All of us are dead now... Yes, every one of us... Cosmo... André... Jonas... Josette... Sandrine... Vera... Fiona... Frank... Latifa... Kacim...

Ah — not you? Really? You're not dead yet?

Thirteenth Day

The Pond

It's a perfectly beautiful day, sunny but not too hot...

Though it's only mid-August, autumn is already setting in...

Look over there — at the foot of the poplar tree — that rain of gold!